CAMAS PUBLIC LIBRARY
D1500286

Echoes of the Lost Order

Echoes of the Lost Order

A Steve and Victoria MacKinnon Mystery

John J. Lamb

Five Star • Waterville, Maine

A Steve and Victoria MacKinnon Mystery.

This novel is a work of fiction. Names, characters, places and incidents are either the product of the author's imagination, or, if real, used fictitiously.

First Edition
First Printing: November 2005

Published in 2005 in conjunction with
Tekno Books and Ed Gorman.

Set in 11 pt. Plantin.

Printed in the United States on permanent paper.

Library of Congress Cataloging-in-Publication Data

Lamb, John J., 1955–
Echoes of the lost order / by John J. Lamb.—1st ed.
p. cm.
ISBN 1-59414-321-8 (hc : alk. paper)
1. Lee, Robert E. (Robert Edward), 1807–1870—Manuscripts—Fiction. 2. Manuscripts—Collectors and collecting—Fiction. 3. Historical reenactments—Fiction. 4. Police chiefs—Fiction. 5.Virginia—Fiction. 6. Theft—Fiction. I. Title.
PS3612.A5457E27 2005
813′.6—dc22 2005024285

For my beloved wife, Joyce

One:

All Quiet Along the Potomac

Stephen MacKinnon opened his pocket watch. It was 10:13 a.m. and, as usual, the attack was late. Snapping the scratched lid shut, he surveyed his small command. Just over twenty Union troops were lounging on the grass near their stacked rifles. They'd learned the first and most important rule of the infantry: never stand when you can sit. Some of the soldiers were chatting and one or two were gnawing on hardtack, but most, like MacKinnon, were content to simply rest in the shade and watch the wide, murky Potomac roll past.

The broad-shouldered Federal officer was a study in martial elegance gone to seed. MacKinnon's dark blue officer's frock coat was faded and dusty, his trousers dirty, and his knee-high boots were caked with drying mud. Around his waist he wore a wide leather belt, upon which hung a battered scabbard containing a saber and a Colt .44 caliber revolver in a flap holster. Unlike so many other officers, MacKinnon wore no facial hair. This was a minor concession to vanity since, although he was only forty-two years old, his whiskers were already iron gray.

He took a sip from his canteen and tasted rust, then poured some of the tepid water into his woolen kepi and placed the blue uniform cap back on his head. It was ungodly hot and humid. Having spent most of his life in the semi-desert of Southern California, MacKinnon had smugly imagined he was a veteran of August heat, but that was before he'd come east to tidewater Virginia. This was his second summer in the Old Dominion State and he still hadn't entirely adapted to the torrid, sultry climate.

From the other side of the woods, a shot sounded and then another. The dull pops grew into a scattered sputtering, and MacKinnon knew that the Union skirmishers had at last bumped up against the Confederate line. Wispy tendrils of leaden-colored smoke drifted back through the pine trees, and he began to smell the rich, acrid aroma of burnt gunpowder.

It won't be long now, he thought, lighting his briar pipe. Into the woods they would march, but he knew that before the Federal battalion had advanced much more than twenty-five yards into the dense underbrush, the formation would swiftly lose cohesion. They would push forward in dribs and drabs until they wandered into the inevitable flaming volley. MacKinnon took a deep pull from the pipe and grimaced. In his mind's eye, he could already see the red Confederate battle flags, the yellowish-white flash of musket fire, and hear the keening Rebel yell. Then the digital telephone in his haversack trilled, and he dug the device from the tar-coated canvas bag.

"This is Chief MacKinnon."

"Sorry to disturb you, Chief, and I know you left me in charge, but we've got a little problem over here in the parking lot," said Sergeant Ronald Sayers, of the Talmine Police Department.

MacKinnon sighed. If there was anything he'd learned in his nearly twenty-one years as a cop, it was that, in police work, the minor obstacles were often more time-consuming and difficult to resolve than the big issues. Striving to keep his voice patient, MacKinnon said, "If it's a little problem, why do you need me, Ron?"

"Well, we've got some protestors here who want to go out

onto the battlefield and demonstrate against guns. They also say they aren't going to pay to get in." Sayers sounded a little flustered.

"Protestors. How many?" MacKinnon asked, noticing that some tourists were snapping photographs and shooting videos of him. He supposed the sight was incongruous: a Civil War-era Union officer talking on a wireless phone.

"I don't know . . . maybe a dozen, a few college kids and some old hippies, but they're pretty noisy. They've got signs, and one of the Richmond TV channels has a reporter here and they're shooting video of them. I expect it'll be on the news," said Sayers. "It might be good if you came here and sorted this out."

"I'll be right over." MacKinnon shut the digital phone off and replaced it in his haversack.

He felt both annoyed and vindicated. Officially, it was his day off and it was vexing that Sayers had intruded on his leisure time as a consequence of his inability to make a difficult decision. The sergeant was the poster child for terminal analysis paralysis. At the same time, the episode demonstrated why MacKinnon had been selected to be chief of Talmine's police force over the homegrown and ambitious Sayers.

His second-in-command was a good enough cop—smart, safe, and diligent—but when things got sticky and there was the risk that a decision might injure his chances for career advancement, Sayers was all too willing to hand the problem to his boss.

Even after nearly a year and a half, MacKinnon still found it amazing that he'd been offered the chief's position of the five-officer force. Prior to coming to Virginia, MacKinnon had logged just over nineteen years with the San Diego Police, where he'd established a reputation as one of that department's most skilled and respected homicide detectives.

But one evening he'd seen the small advertisement for the Talmine Chief's job in a cop magazine. Earlier in his career, MacKinnon would have snickered at the idea of pulling up stakes and moving to a small town, but by 2002, he and his wife, Victoria, were thoroughly disenchanted with the tarnished Golden State. Put too many rats in a cage, MacKinnon remembered telling Vic after working a particularly gruesome multiple homicide, and they begin to kill each other.

Investigating the Virginia town further—first on his computer atlas software and then on the Internet—MacKinnon found himself growing increasingly interested. Talmine was the county seat of rural Brookesmith County and was about ninety road miles southeast of the District of Columbia, on the Potomac River side of Virginia's "Northern Neck." Crime was low, the population was less than 3000, and best of all, there were dozens of Civil War battlefields within easy driving distance. For MacKinnon, who was an avid history buff and Civil War reenactor, the last fact was the ultimate attraction.

He'd talked the matter over with Victoria, who also liked what she saw, and encouraged him to submit an application. However, neither one actually suspected that MacKinnon stood any real chance for the job. After all, he was an outsider from the People's Republic of California—Babylon on the Pacific. Yet six weeks, three trips east, and seven interviews later, MacKinnon was notified that he'd edged out two local lawmen (one being Sayers) for the chief's position.

Although his peers at SDPD thought he'd lost his mind, MacKinnon instantly accepted the offer, along with the collateral cut in wages, realizing that sometimes the quality of life couldn't be measured solely by the size of a paycheck. Meanwhile, Victoria resigned from her longtime position as a civilian crime analyst with the San Diego Police. Before another month passed, the couple was setting up house in Talmine. Although the following fifteen months had been challenging, MacKinnon had never been happier. Life was good in Virginia, and he'd slowly established a strong reputation among the citizens as a chief who managed to blend the best elements of traditional and progressive styles of policing.

And, as the chief, it was time to go to work, which meant he might miss the impending battle.

"First Sergeant!" barked MacKinnon.

A bearded, burly man in a blue uniform responded at a trot. In real life he was Mark Weiss, the owner of the local Internet service provider, but on summer weekends he was the top enlisted man in Company D, Eighth Ohio Volunteer Infantry. A refugee from suburban Montgomery County, outside Philadelphia, Weiss had relocated to Talmine a year earlier than MacKinnon. He'd also been one of the first enlistees in the chief's initially-unpopular Yankee hobby group. Despite the passage of nearly one hundred-forty years, Federal blue uniforms still weren't enormously welcome south of the Mason-Dixon Line, but Weiss had observed that, with his pronounced Philadelphia accent, no one was ever going to believe he was a Rebel.

Weiss snapped to attention and said, "Sir?"

"Mark, I've got to go take care of a problem, so you're in command until I return," MacKinnon said. "Make sure the boys drink plenty of water, and tell Private Holm if I see him playing that bloody Game Boy in ranks again, there will be hell to pay."

"My pleasure, sir." Weiss flashed a wicked smile and snapped a salute. He was a hardcore reenactor and had no patience for farbs, the hobby's scornful label for inauthentic soldiers. No doubt, Weiss would assign Holm some thoroughly unpleasant task, such as water detail. Perhaps a half-mile march in the broiling heat, burdened with a dozen heavy canteens, would finally dissuade the kid from bringing his video game onto the battlefield, but MacKinnon was skeptical.

Pausing to extinguish the pipe, he walked out into the harsh sunlight. MacKinnon blinked and wished he'd worn his broad-brimmed slouch hat, for the cap-like kepi provided no protection against the sun. Sweat began to dribble down his back, and he wondered anew if his beloved hobby wasn't actually an outlet for latent masochism. There was something a little crazy—no, make that very, very crazy, acknowledged MacKinnon—about choosing to wear a heavy woolen uniform on one of the warmest days of the year. Yet he drew some solace from the fact that he wasn't the only costumed lunatic in attendance that Saturday morning in Brookesmith Municipal Park.

Over eight hundred Union and Confederate hobbyists, some from as far away as Toronto, Canada, had assembled in Talmine for the weekend to wage a mock and historically fake battle. The truth was there had never been any fighting in or around the tiny river settlement during the Civil War, but this hadn't prevented the town council and Chamber of Commerce from sponsoring a battle reenactment. The noisy events attracted tourists and their money.

For the spectators, the battle reenactment was a garish and noisy form of entertainment and an opportunity to see the mock soldiers who had imparted authenticity to films like *Dances With Wolves* and *Glory*. Like most reenactors, MacKinnon had initially been attracted to the unorthodox hobby as a consequence of his fervent interest in the Civil War. He'd read hundreds of books and studied maps; he'd toured the pastoral battlefields and wandered through museums, but simply possessing the intellectual knowledge about the battles and how they were fought just wasn't enough. It was like being shown a photograph of freshly-picked raspberries and asked to imagine their tart taste. So, MacKinnon had taken up the hobby in the hope of experiencing, even distantly and artificially, some sensory fragment of the most lethal and passionate of American wars. Yet, he was also honest enough to admit that the primary attraction of the battles was that he could partake in a vast, adult version of the boyhood game of war. Even better, you had a real gun and weren't going to be scolded by a neighbor for running through a flowerbed.

We're really just a bunch of kids, thought MacKinnon, *and that's not necessarily a bad thing. If growing up means cementing your fat ass to an easy chair and watching puerile crap like "When Animals Attack, Part III" on TV, give me this sort of immaturity any day. We may look silly, but at least we're alive.*

MacKinnon made his way past the bone-colored canvas tents of the Union camp and southward along the trail that bordered the sluggish waters of Ezekiel's Creek. A column of Union soldiers wearing the distinctive tall, black, -felt hats of the Iron Brigade marched past, as their drum and fife section played "Hell on the Wabash." Across the field, a troop of Confederate cavalry cantered up a low, grassy hill. The gunfire still sputtered from the woods, but had receded in intensity, which meant the skirmishers were beginning to withdraw in advance of the main attack. *If I hurry,* thought MacKinnon, *I might make it back in time to lead the company in the assault.*

Ahead, he could see the parking lot was packed with cars and spectators. MacKinnon wasn't an expert at determining crowd size, but the attendance had to be at least 5,000. The merchants would be ecstatic, as would be the local politicians; but it also meant additional work under a broiling sun for his officers and the deputies that Sheriff Tom Jarboe had loaned him for the event. MacKinnon made a mental note to remind Sayers to ensure that all officers got at least a half-hour meal break.

He found Sayers near the temporary admission booths at the entrance to the park. As usual, the tall sergeant looked like a caricature of a tough rural cop, with his gleaming, black-leather gun belt, tight-fitting blue uniform, spit-shined combat boots, and felt Smokey Bear hat dipped forward over his eyes. Completing the image was the carefully trimmed brown moustache and the inevitable mirrored Ray-Ban aviator sunglasses. Sayers was also wearing his Arnold Schwarzenegger/Terminator professional frown—an emotionless glower that MacKinnon suspected the sergeant diligently practiced every morning in the bathroom mirror.

Just beyond the admission booths stood a cluster of fatigued-looking people, bearing hand-painted signs declaring the irredeemable wickedness of firearms. It was obvious the protestors were wilting in the enervating heat. One young woman, who wore a tee shirt bearing faux blood-spatters, an image of an AK-47, and the message: "Repeal the Second Amendment," was briskly squirting her compatriots with water from a spray bottle. Beside the small, sweating group was a female television reporter, drinking pricey glacier water from a sports bottle, and her bored-looking video camera operator.

Sayers saw MacKinnon and looked relieved. "Thanks for coming, Chief."

"You called me for *this?*" MacKinnon asked. "Ron, if you'd just given them another fifteen minutes, half of them would have been down with sunstroke and your problem would have been solved."

"Sorry. The mayor saw them and started to get worried," said Sayers sheepishly.

"Mayor Dumfries is always worried," MacKinnon grumbled. He left unspoken the second half of the statement: *and she's always on the lookout for some fresh way to make me look inefficient.*

MacKinnon's relationship with the mayor had begun to deteriorate just before Christmas. One of his officers stopped and arrested a member of the mayor's "Women's Vision 2000" organization for DUI as the lady tried to drive home from the club's Christmas party. The woman's blood alcohol count had been .19, over twice the legal limit. Even worse, she'd slapped the cop as he'd tried to handcuff her and then urinated in the back seat of the police cruiser. Shortly thereafter, Mayor Dumfries had appeared at the police station and tried to bully the officer into dropping the charges. He refused and called MacKinnon at home.

MacKinnon remembered the tempestuous meeting in his office. Dumfries had been wearing a low-cut blue gown and reeked of booze herself, causing MacKinnon to wonder if she'd driven to the police station. She began by appealing to his Christmas spirit and, when the mayor discovered MacKinnon was Scrooge reincarnated, she reminded him of the "political realities" of the situation, which apparently meant Jean Dumfries' friends were free to break the law. The mayor was furious when MacKinnon stood by his officer and said the woman would be booked like any other person. He'd tried to explain that the moment cops began using a double standard, they no longer had the moral authority to police the public, but he might as well have been speaking in Tahitian. The only thing Jean Dumfries cared about was that she wasn't getting her way, and she wasn't about to forget, much less forgive, MacKinnon's lack of cooperation.

From that point forward, he'd had nothing but subtle grief

from the mayor and, worse still, Victoria had also become a target. His wife was treated as a pariah by much of the self-anointed social elite of Talmine, which didn't really bother Victoria because she thought the Dumfries faction were a bunch of stuck-up, anal-retentive snobs anyway.

Oh, the joys of small town politics, thought MacKinnon.

He exhaled slowly. "Before I deal with this little crisis, give me an update on traffic."

"It's still pretty much gridlocked back to Old Tavern Road, so downtown's a real mess," said Sayers.

"What's the problem?"

"Well, we ran out of parking here and had to start funneling the cars back into town," explained Sayers. "But nobody wants to walk a quarter-mile in this heat to get to the park, so they just loop around and come back."

MacKinnon visualized the city map and said, "All right, I want you to block off River View Drive at Addison Farm Road and start directing the traffic toward the high school. Let them park on the football field. That may cause some unhappy faces with the school board, but we've got to keep the road open in case the fire department or rescue squad has to respond to the park."

"I'll get right on it."

"And one other thing, Ron. Make sure our people and the deputies get relieved for meal and latrine breaks."

"Yes, sir."

When Sayers finished issuing the new instructions over his portable radio, MacKinnon hooked a thumb at the demonstrators and asked, "So, who's their leader?"

"His name is Anthony Blay." Sayers pointed to a chunky, middle-aged man with long, wavy gray hair tied in a ponytail, and whose face was coated with so much sunscreen he looked like an overfed street mime.

"Haven't heard of him. Local?"

Sayers consulted his notebook. "Nope. He's from Falls Church and says that he's been on the 'Larry King Show.' "

"Oh my, a celebrity. My heart's *all* aflutter," said MacKinnon. "Well, bring him over and let's see if we can sort this out."

Sayers walked to the group and spoke briefly with Blay. The activist handed his half-consumed, two-liter bottle of Dr. Pepper to another protestor and followed the sergeant inside the park.

"All right, Mr. Blay, here's the chief. You can explain your problem to him," said Sayers.

Blay owlishly looked the costumed MacKinnon up and down. He snorted. "You're kidding. This is your Chief of Police?"

"I'm Steve MacKinnon and, yes, appearances notwithstanding, I'm the chief." He produced his badge case from his haversack and held it open, so the activist could examine the shield and identification card. "Now, how can I help you?"

The reporter and camera operator moved closer as Blay began his sermon, "We represent the Northern Virginia Citizens' Alliance to Combat Gun Culture, and we've come to protest this idiotic celebration of guns. But your sergeant has violated our rights by refusing us the right to assemble. The First Amendment of the United States Constitution gives us the right to—"

"To assemble. Yes, I have some passing acquaintance with the Constitution so, please, spare me the rest of the lecture, because it has absolutely no bearing on the legality of this protest. The fundamental question is: Do you have a parade permit?"

Blay hesitated before answering. "Well, no."

"I didn't think so, or else I'd have remembered seeing the

application," said MacKinnon. "Any particular reason why you didn't apply for one?"

"Because you would have denied our application." Blay's voice quavered with bellicose self-righteousness.

"That's possible, but I guess we'll never know, because you didn't bother to play by the rules." MacKinnon spoke in a mild, accusatory tone, as if Blay were a small child caught in the commission of a petty offense. "If I also understand correctly, you want to come into this special event without paying."

"We have a right to assemble; a right to have our voices heard," said Blay.

"You're absolutely correct, and I wouldn't dream of infringing upon that right . . . so long as the exercise of your rights doesn't interfere with other folks' rights. But in order to get into the reenactment, you and your friends will have to pony up five bucks each, just like everybody else."

"But we have the right to assemble in the park."

"You bet. And you can assemble in the park, right after you pay the admission," said MacKinnon, flashing a wintry smile.

"And what if we refuse?"

MacKinnon's grin became wolfish. "And force your way in? Oh, that would be . . . imprudent. If you are silly enough to do that, I'll book you for criminal trespass and attempted theft of services. True, you'll be out of jail in a couple of hours, but the reenactment will be over by then and you'll have driven all this way just to sample the lunchtime haute cuisine of the Brookesmith County Gray Bar Hotel. I hope you like bologna sandwiches."

Blay studied the Chief of Police's blue eyes and decided MacKinnon wasn't bluffing. "But if we pay, we can protest?"

"To your heart's content, but not on the battlefield. You

see, unlike your organization, the hobby groups went to the trouble of securing a special events permit. They've reserved the park, and I'm certain you and your ethical associates wouldn't want to violate their rights, would you?" MacKinnon tried not to smile at the sight of Blay looking as if he'd swallowed something very unpleasant. "But, I promise I'll find a place for your group where you can be seen."

"You promise?" Blay said doubtfully.

"Cross my heart; hope to die; stick a needle in my eye," MacKinnon deadpanned. "Talk it over with your group and let me know what you decide."

While waiting for Blay, MacKinnon dug his pipe from his pocket and lit it. He hoped there weren't any anti-tobacco puritans nearby, for he definitely wasn't in the mood for another priggish lecture. Then MacKinnon noticed the reporter give a hand signal to her cameraman to pack up. It was obvious there wasn't going to be any violent showdown between police and protestors, so it was time for the video vultures to search out a fresh tragedy. MacKinnon thought it was pathetic that the unofficial motto of modern electronic journalism was, "If it bleeds, it leads."

Apparently there wasn't a surplus of spare cash among the demonstrators, or perhaps it was just too damn hot to stand in the sun, because, in the end, only five activists bought admission tickets while the rest scurried for the refuge of their air-conditioned cars. The chief led the weary group across the parking lot to a naked, grassy clearing just behind and downwind from a battery of four Union cannons. The artillerists watched in puzzlement as MacKinnon told the protestors that their demonstration would be limited to this small bit of grassland.

Blay wasn't happy with the location. "There isn't any shade here."

It was everything MacKinnon could do not to chuckle. "I know, but I thought that since you feel it's wrong for people to own handguns, you'd likely also believe that they shouldn't have artillery either."

"Those are real cannons?" Blay peered with astonishment at the big guns.

"Napoleon twelve-pounders—they'll throw a shell just about a mile."

"And it's legal for them to have cannons?" asked Blay in disbelief.

"Yup. Who needs an assault rifle when you own one of those babies?" MacKinnon replied. However, when he resumed speaking, his tone was stern. "Now, you and your people can stay here until the end of the reenactment, but remember what I said about behaving. If you start harassing anyone or interfering with the reenactors, you'll hit the pit so quickly your eyes will spin. Are you absolutely clear on that?"

Blay squinted up at the sun and grumbled, "We understand."

"Good. Enjoy."

MacKinnon then walked over to the cannons and found the battery commander, Bruce Putnam. The artillery officer, who in real life was a high-ranking executive in a major District of Columbia bank, frowned at the now-chanting protestors and muttered, "Mac, you mind telling me what we did to deserve this?"

"Sorry, Bruce, but I had to put them somewhere and, since they're here to protest against the ownership of guns, I thought they might benefit from being in proximity to your Napoleons."

"Do they have any idea of how loud the guns are?"

"Good God, I hope not." MacKinnon sounded worried. "It would spoil the fun."

Putnam's face brightened. "Oh! Now I get it."

"You're a bright fellow. I thought you might."

At that moment, a panting, tubby orderly with a face the color of raw beef jogged up and saluted Putnam. *The fellow looks bad,* thought MacKinnon, and tried to guess which the orderly would do first—deliver his message or succumb to heatstroke.

Finally, the messenger gasped, "Lieutenant Putnam, the colonel sends his respects and says you can open fire when ready."

"Sorry I can't stay for the festivities, Bruce," said MacKinnon.

Putnam grinned and waved farewell. As MacKinnon departed, he heard the battery commander shout, "Battery H, on my command: volley fire! Fire!"

The four brass cannons roared, belching forth flame and smoke. After a moment, the Confederate artillery replied, adding to the hellish din. As the gunners reloaded, MacKinnon could hear every car alarm for a half-mile shrieking in protest. Meanwhile, the stunned protestors were clutching their ears and gaping in disbelief at the thunderous guns. Then the activists were hidden behind a dense, drifting cloud of white smoke. *Problem solved,* thought the chief.

By the time MacKinnon returned to his company, the soldiers were standing in a battle line and awaiting the order to advance. It was the first battle for some of his new troops, so it was important that he provide some final instructions.

"All right, lads, since we have some fresh fish in the ranks, let's go over the rules one more time." MacKinnon had to shout to be heard over the swelling roar of battle. "First, be safe. This is a hobby, not a real war. Second, remember we're supposed to lose this first battle, so when it comes time to die or skedaddle, do it and resist the temptation to behave like

Rambo. Third, shoot high. Even though we're firing blanks, the gunpowder puts out a sizeable flame and you could very easily set someone on fire. Any questions?"

There weren't any, and a moment later a mounted officer reined his skittish horse to a halt before the two hundred soldiers of the attack force. His shouted command echoed down the line: the battalion would advance into the woods. The drums and fifes began to play "Old 1812" and the color guard took up its position in front of the Union column.

MacKinnon drew his saber from its scabbard, pointed the blade toward the trees, and shouted, "Company D, forward march!"

With each step into the woods, modern reality seemed to evaporate. From behind, MacKinnon could hear the grunts and curses of his men as they struggled through the thorny vines and brush. Ahead, he could hear gunfire and, more distantly, a brass band playing "The Bonny Blue Flag" with more zest than skill.

This is the best part of reenacting, thought MacKinnon. The cacophonous noise, brambles snagging your uniform, the bitter taste of gunpowder, and your vision reduced to an ever-narrowing field of fire; it was as close as he could ever come to experiencing the violent universe of the Civil War soldier. Furthermore, there was a delicious tension in knowing that all hell was going to break loose in the next few seconds. It was a giddy, breathless sensation akin to the way he used to feel just before kicking in a door to serve an arrest warrant on a murder suspect, but with one vital difference: there wouldn't be any genuine bullets fired here.

Suddenly, there was a crash of gunfire to the right and slightly to the rear. Peering through the underbrush, MacKinnon realized that his company had overlapped the end of the Confederate line and hadn't yet been spotted.

Well, he thought, *I know we're supposed to lose, but there's no law against giving the Rebs a good hiding first.* Quickly halting the troops, MacKinnon had them perform a right wheel so that they could attack the Confederates on their unprotected flank. By now, his soldiers could also see the exposed Rebel line and were already picking out their targets.

"Fire by company! Ready! Aim! Fire!" bellowed MacKinnon, the last command obliterated by the simultaneous discharge of twenty-three Springfield muskets.

"Load!" MacKinnon shouted. "Quickly! Fire at will!"

Through the cloud of smoke, MacKinnon saw that two Confederates had deigned to die—one man catapulting himself backward as if he were a refugee from a Spaghetti Western. But the remainder of the Rebel force was apparently wearing imaginary Kevlar body armor, for they were still standing despite the withering volley. The battle scenario called for the Union troops to push the Confederates from the woods and then be swept away by a crushing counterattack. Yet these Rebels were apparently ignorant of the script or had chosen to defy it, because they showed no inclination to withdraw from their position.

Weiss leaned close and shouted, "Christ almighty, does it get any more farby than this? You could drive wooden stakes through their hearts and those fellas still wouldn't die."

"So, what else is new?" MacKinnon yelled back in disgust. "But if we push them, you know there'll be hand-to-hand combat and I'm not in the mood to take one of our boys to the emergency room because some buffoon wants to play World Wrestling Federation. Let's fall back a little and go around them."

MacKinnon ordered his men to withdraw and again set them in motion through the woods. Some of the other Union units had done the same, and the scattered battle line assembled on the far edge of the grove. MacKinnon halted his men and dressed their ranks. Ahead, he could see gray troops servicing the artillery and a fresh battalion of Confederate infantry deploying from marching column into battle line at a jog. On the hill behind the Rebel force were thousands of spectators.

"All right, boys, this is where we get smashed. When we come out of the trees, they're going to let us have it, so run or die. Don't behave like those morons back there," commanded MacKinnon as he motioned with his saber in the direction of the bulletproof Rebels who were still resisting in the woods. Then he turned to face the clearing, pointed his sword at the Confederate ranks, and yelled, "Company D, charge bayonets!"

The troops of the front rank extended their four-foot-long Springfields forward into the charge position, while the rear line shifted their rifles to "port arms." All along the line, the men were shouting with a fierce, barbaric joy.

"Forward, march!"

They emerged from the woods at a steady tread and, although MacKinnon knew this was a sham fight, he could still feel an unpleasant sensation in the pit of his belly as he saw the Rebel troops prepare to deliver a volley. Every time he did this, it imparted a renewed reverence for those long-dead soldiers who had struggled to overcome their terror and advance into the maelstrom of the battlefield.

"At the double quick, boys! Charge!" MacKinnon screamed.

The troops let out a fresh guttural shout and began to trot toward the waiting Rebels. They were about thirty yards away from the Confederate line when MacKinnon heard someone shout, "Fire," and the cosmos dissolved into the roar of muskets, flickering tongues of yellow flame, and dense clouds of white smoke. He pitched forward and fell heavily to the ground. Perhaps if his troops saw his example, they too would become mock casualties. A moment later, MacKinnon lifted his head slightly and glanced to the rear. Half his company was down and the rest were fleeing back into the woods in a panicked rout. He'd never been so proud of his men.

The Confederates were also impressed with the slaughter, and several of the Secesh troops complimented MacKinnon and his men as they carefully stepped over the fallen men on their way to the woods, in pursuit of the broken Union force. He heard the eerie wail of the Rebel yell, and their opponents were gone. Then MacKinnon began to quietly curse. His digital phone was ringing again.

Rolling onto his side, he pulled the phone from his haversack and snarled, "MacKinnon."

"Uh, Chief, sorry to call again, but we've got a real big problem." It was Sayers again and he sounded excited.

"What is it, Ron?" MacKinnon said, recovering his temper.

"It looks like there was some kind of accident over in Crumper's Woods," said Sayers.

MacKinnon climbed to his feet. "What kind of accident?"

"They just found a dead reenactor."

"Sunstroke or heart attack?"

"Neither," replied Sayers. "It's a woman, and Officer Williams says it looks like she's been shot in the head."

Two:

The Unknown Soldier

Sayers led MacKinnon into Crumper's Woods. Seen from the air, the gloomy forest was vaguely crescent-shaped and extended from northwest to southeast across some three hundred acres. About a third of the timberland was inside Brookesmith Park, where the trees grew almost to the river's edge. For countless summers, Crumper's Woods had been a popular retreat for young and ardent couples. As a consequence, local wags had nicknamed the forest "Humper's Woods."

As they walked along the trail, MacKinnon elected to use his phone rather than Sayers' radio to call police dispatch, for there was no point in announcing the shooting over the airwaves just yet. He'd been a cop long enough to know news agencies routinely monitored police radio frequencies for just such messages and that inevitably would result in reporters descending on the woods, eager for video of the body and a maudlin sound bite. This, in turn, meant MacKinnon would have to juggle the resources of his already overburdened force to protect the death scene from the journalists. *Their ignorance is my bliss,* thought MacKinnon.

Connecting with Julie Crozier, the police dispatcher, MacKinnon asked her to contact the County Coroner and advise him of the death. Next, the chief requested a camera and evidence-collection kit be brought to the scene. Julie acknowledged the instructions, but reminded the chief that all his officers were currently working traffic control, so there would likely be a delay before she could find someone to deliver the forensic equipment.

After proceeding on the path for about two hundred yards, MacKinnon and Sayers at last came upon Officer Deshawn Williams. The young African-American patrol cop was jotting down information in his notebook as he questioned a wan-faced and bearded white reenactor wearing the uniform of a Confederate general. *Now there is a sight from a white supremacist's worst nightmare,* thought MacKinnon with a silent chuckle.

Williams had been the only new officer thus far added to the force under MacKinnon's tenure as chief and the hiring had created a slight stir among the citizens, for he was the first African-American cop to ever wear the badge of the Talmine Police. Some of the white residents were certain Williams had been hired to satisfy imaginary racial quotas, while a few from the minority African-American community were equally suspicious that Williams was a token who'd be driven from the department in short order. MacKinnon had heard all the conspiracy theories and was wryly amused. There was only one reason he'd hired Williams, and that was because the former Marine military policeman had the potential to someday be a very good cop.

"Morning, Deshawn. What do we have here?" asked MacKinnon.

"Morning to you, Chief. Got a dead woman—looks like one gunshot wound to the head. A *big* gunshot wound," Williams replied. He pointed toward a human form lying on the ground about fifteen yards away.

The corpse was imperfectly concealed beneath a mound of sassafras branches and blackberry brambles, but enough of the body was visible for MacKinnon to see the victim was dressed in a Rebel uniform. An accidental shooting, he wondered? In spite of all the strenuous safety precautions taken by event organizers, it occasionally happened, for there was no way to completely safeguard against human idiocy. Indeed, MacKinnon had witnessed a hobbyist shot and wounded with an "unloaded" pistol at the Gettysburg reenactment back in 1998.

Well, we'll know presently, he reflected, *but if she was the victim of an accidental discharge, can anyone say, "Seven-figure, wrongful death lawsuit?"*

"And who is this gentleman?" MacKinnon inclined his head toward the reenactor.

"Mr. Carnes, Joseph Carnes. He found her," said Williams.

"There was nothing I could do. I thought about trying CPR but . . ." Carnes let the mournful sentence hang.

"I'm certain you did everything you could, sir," MacKinnon said. "Mr. Carnes, I'd like to talk to you in a few minutes, but can you excuse us for a moment?"

Stepping cautiously to avoid obliterating any shoe impressions, the trio of cops approached the body and MacKinnon crouched to take a closer look. The woman lay on her back with her head tilted slightly to the right and upward, as if flinching to avoid a blow. Her right arm was draped over her chest and the left was extended away from the body at about a forty-five-degree angle. A Confederate forage cap rested on the ground just above her head, like a deflated gray halo.

Next, MacKinnon examined the woman's face. She was a Caucasian female, approximately twenty-five years old, with light brown hair and dark brown eyes. The orbs were dull, and peered into nothingness. MacKinnon had sometimes heard eyes referred to as the windows of the soul. If so, it was obvious that nobody was home at this house.

He shifted his gaze to the pathetically fake beard and moustache that hung from the woman's left ear. It wasn't uncommon for female reenactors to rely upon makeup and false whiskers to disguise their sex on the battlefield. Sometimes the effect was quite convincing, but more often it looked ludicrous. These whiskers belonged in the latter category. Up close, the counterfeit beard wouldn't have deceived a blind man, but perhaps at a distance the woman might have passed for a male.

The cause of death was instantly identifiable. There was a large and roughly circular hole just above her left eye. *The wound is certainly too big to have been caused by a modern rifle or pistol,* thought MacKinnon. Peering more closely, he saw there were powder burns and black stippling around the gory crater; unmistakable evidence the murder weapon had been discharged very near the victim's head.

"Sweet screaming Jesus," murmured Sayers. "What do you think did that?"

"Whatever it was, the round was low-velocity because there doesn't appear to be an exit wound," MacKinnon said thoughtfully, as he bent further to examine the visible portion of the back of the woman's head.

"Black-powder gun?" asked Williams.

"That would be my guess, but we'll have to wait for the autopsy and chemical analysis of the powder residue to be certain," MacKinnon answered. Since black powder burned more slowly than modern gunpowder, the discharged bullet traveled at a relatively low speed. This translated into a reduced potential for a through-and-through wound. He added, "Of course, even if I'm right, it isn't much help at the moment."

Talmine was a peaceful place; therefore, it had been nearly two years since he'd last scrutinized a victim of violent death, yet MacKinnon was surprised to discover his observational skills were still keen. Little things about the body began to catch his eye.

For starters, the victim's face was abnormally pale, which indicated that the process of postmortem lividity was well underway as her blood drained down to the lowest parts of the body. *This is strange,* thought MacKinnon, since lividity usually took some time to become noticeable. It also forced him to abandon his original theory that the killing had occurred sometime during the reenactment battle. She'd expired before the combat, a fact that also decreased the chances that the death was the result of an accident.

Reaching down, MacKinnon touched the woman's cheek. The flesh was cool. She'd been dead for at least an hour or more. *No, it didn't happen during the battle, because she's been here a little while,* deduced MacKinnon.

He stood up to resume his visual inspection and noted another peculiar element: the victim's dark gray uniform looked almost brand-new. This meant she was probably a novice reenactor, because one of the first things hobbyists did was trash their uniforms to attain the begrimed appearance of a seasoned campaigner. Her coat was a Richmond Depot shell jacket, MacKinnon noted, worn over light blue Federal trousers—a familiar combination among Rebel hobbyists recreating units from the Army of Northern Virginia.

Yet, the chief realized that the victim's uniform wasn't complete. Although his view was somewhat obscured by the foliage and the position of her body, he could see that the only equipment worn by the victim was a new, white-canvas haversack. If the woman had been participating in the reenactment battle, she should have been wearing a cartridge box on a leather shoulder strap and a waist belt to carry her bayonet and pouch for percussion caps, but there were no signs of those items. *Nor did she carry a canteen, which was a damned odd thing to do in this heat,* thought MacKinnon.

The longer he looked, the more perplexed MacKinnon grew. Another thought intruded: *if she was an infantry reenactor, and the uniform indicated she was, where was her rifle? Had it been stolen? And if so, was it the murder weapon?* He glanced again at the large gunshot wound and wondered if the hole hadn't been caused by a .58 caliber, one-ounce, lead Minie bullet. MacKinnon was impatient for answers, but it was too early to speculate.

It was quiet in the woods, and then he heard a mockingbird somewhere overhead begin a melodic repertoire of birdcalls. The victim's shoes were the final, incompatible piece to the puzzle. Instead of authentic leather brogans, she wore black tennis shoes. Try as he might, MacKinnon couldn't imagine any of the fanatically authentic Confederate reenactment companies allowing someone this painfully counterfeit to fall in among their troops. She would have been laughed out of camp.

"You want me to check her pockets for ID?" asked Williams.

"No. The first lesson in Homicide one-oh-one is that we don't start moving the body until we've taken our crime scene photographs and the coroner's had a chance to take a look," MacKinnon replied.

"Homicide? Isn't it possible this was an accident?" asked Sayers.

"Considering it was almost a contact shot and how much effort was invested to hide the body, not bloody likely," said MacKinnon. There was a long pause, and then he continued, "Nope, this was a murder."

"So, do you want to call the State Police yourself, or do you want me to handle the notification?" Sayers was already pulling his portable radio from its belt holder.

"Neither, and stay off the radio about this business,"

MacKinnon replied. "Ron, is there anything in our rules and regulations where it's carved in stone that we hand all major felony investigations over to the State Police?"

"No, but we've always done it that way."

"Well, brace yourself, Sergeant, because I'm about to recklessly break with tradition. I don't know about you, but I think it's well past time the Talmine Police Department began taking care of their own business. And this dead young lady is definitely our business."

Sayers frowned. "The mayor isn't going to like it."

"Fortunately, that's not your concern, Ron." There was an unmistakable note of warning in MacKinnon's voice. Suddenly, he was weary of Sayers' continuous politicking for his job, particularly when the maneuvering occurred over the body of a woman with her brains blown out. MacKinnon continued, "I'm running this police department, and I'll be damned if we're going to continue to rely on the Virginia State Police to do our work."

Yet MacKinnon silently acknowledged that his decision was in part motivated by a less noble reason than serving the town's citizenry. Although one of his goals was to make his police force self-sufficient, it was also a fact that MacKinnon missed the intellectually challenging and exacting work of the homicide squad and was anxious to sink his teeth into a real investigation. He knew the motive was selfish, yet there was something inside of him that instinctively rebelled against the idea of handing the murder over to another agency, for it would have meant admitting failure. He'd never jettisoned an unsolved homicide case and wasn't about to start now.

Finally, he said, "Deshawn, have you ever managed a homicide scene?"

"No, sir."

"Well, there's no better time than the present to learn.

You're now my incident commander. Make a note of the time we arrived, and from this point forward I want you to keep a log of anyone who comes in or out of the crime scene."

"What about me, Chief?" Sayers asked plaintively. The sergeant had reconciled himself with amazing speed to the idea of investigating the murder, and was obviously crestfallen at being denied what he clearly considered was a reputation-enhancing job.

"I know you want to help, Ron, but you're too valuable to be used as a scribe and glorified gofer. I'm going to need you to continue handling the reenactment and coordinate other elements of the investigation while I process the scene," replied MacKinnon, hoping to salve the sergeant's injured feelings. "In fact, the first thing I need done is for you to personally contact the event organizers and tell them that the battle scheduled for two o'clock is postponed indefinitely."

"Should I tell them why?"

"Just say that there's been an accident and leave it at that for now. Next, I want the organizers to conduct a roll call of all the Confederate units. If there's anyone missing, male or female, I want to know instantly. Finally, I want all the troops from both sides to remain in their camps. I don't want anyone leaving the park until we've had a chance to look at their IDs and take their information down."

"There are over eight hundred reenactors here," Sayers bleated.

"Which also means about eight hundred black-powder firearms, any one of which could be the murder weapon—so, we've got to talk to everyone. Oh, and one other thing: ask the organizers for all the event registration forms and, if they get balky about it, seize them as evidence. We're going to want to match that information with the data we collect from the ID cards. Welcome to the wonderful world of homicide investigation, Ron. Are we having fun yet?"

Shaking his head in disbelief, Sayers departed, promising to keep MacKinnon advised of his progress.

MacKinnon turned to Williams. "This guy Carnes, what do we know about him?"

"Got a New York DL," said the patrol officer, opening his notepad. "It's valid, and I ran him for warrants. He's clean in Virginia and through NCIC."

"What else?"

Williams consulted his notes. "He lives in some town called Saugerties. I guess it's up the Hudson about a hundred miles from New York City. Anyway, he's thirty-five and says he owns an antique shop there—Carnes' Antiques and Collectibles."

"Imaginative name. What did he say happened?"

"The *Reader's Digest* version is that he came back into the woods to take a piss, because there were too many people in line for the port-a-johns. He thought he heard a shot, but didn't think anything about it since there were guns going off all over the place. Anyway, he found her a little later. He says he got close enough to see she was dead and then ran to find a cop."

"Which was you." MacKinnon squinted back toward the Confederate camp in the park. The tents were just barely visible. "Unless he's excessively modest, that's a mighty long way to walk when nature is calling. What would you say, two hundred yards? And there are any number of big trees between here and the camp. Why come out this far?"

"I wondered about that too, so I asked him. He told me that he ran into a man and a woman back along the trail and had to go farther into the woods."

"Now, that is interesting. Come on, let's go talk to Mr. Carnes again."

MacKinnon reintroduced himself to Carnes and asked the witness to repeat his story. The account was unchanged and MacKinnon said, "This shot you heard, could you tell what direction it came from?"

"I wish I could tell you it came from here, but I can't. In fact, the more I try to remember, I want to say that the sound actually came from over that way." Carnes pointed to the north and away from the body. "But there was a lot of gunfire, because the battle was still going on."

Well, that cleared one thing up, thought MacKinnon. He'd been instantly doubtful of Carnes' initial claim of hearing a gunshot from the scene, for he already knew the woman had been dead before the battle began. The error was understandable, however. Witnesses wanted to be helpful, and that assistance sometimes included the insertion of imaginary elements. "And these people you saw along the trail, the man and woman, which way were they coming from?"

"Out of the woods, from this direction," said Carnes.

"How were they dressed? Were they reenactors?"

Carnes shook his head. "No, they had on modern clothing. The lady was wearing a blue skirt and white blouse, and the guy had on khakis and a polo shirt."

"What color was the shirt?"

"Maroon or red. I gave your officer descriptions of both of them."

"Were these people doing anything you considered out of the ordinary?"

"No." Carnes chewed his lip for a moment. "They were just walking along, but they were in a hurry. She may have said something to him, but I wasn't close enough to hear anything."

Hurrying after committing a murder? *It is an interesting lead,* thought MacKinnon, *so long as this witness isn't mistaken or lying.* Maybe it was unfair to again automatically doubt Carnes, for he seemed earnest and his story made sense. But after twenty-one years in police work, MacKinnon had learned that when it came to violent death, his fellow creatures were either very bad witnesses or very good liars. It was a jaundiced view of humanity and an element of his personality he wasn't very proud of, but it was an attitude borne out by bitter experience. MacKinnon would therefore withhold final judgment on the statement until all the facts were in hand.

MacKinnon asked, "Do you think they saw you?"

"No. You see, I'd just gotten my trouser buttons undone when they came along the trail, so I ducked into some bushes," Carnes said with an embarrassed smile.

As they talked, the chief conducted a surreptitious inspection of Carnes and was impressed with his authentic appearance. It was obvious that quite a bit of time, research, and money had gone into the creation of the uniform. The antique dealer wore gray woolen trousers tucked into knee-high cavalry boots and a gray frock coat with three stars on each erect, buff-colored collar. The ornate loops of gold braid embroidered on both the sleeves signified this was the uniform of a high-ranking officer. Carnes wore a brown belt with a saber on the left hip, and on his head was a gray kepi decorated with an intricate cruciform design of gold embroidery.

But there was no holster and pistol, MacKinnon noticed, not that the absence was necessarily odd; historically, many Confederate officers had limited their personal armament to swords. He gestured to the man's costume and said, "Dynamite impression. Are you portraying a generic Reb officer or someone in particular?"

"Actually, I'm supposed to be D. H. Hill," Carnes replied.

An intriguing choice of historical personage to portray,

thought MacKinnon. The brother-in-law of Stonewall Jackson, David Harvey Hill was an intelligent, skilled, and aggressive soldier, but he had also possessed an acid tongue and proclivity for dissension that had caused a series of conflicts with his superiors. Indeed, the willful Hill had even managed to infuriate the normally serene Robert E. Lee.

MacKinnon found it a little odd that the congenial-appearing Carnes should have elected to portray such a sarcastic and disagreeable character. It caused him to wonder if there might be more to the witness than first met the eye. He decided to find out. "Kind of strange that I've never seen you at other reenactments."

"Not really. Most of the events I attend are in upstate New York and New England. I have a very low tolerance for Interstate 95, and Virginia is a long drive. In fact, the only reason I'm down here is because I'm mixing business with a little pleasure."

"That's right, Officer Williams told me you were an antique dealer." MacKinnon decided it wouldn't hurt to confirm the witness's background. "I'd imagine you would specialize in Civil War artifacts."

"Obviously," said Carnes, and although MacKinnon wasn't certain, he thought he heard a tinge of D. H. Hill-quality sarcasm in the voice. "But I don't limit myself to them."

"Still, maybe you can offer me a little professional advice," said MacKinnon.

"I'll try."

"I've got a Clauberg I'm thinking about selling."

Carnes did not hesitate. "What model?"

"Eighteen-forty."

"Heavy cavalry saber?"

"Right."

"With scabbard?"

"Yes. The blade isn't in bad shape, but the scabbard has a few dings in it."

"Any history?"

"It belonged to an officer in the One-fifty-seventh New York and I bought it from the family."

"And you're sure it isn't a repro?" asked Carnes. "You can't believe the number of excellent quality fakes I've seen in the past few years."

"I had it examined by two experts and they both said it's genuine."

"I'd be hesitant to decide without actually seeing it, but five hundred dollars wouldn't be out of line," Carnes said thoughtfully. He reached into his coat pocket, removed a business card, and handed it to MacKinnon. "If you do decide to sell, give me a call first. I'm always on the lookout for sabers, and I'll offer you a fair price."

"Thanks. I'll keep that in mind," said MacKinnon, taking the card.

He was now satisfied that Carnes was either an antique dealer or an aficionado of historical edged weapons. The witness hadn't fumbled even for a second in identifying the Clauberg as a Civil War-era saber and had suggested an accurate price for the sword. Indeed, based on his own Internet research, MacKinnon had already decided to list the saber for sale at six hundred dollars and accept the best offer above five hundred.

There was a moment of silence and then MacKinnon said, "It wasn't war, it was murder." The words were D. H. Hill's, delivered in 1862 to describe a bloody Confederate defeat during the Peninsula Campaign near Richmond.

Carnes nodded and looked mildly surprised. "Malvern Hill. You know your history, Chief."

"And this isn't war, it's murder," MacKinnon said, inclining his head toward the body. “Have you ever seen this woman before?”

“Never.”

“Did you kill her?”

If the first question had surprised Carnes, the second poleaxed him. “I don’t know what you’re trying to say, but if you’re accusing me of murder, you’d better go damn carefully, Chief.”

“No, I’m not accusing you of murder, Mr. Carnes,” said MacKinnon, noting with satisfaction that he’d been right—there was a solid framework of iron behind the witness’s affable façade. “The fact is, I don’t have the slightest idea of who did this, and I want to eliminate you as a possible suspect. I’m sorry if you took it wrong, but I expect to ask that question to a number of people before I’ve finished.”

Carnes looked slightly mollified. “Well, of course I didn’t kill her.”

“That’s good to hear. I have one other request, however.”

“What’s that?”

“I’d like Officer Williams to pat you down for weapons.”

“I don’t suppose it would make a difference if I refused to cooperate.” There was an arrogant amusement in Carnes’ voice.

“No, it wouldn’t. In fact, there’s an excellent chance it might be painful,” said MacKinnon. “Williams, do the honors.”

Williams patted Carnes down and announced, “He’s clean.”

“Chief, if I were you, the first thing Monday morning I’d enroll in whatever passes for a junior college down here and start learning a new vocation,” Carnes said as he smoothed the wrinkles from his coat.

“Oh, dear. Here comes the ritualistic threat to sue me.”

"Laugh if you want, but when my attorney finishes with you and this town, you won't have a job," Carnes snarled. "Where I come from, the police aren't allowed to manhandle law-abiding citizens."

"Sorry I didn't show the appropriate amount of abject terror, Mr. Carnes, but if I had a dollar for every person who threatened to sue me over the past twenty years, I'd be a very wealthy man." MacKinnon examined the business card. "Thank you for your time and, if I do have any further questions, can I contact you at this number?"

"If you do, you can expect to hear from my lawyer even sooner," Carnes called over his shoulder as he stalked down the trail.

Once the witness was out of earshot, Officer Williams asked, "You don't think he did it, do you, Chief?"

"Too early to tell. Right now, I'd say no, but . . ."

MacKinnon's telephone rang. It was Sayers, reporting that the battle had been postponed and the event organizers were personally checking the attendance rosters against the troops actually present. He had the registration forms and also informed MacKinnon that messengers had been dispatched to all the reenactment units with instructions to remain in camp until further instructed. But there was trouble looming. Mayor Jean Dumfries had learned of the postponement, and the despot of local politics was unhappy. Worse yet, she wanted to talk with MacKinnon.

Suddenly, Dumfries' contralto voice was on the line. "Chief, I don't mean to micro-manage, but I hope you realize what you're doing."

"Yes, ma'am. I'm investigating a murder."

"And you're also disrupting an event that cost this town and its business community thousands of dollars in advertising and merchandise."

MacKinnon rolled his eyes. "Yes, well, I apologize for that, Mayor, but it wasn't my idea for someone to kill this woman."

"Sergeant Sayers told me about the body. Are you sure it wasn't an accident or suicide?"

"There's a very tiny chance it could be an accident, but based on my experience, I don't think so. And as for a suicide, it's kind of hard to shoot yourself in the head and then hide the gun."

"So, why haven't you called the State Police?"

"Because we're perfectly capable of conducting the investigation ourselves. Besides, even if we called the State Police, I can't possibly imagine their detectives ruling this anything but a homicide, and then they would do precisely the same things I'm doing, only an hour later."

"But is it possible to stage the second battle?" Dumfries' question sounded more like a command.

"Mayor, please listen carefully. Someone is shooting real bullets out there, and now we've got a dead body. Maybe we have some loon who thinks he's still fighting the Civil War; or it could be we've got someone here who really doesn't like the Confederate battle flag; or perhaps it was just a horrible accident. Right now, I don't know which it is, but if you decide to stage that battle, are you prepared to personally take the chance the shooter isn't going to do it again?" MacKinnon didn't wait for her answer. "Look, I know the merchants are going to be hurt by this and I'm sorry, but you hired me to protect the citizens of this community and that's precisely what I'm trying to do."

"You really feel there is a risk of another shooting?" asked Dumfries.

"I wouldn't want to bet the town treasury against it happening. And that's what we'll be doing, if we let those fellows start blasting at each other before we get some idea of what happened here. If we have another person shot, the civil lawsuit will kill us."

"Fine. I support your decision for now, but you and I are going to talk later." Dumfries' tone was chilly.

When Sayers returned to the phone, the sergeant had one other bit of information: Victoria was on her way out to the woods with the requested camera and evidence-collection gear. MacKinnon commended Sayers for his swift work and disconnected, but no sooner had the chief hung up than the phone rang again. This time it was Dr. Allen Morris, the Brookesmith County Coroner, who said that he would be en route from his home and expected to arrive in about a half-hour, barring delays in traffic.

"Chief, your wife is here," said Williams.

Weighed down with a knapsack, a metal camera case, and a plastic fishing tackle box that contained the evidence-collection equipment, Victoria MacKinnon was the most beautiful porter the chief had ever seen. Although she was nine months older than MacKinnon, Victoria's appearance was far more youthful than that of her husband. With bright blue eyes and cherubic features, she had the sort of friendly face that provoked strangers to stop her on the street and ask for directions. Moreover, Victoria was endowed with a splendid, buxom figure, the sight of which, even after six years of marriage, still utterly entranced MacKinnon. This afternoon she wore her shoulder-length curly blonde hair pinned up in back, and was dressed in white shorts and a green tee shirt decorated with appliquéd teddy bears marching in single file across her chest. *Lucky bears,* thought MacKinnon.

He remembered the first time he'd met Victoria, back in 1993. He had visited the SDPD crime analysis office in search of statistics on a series of assaults against gay men in

Balboa Park. As Victoria typed the search parameters into the computer, she'd caught him, *flagrante delicto,* trying to look down her blouse. Instead of being offended and threatening him with a sexual harassment complaint, Victoria had giggled while his face turned red and he stammered an apology. It was the inauspicious beginning of a romance.

At the time of their meeting, MacKinnon had been a grim and increasingly callous cop who'd come to view life as a brief and pointless stroll through a madhouse. Too many years of investigating drive-by shootings, babies shaken to death, husband and wife murder-suicides, and senseless dope killings had, like an attack of dry rot on the wooden framework of a house, slowly undermined his capacity to believe that any human endeavor had genuine meaning. MacKinnon's creed back then was as simple as it was ugly: You were born, you died, and, if you were lucky, you didn't hurt too much between those two events. He'd been a proud cynic, never realizing that he'd come to treasure his caustic attitude as a miser did his wealth.

Furthermore, after one calamitous marriage, MacKinnon had solemnly sworn that he would never be so damnably foolish as to fall in love again. As a consequence, the early months of the relationship were tempestuous and often tearful. Sometimes MacKinnon tried to envision how his life would have turned out if Victoria hadn't persevered, and the exercise unfailingly chilled him.

Yet Victoria had persisted, for she briefly glimpsed in MacKinnon something he'd gone to a great deal of effort to conceal behind a carefully crafted façade of cold cynicism: a kind and tender heart. And being stubborn and a little selfish for the hidden MacKinnon, Victoria had employed every gentle weapon at her disposal to erode that bitter mask. In the end, he succumbed to her flower garden, teddy bears, golden retrievers, and cats rescued from the animal shelter, slowly learning that it was possible to live a joyful life.

"Hi, honey. Hi, Deshawn," Victoria called.

"Morning, Mrs. MacKinnon," said Williams as he rushed to take the equipment from her hands.

"Hi, sweetheart." MacKinnon gave his wife a kiss on the cheek. "What are you doing out here?"

"Well, I'd stopped by the station to see if Julie needed some lunch, and she told me what was happening," answered Victoria. "The poor girl was in panic mode. There were no cops available, and she didn't know how she was going to get this stuff out to you, so I volunteered. And I knew you hadn't eaten, so I brought you some lunch."

"Remind me to put you in for a citizen's commendation."

"Hungry, Deshawn? I brought plenty." Victoria removed a nylon knapsack from her shoulders and produced a ham and cheese sandwich inside a Zip-Lock plastic bag.

"No, thanks."

She handed the sandwich to MacKinnon. "Eat this while you have a chance. From what I hear, you're going to be out here all afternoon, and you know how you get when you don't eat."

MacKinnon pretended to be annoyed. "No, how do I get when I don't eat?"

"Grumpy. Very grumpy. Everybody knows that," Victoria blithely replied.

MacKinnon felt his cheeks begin to flush, because it was true.

Williams began to chuckle, then cleared his throat, and said that he would go to the head of the trail and await the arrival of Dr. Morris.

"You embarrassed Deshawn," said MacKinnon.

"I embarrassed you. Deshawn thought it was funny," Victoria replied. "So, what do you have?"

"A One-eighty-seven. No, check that," said MacKinnon, realizing that from long experience he'd accidentally cited the California penal code definition for murder. "A Section Thirty-one. Doesn't quite have the same ring, does it?"

"No. I've got another question."

"I'm all ears."

Victoria tugged at his sleeve. "It's ninety-three degrees, the humidity is eighty-four percent, and I'd like to know why my husband is wearing a woolen coat."

"I'd forgotten all about it. Jesus, no wonder I'm roasting." He quickly undid the buttons and removed the frock coat.

Victoria looked toward the body. "This is your first homicide victim since we left San Diego. Are you going to bully everyone until you solve it?"

"I don't bully," he meekly protested.

Victoria fixed him with those lustrous eyes and said, "Darling, I love you more than life, but the truth is you are an obsessive tyrant when you're working a murder, and the poor people of Talmine are about to discover that fact."

Three:

The Residues of Murder

In her new life, people knew Victoria MacKinnon for her membership in the local quilting club, volunteer work at the animal shelter, and lately, a decadent hazelnut and Frangelico cheesecake that had won an honorable mention at the Brookesmith County Fair. Most residents were vaguely aware that she'd worked at the San Diego Police Department with her husband, but few realized that she was a veteran crime analyst whose diligent work had helped solve a number of major cases. Only MacKinnon knew that his wife, in her own way, was just as skillful an investigator as he was. For that reason, he was glad she'd have the opportunity to see the crime scene before he began to collect the evidence.

"Any idea of who she is?" asked Victoria, glancing at the body.

"Not yet."

"She's so young—not that there's a good age to be murdered, I suppose. Any decent leads?"

"Detectives baffled—vow arrest," said MacKinnon, citing the stock American newspaper headline for stories about unsolved murders.

"That bad, huh?"

"Yep. Right now, the only thing we have is that the guy who found the body claims he saw a man and woman coming from this direction, but our witness doesn't exactly inspire my confidence."

"How do you mean?"

"I don't know. There were times when I had the unmistakable feeling that I was being jerked off, and that he knew that I knew it, and it amused him." MacKinnon opened the metal case, took out the Polaroid camera, and checked the picture counter. "Who says miracles never happen? There's actually a full cartridge of film in this thing."

"No miracle. I checked it before I left, and it was empty," Victoria said. "In fact, I couldn't find any Polaroid film in the equipment closet, so I stopped at Harmon's on the way and picked up a fresh box. The Town of Talmine owes us fourteen dollars and twenty-seven cents."

"Thanks. Was there plenty of thirty-five mil?" MacKinnon bent low over the body and focused on the woman's face. "Say cheese."

"Honey, has anyone ever told you that you can sometimes be really gruesome?" teased Victoria.

"Not in the last hour."

Victoria shook her head and smiled. She'd been around homicide cops long enough to know that most successful investigators were those who maintained a sense of the absurd in the face of violent death. Sometimes it was the only defense against despairing over people's infinite capacity for cruelty. She said, "To answer your question, there were three rolls of color, thirty-six exposures each."

"Ought to be enough." MacKinnon shot a picture and then turned to his wife. "What are you doing the rest of this afternoon?"

"I was going to finish the new bed ruffle, but I have this feeling my plans are about to change." But Victoria did not sound very disappointed.

"Oh, yeah, as if you'd rather play Susie Homemaker than help with a homicide. Vic, my love, I know you better than that. Wild horses couldn't keep you from getting involved, and I intend to take full advantage of your unsavory interest in murder." MacKinnon took several close-up photographs of the victim.

"You've always known how to sweet-talk me."

MacKinnon handed her three photographs. "So, how would you like to do me two very big favors?"

"You want me to take these pictures to Ron, so he can start showing them?"

"Correct. Maybe someone will recognize her or, more likely, that hideous beard. Then I'd like you to go to my car—it's parked near the gate—and get the laptop and some spare disks from the trunk." MacKinnon handed her the keys. "While I take care of processing the scene, I need someone to start making a list of every reenactor who's here today."

Victoria was dazed. "Honey, you're talking about interviewing hundreds of people."

"Not full interviews," he countered. "But I do want a complete database on all the reenactors. I need someone to check ID cards and see if anyone wants to cop to being a member of the Manson Family."

"The someone being me?"

"I'll get you some help." MacKinnon tried to sound encouraging. "Sayers and whoever he has available can collect the information, and I think Officer Venard keeps a laptop in his patrol car, so that should speed things up. I'll want personal information and some sort of listing on their gun . . . caliber, serial number, and so forth. Oh, and one other thing . . ."

"I knew there would be."

"I'm going to call Sayers and have him put out a request to the reenactors, asking them to loan us any pictures or videotape shot on the battlefield today. In spite of the rules, there are always lots of cameras out there, and maybe we'll get lucky and find something useful in one of the pictures. As an enticement, we'll offer to pay for the development of the film and mail it to them when we've finished."

"Which also means you'd like me to create an evidence log for the film," said Victoria. From her long experience in police work, she knew that evidence was of absolutely no value, unless there was a documented chain of custody.

"Right. Take a couple of property receipt books, and I'll get someone to bring you about two hundred paper lunch sacks for packaging the film and cassettes."

"Two hundred?" Victoria said with a mock wail.

"I'm hoping there'll be more, but two hundred will be a good start."

"So long as you aren't the one filling out all the forms," Victoria reminded him.

"One of the perks of being the chief." He reached out to gently tug on a ringlet of her blonde hair. "And I'll remind you of the inequity of the work assignments when I'm camped out in my office, writing a seventy-page report."

Victoria looked at the body, and suddenly there was no trace of humor in her voice. "You're going to catch the guy who did this, aren't you, Steve?"

"I'm gonna try."

"Good, because I hoped we'd left this behind when we left California."

"People get murdered in small towns too."

"But not our small town," said Victoria. "Okay, I'm going to go get to work. Love you, darling, and Ron will call if we come up with anything."

"Love you too," he said as he watched his wife go back down the trail.

After calling Sayers with the fresh instructions, MacKinnon went to work. However, processing this crime scene was going to be a little different from the homicides he'd worked in San Diego. In the past, he'd had a team of evidence technicians to do the painstaking and boring work so vital to a murder investigation. However, in Talmine he would have to accomplish most of the tasks himself.

He took a small magnetic compass from the evidence box and aligned himself to north. Then he took a steno notepad and pencil and began to sketch an overhead representation of the body and surrounding terrain. These drawings would later be paired with measurements, to create a detailed diagram of the crime scene. On the sheet, he also noted the wind direction, weather conditions, and an estimate of the air temperature.

Preliminary notes completed, he loaded the 35mm camera and took a series of orienting photographs of the dead woman. However, before approaching the body to take close-up pictures, he conducted a thorough inspection of the soil adjoining the corpse, looking for shoe impressions and any other evidence that needed to be photographed or otherwise collected before he began disturbing the ground around the victim. Despite the thorough search, he found nothing.

Next, he took a series of detailed photographs of the victim from all directions. When he finished, he began to carefully remove the foliage covering the body and placed each branch separately inside plastic trash bags. He didn't consider it likely, but there was the faint chance the State Police's crime lab could recover some trace evidence from the vegetation or perhaps a latent fingerprint from the leaves. *And as long as you're wishing, why don't you send a letter to Santa asking for a pony for Christmas,* he sourly reflected, knowing that, both figuratively and literally, he was clutching at straws. Officer Williams and Dr. Morris arrived as he completed the second set of photographs of the now-uncovered victim.

With his plump, florid face, white hair, and merry eyes, Allen Morris was the archetypal country doctor, lifted straight from an early and treacly Norman Rockwell illustration. Yet appearances were deceiving. A retired Army officer, Morris had spent the final portion of his twenty-eight-year military medical career assigned to the Walter Reed Army Medical Center in Washington DC. Nor did Morris dress the part of a high-ranking county official. Today the coroner was togged out in faded blue jeans, a yellow King's Dominion Amusement Park souvenir tee shirt, battered tennis shoes, and a ratty Washington Redskins ball cap.

Morris wiped his moist brow with a handkerchief. "Hello, Steve."

"Al."

"You were lucky to get me. Wife and I were about to take a ride up to the mall in Fredericksburg." Morris set his briefcase down. "Patti told me she was going to make me live in the garage, if I didn't get some new clothes."

"Can't say I really blame her. Every time I see you, I expect to see you pushing a shopping cart full of aluminum cans, with a 'Will Work for Food' sign attached."

"You have absolutely no idea of how strange a complaint about my appearance sounds, coming from someone dressed as if he were a refugee from a John Ford western," Morris retorted. "Besides, after wearing that goddamned Army monkey suit for twenty-eight years, I'm entitled to dress the way I please."

"Which is like a skid row transient. Maybe I'll feel the same way when I become elderly."

"Steve, you can kiss my wrinkled ass," declared Morris, but there was no rancor in his voice. MacKinnon and the coroner were actually very good friends who happened to revel in the adult male ritual of exchanging casually malicious insults. Morris opened his notebook. “Do we have a name on the victim?”

“Jane Doe, for now,” said MacKinnon.

“Time of discovery?”

“Right around eleven-ten.”

Completing his notes, the coroner approached the body and whistled tunelessly as he surveyed the corpse. Then, retrieving an old Polaroid camera from his briefcase, Morris snapped several pictures of the body and then pulled on a pair of latex gloves. The coroner knelt to examine the woman. Peering at the gaping hole, he gently inserted his thumb into the orifice and grunted. At last he said, “Somebody was using a street howitzer. This is almost big enough to have been caused by a shotgun, except the perimeter is too round and regular and the back of her head is still here. Any idea of what caused it?”

“My guess is a black-powder weapon,” said MacKinnon. “Possibly a .58 caliber rifle slug from a Springfield or Enfield.”

“My, the things you reenactor fellas do in the pursuit of realism,” said Morris with a dry chuckle. He took the dead woman’s chin in hand and tried to rotate the head. “This happened a little while ago. You’ve got the beginnings of rigor.”

MacKinnon nodded. “I figured as much, but I didn’t want to touch her until you got here.”

“I appreciate that.”

Working deliberately, Morris searched the woman’s uniform. He found nothing until he reached into the right front trouser pockets and removed a key ring. He handed his discovery to MacKinnon.

There were only two keys on the ring, both for a GM auto or truck of recent make. Attached also to the ring was a clear plastic sheath that housed a small cardboard tag bearing the logo of a rental car agency. MacKinnon examined the tag and saw that it contained handwritten information about a vehicle, a red 2002 Pontiac Bonneville with Virginia license plates.

"Anything else?" he asked.

Morris frowned. "Nothing."

MacKinnon tossed the key ring to Williams. "Deshawn, run the plate for wants and registration."

"I'm on it," Williams said eagerly.

Looking down, MacKinnon saw that Morris had completed his inspection of the woman's front pockets and was about to turn the body. He knelt to assist the coroner, but as they started to roll the woman onto her right hip, MacKinnon said, "Whoa! Hang on, Al. I'll need a picture of that."

"Of what?"

"The haversack. See? It's been turned inside out." MacKinnon pointed to the inverted canvas bag. "Up until now she'd been lying on it, so I couldn't see it."

"So, somebody searched her," said Morris.

"And from the position of the body, we can safely assume that it happened before she was shot." MacKinnon took several photographs of the haversack.

"Robbery?" Morris sounded doubtful. Other than domestic assault and the occasional bout of fisticuffs at the local bar, violent crime wasn't a common facet of life in Talmine.

"You tell me what else it could mean."

Williams' radio squawked. The officer acknowledged the message and then turned to MacKinnon. "Chief, the car comes back to the rental office at Baltimore-Washington International. No wants, and it isn't reported stolen."

"BWI?" questioned MacKinnon. "Tell Julie to get me the phone number for their customer service desk there, and make sure she understands I don't want some eight-hundred number that shuttles me into voice-mail hell."

"Yes, sir."

The information about the vehicle was promising. Unless the car rental agency decided to be balky over the release of information over the telephone, MacKinnon would soon know who had rented the Pontiac. The chances were fairly good it was the murder victim and, if so, it meant that she'd have presented a driver's license and credit card at the time she signed the rental paperwork. Having her name would be the first big step in moving forward with the investigation.

A pair of EMTs from the local ambulance service arrived, pulling a metal gurney behind them. Once Dr. Morris was finished with his preliminary examination, they would transport the corpse to the coroner's office in the basement of the County Government Building in downtown Talmine. One of the attendants unfolded a heavy, zippered, plastic bag while the coroner filled out the identification tag.

Williams approached and said, "Julie's working on getting you the number, Chief, and there's a Maryland cop here who'd like to talk to you."

"Maryland? He's just a little far from home isn't he? Did you check his badge and department ID?"

"Yes, sir, and the info from his DL." Williams tapped his notebook, indicating he'd committed all the data to paper.

"Good. What does he want?" asked MacKinnon.

"He says he might have some information for us."

MacKinnon glanced at the newcomer, who might as well have been wearing a button on his chest that read, "off-duty cop." The man wore a military-style haircut, a sparse moustache, blue jeans, and a baggy Baltimore Ravens football jersey. Although the light was subdued in the woods, the cop concealed his eyes beneath a pair of rainbow-tinted, reflective Oakley Blades. At first, MacKinnon considered telling Williams to get the man's phone number, so that he could talk to him later. One of the favorite pastimes of off-duty cops was "helping" at a crime scene, and the chief had better things to do than provide entertainment for a kibitzer. But the facts—the detective was from Maryland, and the car keys were from BWI—were far too synchronistic to be ignored. MacKinnon believed in many strange things, but this sort of coincidence wasn't one of them. Finally, he said, "Let's find out what he knows."

A moment later, Williams made the introductions. The cop removed his sunglasses and extended his hand. "Chief MacKinnon? I'm Detective David Benham, Sharpsburg PD."

As they shook hands, MacKinnon inspected the investigator more closely. Although Benham looked to be only in his thirties, there were baggy furrows beneath his watery eyes, his complexion was sallow, and there were the beginnings of a fine rum-blossom floral display on his nose. It didn't take the observational skills of Sherlock Holmes for MacKinnon to deduce his visitor was overly fond of the bottle.

"What can I do for you?" asked MacKinnon.

There was a forced casualness to Benham's next words. "I was working an embezzlement case and ended up down here on a rolling surveillance. I lost the guy in the crowd, and then I heard that someone got shot in the woods, so I thought I'd check with you."

"Sharpsburg. That's over a hundred miles from here, isn't it?"

"About. Why?"

"It's just kind of odd for a rolling surveillance to go that far, and across state lines. And it would have been nice to let us know you were operating in our town."

"You're right, and I'm sorry for not checking in, but this is kind of a special case." Benham was nervously apologetic. "There was a big loss, and we've had a lot of pressure from city hall to keep the investigation quiet. The victim was a local charity organization, and the guy who we think embezzled the money is the brother-in-law of one of our local politicians."

"Why aren't you following your suspect now?"

"Like I said, I lost him in the crowd, so I decided to keep an eye on his car," Benham replied. "But then I saw the ambulance arrive and heard some people saying that the battle was postponed because someone was found shot in the woods. Your officers wouldn't tell me anything, so I assumed the worst and came to check and see if the victim is my mope."

"Sorry to disappoint, but our victim is a woman," said MacKinnon, wondering how much of Benham's story to believe. It was possible, but unlikely, that the alcoholic detective was the sort of dedicated cop willing to spend his weekend following a crook who, if MacKinnon had learned anything about the protective nepotism of small-town politics, would never be listed in a criminal indictment. Furthermore, there was something about Benham's demeanor that suggested suppressed panic.

"Oh, that's a relief," said Benham, sounding anything but relieved. "Could I take a look at her anyway?"

"Sure, why not?" MacKinnon nonchalantly replied, thinking: *Fact is, pal, I want you to look at her, because you're way too hinky.* He led Benham to the victim, who was being roughly shoved inside the zippered plastic bag. MacKinnon called to the attendants, "Hold up there a second, guys. I need this man to take a look at her."

The woman's long auburn hair had fallen over her face, and MacKinnon reached down and gently pulled it to the side. He glanced sideways at the Sharpsburg cop, who had replaced the sunglasses over his eyes. MacKinnon thought: *my friend, if you don't know this woman, then I'm Pee Wee Herman.* Finally, he asked, "Ever seen her before?"

Benham bent forward a little to look at the body. "No. I wish I could help, but no."

"Are you sure?"

"Of course I'm sure," Benham replied a little crossly.

MacKinnon was certain he was lying, but also knew that, at the moment, he couldn't prove it. Furthermore, the untruthfulness didn't necessarily mean that Benham was the killer. MacKinnon was also certain of what would happen if he detained Benham and took him to the police station for a more intense interrogation. The detective would deny any knowledge of the woman, eventually invoking his constitutional rights, and walk from the station a free man because there wasn't a scintilla of evidence to hold him. So, rather than confront the lying witness now, MacKinnon decided to wait until he had more information. For the moment, he'd allow Benham to believe that Talmine's Chief of Police had a room-temperature IQ and had swallowed the flimsy tale hook, line, and sinker—that is, until he could prove otherwise.

"Thanks for taking a look, and now I suppose you're going to have to get back and see if your crook's car is still there," said MacKinnon.

"Yeah, I guess I'd better." Benham looked away from the body and once more took his sunglasses off.

"But if you find he took off, maybe you can give me the plate and description, and we can put out a BOLO," said

MacKinnon. "My cops won't stop it, but we can let you know if it's still in town."

"Uh, I've got the license plate written down in my notebook, back in the car." Benham wore a deer-in-the-headlights expression.

MacKinnon did his best not to sound chiding as he said, "You can call my dispatcher with the plate, but I'm certain you can give me the description. After all, you followed the car all the way down here from Maryland."

"Well, sure. It's a nineteen ninety-seven Mitsubishi Eclipse, blue in color," said Benham. "I'll let your dispatcher know the plate before I head back home."

"Good. One other question: Are you carrying?"

"Not on me. It's in my car."

"Just to eliminate the possibility of bothersome questions from a defense attorney a year from now, do you mind if I make certain of that?"

"Go for it. I've got nothing to hide," said Benham.

It took every ounce of control MacKinnon possessed not to roll his eyes. It was an immutable rule of police work that whenever someone loudly announced they had nothing to hide, it was usually the exact opposite. Benham raised his arms as Williams searched him. It was as the Sharpsburg cop claimed; he was unarmed.

"And what kind of gun do you have in your car?"

"A Glock .40 cal."

"Nice gun. I'm going to send Officer Williams with you to take a look at it and write down the serial number." MacKinnon wasn't asking. The statement was a command.

"Not a problem, and if it turns out my guy is in the wind, I can give your officer the license plate," Benham said.

"That would be excellent. I want to thank you for your assistance, Detective Benham. Have a real safe drive back to

Maryland, and good luck with your case," said MacKinnon, shaking the other's moist hand.

Before leaving with Benham, Officer Williams handed MacKinnon a small sheet from his notebook. It contained the telephone number to the car rental agency at BWI. But before he could call, Dr. Morris approached. Behind him, the ambulance attendants dragged the body-laden gurney down the trail.

Morris motioned with his head toward the departing Benham. "What's up with him?"

"Other than the fact that he's scared, lying, and quite possibly the killer, nothing," replied MacKinnon.

"And you're letting him go?" Morris was incredulous.

"For now. But I think he's bright enough to know that I didn't buy his bullshit and that our next conversation isn't going to be as sociable as the first." MacKinnon pulled his pipe from his pocket and knocked the bowl against his heel to dislodge the ashes. "So, when can we do the autopsy?"

"I take it you'd prefer not to wait until Monday?"

"I want to get it done by tomorrow at the latest."

Morris pretended to be annoyed. "Damn. That means I can't go shopping for clothes with Patti tomorrow, either. How does tomorrow morning at ten sound?"

"I'll be there. And you know, you could still make the mall this afternoon."

"Right. My friend, the paperwork on this body is going to take me at least until the Orioles-White Sox game is over," said Morris, showing a sly grin. "See you tomorrow, Steve."

As the coroner followed the attendants down the trail, MacKinnon called the car rental agency and was gratified not to hear a recorded message that began with the words, "Your call is important to us . . ." Instead, he actually got a living human being, who made it clear that she was not going to tell him anything about the Pontiac, other than the fact it had been rented earlier that morning. MacKinnon patiently explained that he was a cop investigating a murder, and the woman just as patiently explained that company policy prevented her from giving out personal information over the telephone. He was told that if he wanted to see the car rental paperwork, MacKinnon would have to drive up to BWI, and that it probably wouldn't hurt to have a search warrant. It was infuriating, but MacKinnon could understand the need for such rules. After all, anyone could call and identify themselves as the police to get confidential information.

MacKinnon heaved a sigh of frustration and disconnected from the call. It looked as if he would be driving up to Baltimore tomorrow after the autopsy. With the body gone, he decided to give the surroundings one final search. MacKinnon began by inspecting all the standing timber in the immediate vicinity for bullet holes. If the killer had fired more than one round and missed, a projectile might still be recoverable in one of the surrounding trees. But he found nothing.

Next, he got on his hands and knees and began examining the ground near the area where the body had lain. Shifting some decaying leaves, MacKinnon spotted a small, dull white fragment. At first he thought it was a piece of the woman's skull, but when he looked more closely, MacKinnon recognized the object. It was a broken acrylic fingernail. In fact, he could even identify the type: it was a French manicure, one of Victoria's favorite nail styles. Closing his eyes, MacKinnon visualized the victim's hands and recalled that she'd worn no polish on her nails, which meant this half-inch segment of acrylic fingernail belonged to someone else.

Well, that's just what I need, a piece of anomalous evidence to compound the confusion, thought MacKinnon as he photographed the nail. He knelt to collect the evidence and, when he stood, MacKinnon realized that the TV reporter and her camera operator had returned to the park and were videotaping him.

"Chief, I'm Alyssa D'Arcy from Channel Four news, Richmond."

"I know."

"Can you tell us anything about what happened here?" D'Arcy extended the microphone for his answer.

"Only that earlier today there was an apparent shooting death here in the woods and that we're investigating," said MacKinnon, lighting his pipe.

"Was it a murder?"

"I don't know yet."

"We've been told that the victim is a woman in a Civil War costume. Could the shooting be connected with the reenactment here in the park?"

"I don't know that yet, either."

D'Arcy frowned. "Do you know the identity of the victim?"

"Not yet."

"Do you have a suspect?"

"Not yet."

D'Arcy sighed and nodded to the camera operator, who lowered the device. "Jeez, Chief, give us a break here. This is worse than pulling teeth. Off the record, can you tell me anything else?"

MacKinnon smiled. "Ms. D'Arcy, it's a firm rule of mine to never speak off the record and, even if it weren't, I wouldn't do so now because I have a very low tolerance for sneaky reporters. The first time this stunt was pulled on me, you were probably still in grade school."

"Stunt? What do you mean?" D'Arcy tried to sound puzzled, but her cheeks had begun to turn cherry red.

"The stunt where you lower the camera, but keep the tape running so you can record my voice, in the hope I'll tell you something grisly or dramatic," MacKinnon explained in an amused tone. "Good afternoon, Ms. D'Arcy."

D'Arcy was wise enough to know she'd blown it and offered an apology to MacKinnon, who began to pack up the camera and evidence-collection equipment. As the journalists moved farther into the woods to shoot some more video, Williams jogged up and delivered two bits of information. The first was that the rookie cop had inspected Benham's pistol and felt it hadn't been fired recently. The second was that the Maryland detective reported that he seemed to have lost the license number of his suspect vehicle, but promised to call and provide the plate number when he got back to Sharpsburg.

MacKinnon snorted. "Yeah, I'll bet. How are things going in camp?"

"A lot of people in line, but it's moving pretty fast. Your wife and Venard are taking all the information down."

"And it will go even faster when you and I get over there to help. Grab those plastic evidence bags and I'll get the other stuff."

"Yes, sir."

Passing through the camp, MacKinnon saw long lines of reenactors, all waiting to provide their information to the Talmine cops. Victoria, seated behind one of the registration tables, was swiftly typing the data into the laptop. She looked up, flashed a weary smile, and said, "You owe me big time."

"Dinner at the Sutherland Inn?"

"It's a start," Victoria replied.

The harried Sayers saw him, and a look of relief appeared on the sergeant's face. Approaching, he said plaintively, "Chief, I hope you're here for good, because I'm about to blow a goddamn head gasket."

"Not enjoying your stint in charge, Ron?"

"Not today."

Knowing how Sayers coveted his job, it would have been easy for MacKinnon to say something sarcastic, but instead he said, "Well, it looks like you've done a pretty good job."

"Thanks, Chief."

Once Williams had helped him deposit the evidence and forensic equipment in the trunk of his patrol car, MacKinnon sent the rookie officer to assist Sayers. Meanwhile, he went to the tall, conical-shaped Sibley tent that was the event headquarters. Inside he found a collection of Union and Confederate officers and event organizers. There was a debate in progress over whether the rest of the event should be cancelled. One or two speakers wanted to proceed with the reenactment, but most were of the opinion that a resumption of the fake combat would be inappropriate in light of the shooting death.

Furthermore, if the battle flared anew, it would provide ugly fodder for the media, who already were disposed to portray the hobby of Civil War reenacting as a refuge for gun fanatics, closet racists, paramilitary cranks, and social misfits. For that reason, the rest of the event would be cancelled and they'd try again next year. MacKinnon knew that Mayor Dumfries and the local merchants would be furious with the decision, but he couldn't argue with the organizers' logic.

As he left the headquarters tent, MacKinnon's phone trilled. It was Sayers asking him to return to the registration tables. The sergeant reported that the search for witnesses had at last produced some slight success: two people thought they remembered seeing the uniformed young woman earlier in the day.

MacKinnon quickly made his way toward the parking lot

and soon saw Sayers. He was standing next to a pair of Union reenactors who were attired in the gaudy French-Algerian Zouave uniforms that were popular among some regiments during the early years of the Civil War. The soldiers' pants were navy blue and voluminously baggy, secured at the ankles by black leather *jambieres* and white canvas gaiters. Their waists were encircled in red sashes, and their snuggly-fitting and midnight blue coats were lavishly decorated with claret-colored embroidery. Each man also wore a dark blue fez, adorned with a dangling tassel of the same color.

The uniforms were magnificent, thought MacKinnon, *and utterly lethal on the modern battlefield.* Men wearing such brightly-colored apparel made excellent targets, which was one of the primary reasons so few soldiers wore Zouave uniforms by the war's end.

"Chief, I want you to meet Eric Niles and Wayne Bibbs," said Sayers, pointing to the men in turn. "They think they saw our victim sometime around nine this morning."

Niles was the younger of the two—perhaps in his late twenties—and he peered at the chief excitedly through the tiny, rectangular lenses of his replica 1860s eyeglasses. Bibbs looked to be in his mid-forties and wore a thick, brown beard with a shaggy soup-strainer moustache. There were twin red stripes on the older man's sleeves, indicating he held the rank of corporal.

"That girl is really dead?" Niles asked.

"Unfortunately, yes," replied MacKinnon.

"Any idea of what happened?" said Bibbs.

"It's a little early to speculate," MacKinnon said. "So, did you see that girl earlier today?"

"Yeah. At least I think so. We were—" Bibbs began, but he was interrupted by Niles.

"We were over on sutlers' row when we saw her. Well, actually, I saw her first," Niles said almost proudly. "God, remember that fake beard that Woody Allen wore in that old film, *Bananas*? She just looked so utterly farby I just couldn't believe it. I pointed her out to Wayne and we just laughed."

"Ever seen her before?" asked MacKinnon.

"Nope," said Niles.

"Never," said Bibbs.

"What was she doing when you saw her?"

"Just wandering around the tables looking at stuff," Niles replied.

"Which tables?"

"Those over there." Bibbs pointed toward a merchant's stall beneath a large tent canopy.

MacKinnon glanced at Sayers. "Ron."

The police sergeant nodded. "I'll go and show them the picture."

MacKinnon turned his attention back to the reenactors. "Was she alone?"

"Yeah, seemed to be," said Niles, and Bibbs nodded once in silent agreement.

"Did you see her talking to anybody?"

"No," both reenactors answered in unison.

"What happened after that?"

"Nothing. That's the last we saw of her," said Niles. "Right about that time, we split up. I headed back to camp because they were starting to sound assembly, and Wayne went to his car."

"Why was that?" asked MacKinnon, turning to the older man.

"I'd just bought a Model 1855 bayonet from one of the sutlers, and there was no way I was going to leave it in my tent during the battle." Bibbs flashed a rueful smile. "The last time I did something stupid like that, I had an authentic brass cartridge box plate stolen from my knapsack. There's just too many light-fingered guys out there, and the hell of it is that some of them are wearing blue uniforms."

"Which is a shame, but at the same time it's also kind of realistic," MacKinnon said. "We'd like to think that the soldiers were all heroes, but every regiment had its share of thieves."

"Yeah, and wouldn't it be nice if we could be really authentic and hang them by their thumbs, or make them march around wearing a wooden barrel when we catch them?"

"I'm afraid the Supreme Court would consider that cruel and unusual punishment," said MacKinnon with a chuckle.

"Hell, Chief, it ain't punishment unless it's cruel and unusual," Bibbs said sourly.

"Before I forget, back to the woman. Can either of you guys remember whether she was carrying anything in her haversack?" MacKinnon asked.

"I didn't notice anything, but then again the only thing I was looking at was that fake beard and those black sneakers," said Niles.

"Same here," said Bibbs.

MacKinnon hooked a thumb toward Bibbs' uniform. "So, what unit are you guys with?"

"Seventy-sixth Pennsylvania Infantry—the Keystone Zouaves," Bibbs replied. "Our group is headquartered up in Emmitsburg, but we've got members from all over northern Maryland and southern Pennsylvania."

"Well, I guess I'd better let you guys get on the road then," said MacKinnon. "You've got a long drive ahead of you."

Bibbs said, "Actually, most of us won't be going home until next weekend. Our company is doing our annual tour of the Virginia battlefields. We started down at Petersburg and we've been working our way north, camping out along the way. Tomorrow, we'll head up to Chancellorsville and go into camp. We're scheduled to put on a living history demonstration at the National Park for the rest of the week."

"Wow. You guys must be hardcore," MacKinnon said admiringly. "From what I've heard, the National Park people only let the most realistic units camp out on the battlefields."

"We try," said Bibbs with ill-concealed pride. "We've got a good bunch of guys."

"Gentlemen, thanks for your time, and in the unlikely event I have any other questions, I'll give you a call," said MacKinnon, shaking hands with both men.

By 4:00 p.m., nearly all of the reenactors had passed through the identification checkpoint, and no one else admitted to recognizing the dead woman from the photographs. Traffic was slowly flowing from Brookesmith Park, and in the parking lot glum tradesmen disassembled sales booths and loaded trailers with merchandise. Talmine's inaugural "Civil War Days" was an utter bust, and MacKinnon knew he'd be blamed for the failure.

With only a few people left in the park, MacKinnon gathered his personnel and briefed them on the salient facts about the shooting and investigation. Next, he assigned tasks. Officer Williams was to take a photograph of the victim back to the police station and make enough color copies to provide every Talmine cop and Brookesmith County deputy sheriff with a picture. A BOLO was broadcast for the Pontiac Bonneville, and MacKinnon instructed that if the vehicle was located, the cops weren't to touch it and that he should be notified immediately. Finally, the officers were also told to check the local motels, restaurants, and businesses to see if any of the merchants remembered dealing with a female dressed as a Rebel soldier.

At the conclusion of the briefing, MacKinnon said, "All

right, you all know as much as I do about this business. Does anyone have any suggestions or questions?"

Officer Keith Booth raised his hand. "Chief, if we see the vehicle moving, how do you want us to handle it?"

"Get a back-up unit rolling, call me, and get the car stopped. If it turns into a vehicle pursuit, you're authorized to follow that Pontiac to hell if need be. I want that car and whoever is driving it, but remember, I also want the driver in condition to talk," MacKinnon warned.

Officer Andrew Venard also had a question. "With all the guys shooting guns out there, could this have been an accident?"

MacKinnon grimaced. "I really don't think so, Andy. But if it was, there's a strong probability that you guys would have a new Chief of Police."

Four:

Storm Line

It was nearly 5:00 p.m. before MacKinnon and Victoria could leave the park. On the drive back, the chief telephoned Harmon's Drugstore and told the merchant that he was on his way over to drop off 143 rolls of film for developing. MacKinnon drove west along River View Drive and then turned left at the town's only traffic signal onto Old Tavern Road, the main commercial thoroughfare of Talmine. Traffic was still fairly heavy, and a considerable number of people were strolling along the sidewalks. Some waved at MacKinnon as he drove past.

And unlike back in California, the citizens are waving at a cop with all their fingers extended instead of just the middle one, thought MacKinnon. Even after nearly a year and a half, the friendly behavior was both slightly alien and refreshing.

Not so many years ago, Old Tavern Road had been a sleepy avenue lined with half-vacant and unkempt brick buildings, but the business district was slowly being restored to its former glory. Most of the structures had been constructed during the town's golden era, from the 1880s to the 1920s, when some of the wealthiest families of Washington, D.C. came to Talmine to escape the Capital's hellish summertime heat. Splendid homes were built, and a small but thriving commercial sector was created along Old Tavern Road. But the Great Depression hit and the suddenly no-longer-rich visitors stopped coming. Sixty years later, the moneyed—this time affluent, young professionals from inside the Beltway—had rediscovered Talmine and the old buildings had new life.

As in most small towns, the businesses on Old Tavern Road reflected the changing mores of American culture. There was Tinsdale's Bait, Tackle, and Hunting Supplies, established in 1926, and its neighbor, Video Addict, with a sign out in front indicating that Sega's newest celebration of bloodshed, carjacking, and dismemberment was available for rent or purchase. On the opposite side of the street was the old Sandbar Tavern, flanked on one side by the upscale Talmine Coffee Emporium and on the other by Byte Me, a computer sales and repair shop. Every time MacKinnon saw the last sign he winced, unable to fathom America's modern love affair with belligerent and tawdry expressions of sleaze. Indeed, if the chief ever caught someone vandalizing the business placard, he honestly didn't know whether he'd arrest the suspect or shake his hand in admiration.

On the next block was the Brookesmith County Courthouse, where MacKinnon would meet Dr. Morris the following morning for the autopsy. Fronted with tall Doric pillars and decorated with friezes of David slaying Goliath and George Washington receiving the surrender of the British at Yorktown, the Neoclassic building was beautiful, so long as you didn't look at the roof, thought MacKinnon. The satellite dish and array of radio antennae atop the courthouse were abominations.

Passing the Lord Sutherland Inn, Victoria said, "We aren't going to get in there tonight. There are people waiting outside for tables."

"Maybe we'll go tomorrow night, then," said MacKinnon as he parked the car outside the drugstore. "When we get home, let's just microwave some of that lasagna from last night and make a salad. It'll be fast and I don't want to waste a lot of time over dinner. I have some serious report-writing to do later this evening."

"Oh no, don't make me eat homemade lasagna," Victoria cried in mock despair. She could take or leave Belgian chocolates and steamed Maine lobster, but Victoria was a rabid devotee of pasta.

"Come along, sweetheart. The sooner we get these chores finished, the sooner we can have dinner." Getting out of the patrol car, MacKinnon opened the trunk and removed two shopping bags full of undeveloped film and disposable cameras.

He had always liked Harmon's Drugstore. With the American flag hung near the front door, polished wooden shelves, and the store's old-fashioned practice of marking the price on merchandise rather than relying on the ubiquitous digital barcode, a visit to the tidy shop was like stepping back in time about fifty years. You could still get a hand-scooped ice cream cone at the drugstore, and the most prurient periodical on the magazine rack was *Family Circle*. There were a few concessions to the new millennium, however. A new computer terminal stood on the pharmacy counter, and an ATM card scanner had recently been installed next to the vintage cash register.

Frank Harmon was handing a double-scoop cone of mint chocolate chip ice cream to a customer, when he saw MacKinnon and Victoria enter. Wiping his hands on a towel, he said, "Hi, Mrs. MacKinnon. Chief, did I hear you correctly on the phone just a minute ago?"

"That's right, Frank."

Harmon looked down at the two shopping bags. "And you want me to do a rush job on how many rolls of film?"

"One hundred and forty-three. And I need them done just as soon as possible, like tonight and tomorrow."

"Is this about the shooting in the park?"

MacKinnon nodded, unsurprised that the news had spread so rapidly throughout the town. "I'm hoping these pictures will help my investigation."

"The big store could probably get them to you just as quickly." The merchant's voice was downhearted. "The big store" was Harmon's disdainful euphemism for the new Food Lion on the outskirts of town. Since opening, the modern supermarket had cut into his drugstore's business.

"That's true, but for purposes of evidence control I want only one person to handle the film and I can't have these pictures getting mixed up with someone else's vacation snapshots," MacKinnon said. He didn't mention there was an ulterior motive. If he were going to spend about a thousand dollars of police department funds developing the film, MacKinnon would rather give the business to a small local merchant like Harmon than a corporate giant.

"I suppose you're going to want some sort of discount," Harmon said, sounding so much like the melancholy donkey, Eeyore, from the Disney cartoon of Winnie-the-Pooh, that Victoria had to cover her mouth for fear of giggling.

"The department will pay full price, Frank. This is a rush job, and I don't expect you to work extra hours and not be compensated." MacKinnon struggled to maintain a solemn facial expression. He too wanted to laugh, because Victoria often referred to the gloomy druggist as Eeyore and MacKinnon knew why his wife looked like she was strangling.

Harmon smiled cautiously and took the bags. "I'll get Karen to take over the counter while I get started on this. Can I call you when I get the first batch done?"

"You've got our home number, and we'll be up until at least eleven tonight," answered MacKinnon.

"You want me to call that late?" Harmon looked doubtful.

"Frank, I need these pictures as soon as possible."

"I'll get right on it, Chief," said Harmon. "Oh, and Mrs. MacKinnon, are you all right? Sounds like you've got something stuck in your throat."

MacKinnon took Victoria by the arm and began to lead her toward the door. "She's fine, Frank. Just allergies, that's all."

Once back in the car, Victoria whooped with laughter as MacKinnon halfheartedly told her to behave. Turning left onto York Avenue, they drove to the old two-storied brick building that was Talmine's "new" police station. Erected in 1927, and the former home of the town's Volunteer Fire Department, the most conspicuous architectural feature of the structure was the fire engine–sized garage door that had been inartistically converted into an exterior wall. But MacKinnon had worked in worse places. Indeed, prior to moving to a modern high-rise in the 1980s, SDPD's headquarters had been a musty and antiquated faux mission-style monstrosity, complete with bad plumbing and rats.

Entering through the back door, MacKinnon's first stop was dispatch, to check in and see if his officers had uncovered any fresh information on either the victim or the missing Pontiac. Julie Crozier had gone home and the new dispatcher was Kathy Sayers, wife of Sergeant Sayers. She said there was nothing new to report.

There was always a feeling of unspoken tension whenever MacKinnon conversed with Kathy, for she'd made no secret of her belief that her husband had been cheated out of the chief's position by a carpetbagger from California. Although she was always polite—in fact, punctiliously so—MacKinnon knew that when Kathy wasn't working, her favorite hobbies were producing and disseminating falsehoods about him and acting as an informant for Mayor Dumfries. In recent months, MacKinnon had been secretly branded a drunk, accused of misspending city funds, and now he was an aficionado of Internet kiddy porn, because he'd given his officers a training class on the subject. This last tale was so outrageous that Sergeant Sayers had nervously apologized for his wife's vicious behavior, but admitted that there was no guarantee he could stop any future episodes.

The only reason MacKinnon ignored the ugly rumors and endured the surreptitious campaign of character assassination was because Kathy was by far the best police dispatcher in the county. Officer safety and efficiency were more important to MacKinnon than his bruised feelings. Yet if he ever found someone with a similar level of dispatching ability, the next time Kathy Sayers slandered him, she would be looking for a new job.

While MacKinnon relieved Kathy for a bathroom break, Victoria began to transfer the evidence from the trunk of the patrol car to the closet that served as Talmine PD's evidence locker. Once Kathy returned, MacKinnon told her that when he had the evidence secured, he was going home, but he wanted to be called immediately if anything came up. Going out to the car, he gathered up the rest of the evidence, the camera kit, and the forensic equipment, and carried them upstairs. Before closing the storage room, he selected ten videotapes at random, placed them in a bag, and logged the evidence out for examination.

"For your viewing entertainment," he said, holding up the large paper sack. He knew his own shortcomings, and one of them was a lack of patience for the vital but frustrating task of analyzing and making sense of minute and seemingly unrelated pieces of information. So he would rely upon Victoria, who loved puzzles, to review the videos and photographs.

"I can hardly wait." Victoria glanced downward meaningfully. "How was the witch today?"

"Full of cloying courtesy, as usual."

"You know, one of these days I'm going to knock that smirk right off her lying face."

"Sweetheart, she isn't worth getting upset over. My guess is that most folks, including Ron, know that Kathy is a two-faced liar. Remember she grew up here, and you don't develop that kind of talent for backstabbing overnight. And if someone actually believes her stories, I can't help that, and I'd only play into her game by responding to her. Now let's go home and get some dinner. I'm not the only one who gets grumpy when I haven't eaten."

Victoria sighed heavily. "Okay. But I still think you should fire her."

"I will when I have someone to take her place."

"I could dispatch."

"I know, and I have absolutely no doubt you'd do a great job. But think of how that would play to the locals, if I fired a hometown girl and replaced her with my wife. Besides, I like having you at home, doing all that foofy stuff like quilting, tending to your flowers and baking cinnamon bread. That was the entire purpose of this expedition to Virginia."

Victoria frowned and said, "I know. But damn it, I don't like her sniping at you."

"Honey, nothing can hurt me, so long as I know that you're on my side." MacKinnon hugged her and then pulled her toward the stairs. "Smile at Kathy as we go by. It'll drive her nuts."

A few minutes later, they pulled into the driveway of their home on Braxton Street, in the western section of Talmine. It was a neighborhood of large nineteenth-century homes and theirs stood mid-block, about fifty yards from the river. Late at night on the porch, MacKinnon could hear the soothing murmur of the rolling waters, a very different noise from the blustery rumble of Pacific Ocean waves. This evening however, the only thing he could hear was the joyous sound of their golden retrievers, Rob Roy and Noel, barking from within the house.

Getting out of the car, MacKinnon paused to savor the sight of his home. Throughout his life he'd lived a California suburban existence in characterless tract houses and apartments that were truly little better than drab stucco-dabbed boxes. But this was a house. Built in 1897, it was a three-story Victorian Queen Anne, painted pale-blue with ivory trim, with a peaked garret and a wide porch. The lush front lawn was dominated by a huge willow oak and decorated with clusters of rose bushes.

It is amazing, thought MacKinnon. The house had been in sad shape when he and Victoria first saw it, but his wife had fallen in love with the forlorn old home and had convinced him that it could be reconditioned. At the time MacKinnon was frankly doubtful, but he'd been happily proven wrong. What's more, he'd been surprised to discover he actually enjoyed the restoration work and that he possessed a previously unsuspected talent with tools. Working on weekends and evenings, he and Victoria had invested hundreds of hours scraping off multiple layers of old wallpaper, painting the interior and exterior, refinishing the hardwood floors, and replacing the rickety stairway banisters. And once the structural work was finished, they'd labored to reclaim the weed-covered yard, planting a new lawn, flowerbeds, and Victoria's beloved rose garden. They'd toiled for nearly a year, but MacKinnon didn't regret a single second of the time invested. He was proud of his home.

Opening the front door, he and Victoria were nearly trampled asunder in a furry stampede of two dogs and five cats. It was past dinnertime, and the animals were pretending they were starving. MacKinnon fed the pets and then retired upstairs to change out of the woolen uniform and take a quick shower. Meanwhile, Victoria prepared dinner.

Fifteen minutes later he reappeared, wearing jeans and an old San Diego Padres tee shirt. He opened a caffeine-free Diet Coke for his wife and a bottle of Stone Indian Pale Ale for himself. Although it was still hot outside, he and Victoria elected to eat on the porch. In the shade, the temperature wasn't too bad, and it was fun to watch the neighborhood kids playing baseball in the street.

As they ate, Roly Polar announced his presence with a purring meow and began rubbing his body against MacKinnon's leg for tidbits. When the goodies weren't immediately forthcoming, the chubby white cat jumped up into MacKinnon's lap to get at the lasagna.

MacKinnon laughed at the cat and gently pushed him to the floor. "Oh yeah, like you really need lasagna. If you keep putting on the tonnage, we'll be able to enter you as a float in the Rose Parade."

Roly briefly glowered at MacKinnon and then went to pester Victoria who, being an easy mark, fed the cat a tiny fragment of melted mozzarella cheese from her fork.

MacKinnon watched the performance, "And you wonder why he's the size of a Hyundai."

"Roly's not fat. He's . . . fluffy."

"Uh-huh. The next time my gut hangs over my belt, remind me to use that excuse." Throughout most of his adult life, MacKinnon had struggled with his weight. For the past four years he had managed to keep his weight at 190 pounds, but he knew that the moment he stopped exercising and paying daily attention to his diet, he'd begin putting the pounds back on with depressing speed.

As they ate, MacKinnon brought Victoria up to date on what he'd discovered at the crime scene.

She took a drink of soda and cleared her throat. "This fellow from Maryland . . ."

"Benham."

"You want me to work up an information package on him?"

"On both him and Carnes, but it can wait until Monday."

"And when we get the pictures back, and tonight, when I'm watching the videos, just what precisely am I supposed to be looking for?"

"Four things." MacKinnon ticked them off with his fingers. "We want any images of the victim, the male-female team in modern clothes described by Carnes, the arrogant Mr. Carnes himself, and Benham."

"I don't have any pictures of Carnes or Benham."

"I know. Carnes left before you got there with the camera and I didn't want to hink up Benham, but I can provide good descriptions. Carnes is dressed as a Confederate general and Benham is wearing a white football jersey with the number four on it and looks like your classic alkie off-duty cop."

"He sounds cute," Victoria said. Neither she nor her husband could abide drunks, particularly if they carried a badge. "Any ideas about the acrylic fingernail?"

MacKinnon wiped his mouth with a paper napkin. "It could mean that there was a female accomplice. Or it might have been there prior to the murder and it's simply a bizarre coincidence that I found it."

"Well I'm impressed that you recognized it as a French manicure."

"Yeah. Frightening, isn't it? I guess it means I've got a terminal case of girl cooties."

"If it were a little darker and the neighbors weren't out, I'd give you some real girl cooties," said Victoria, leaning over to give him a moist kiss on the cheek.

"What a shame that I have to get to work," MacKinnon said. On more than one occasion they'd necked like teenagers on the porch swing, but unfortunately tonight there was no time.

However, before retiring to his office, he devoted a few minutes to throwing a tennis ball to Rob Roy and Noel. The dogs needed the exercise and, just as importantly, he needed the simple companionship of his golden retrievers. Returning to the house, he saw that Victoria was in the living room and was watching the first videotape of the reenactment.

"How's it coming?" he asked.

"I just started it, and I'm already starting to get motion sickness. The guy who shot this must have had cerebral palsy," groaned Victoria.

MacKinnon squinted at the jiggling image on the screen. "Or he makes music videos."

He kissed Victoria on the forehead and went to his office, trailed by Tagger, a sleek charcoal gray cat with silvery paws, and Rob Roy. The room was a haven of unalloyed masculinity in a home where the unifying decorative themes were angels, quilts, and teddy bears. Not that MacKinnon objected to Victoria's beloved country décor, but he derived a quiet satisfaction from the oak paneling, shelves packed with hundreds of history books, and Civil War artwork that adorned his office. His prize possession was the antique Model 1861 Springfield rifle mounted high on the wall behind his desk. The firearm, which was the standard weapon of Union infantrymen during the war, had been a present from Victoria last Christmas, and MacKinnon still marveled at how his wife had manipulated their budget to find the extra $2,700 he knew the gun commanded on the open market.

By choice, his study was the only room in the house where MacKinnon smoked his pipe, so he shut the door behind him and turned on the air filter. He switched on the computer and packed a pipe with shag while the system booted up. Meanwhile, Tagger curled up on the desk and Rob Roy made himself comfortable on the leather wingback chair.

Turning on the radio, MacKinnon frowned. The local classical station was playing a modern, atonal piece that seemed calculated to provoke a suicidal depression. He switched the sound system to the CD mode, and a moment later the speakers erupted with the barbaric and joyful sound of uilleann pipes, bodhrán, banjo, and fiddle playing "The Irish Volunteer," a bellicose song from the Civil War. *Much better,* he thought.

Settling into his chair, he logged onto the Internet and checked his e-mail. There was nothing but a brief message from an old coworker from San Diego PD, indicating he and his wife were going to be taking a vacation on the East Coast in late October and hinting that they'd like to stay with MacKinnon and Victoria for a few days. He would answer the inquiry later.

Before disconnecting from the Internet, he decided to check on one piece of Joseph Carnes' story. The mock Confederate general had claimed he was an antique dealer, and his business card listed both a physical address and Website. But neither meant that Carnes actually operated an antique store. False business cards were easy enough to have printed, and the building address might be nothing more than a mail drop. Furthermore, possession of a Web page didn't necessarily mean there was a genuine business to go along with it.

So rather than type in Carnes' Web address, MacKinnon conducted a search for listings connected with Saugerties, New York. He quickly found a Website dedicated to local businesses, and discovered the Hudson Valley town was an antique hunter's Mecca. Scrolling down the page, he found a listing for Carnes' Antiques and Collectibles on Partition Street and clicked on the icon. A few seconds later, MacKinnon was looking at a color photograph of the shop. The accompanying text indicated that the business specialized in American Civil War uniforms, documents and weapons. Carnes was indeed an antique dealer, but this information did nothing to dispel MacKinnon's vague distrust of the witness.

Disconnecting from the Internet, he accessed the word processing program and began to list the headings of the narrative: Origin of Report, Crime Scene, Victim Description, Witness Statements, Investigative Actions, Evidence, and Preliminary Observations and Conclusions. From long experience, MacKinnon knew he wouldn't finish the report that evening, but he could make a good start. And as he typed, he thanked a merciful God for the invention of the word processor, for he could remember what a demanding chore it had been to write reports on an old electric typewriter.

Just before 8:00 p.m., Victoria came into the office. She carried a steaming cup of decaffeinated coffee and put it on the end table near the window.

"Thanks, honey," he said, without looking up from the computer screen.

"You've got to pay the toll before you get it," Victoria said, leaning close to him.

Recognizing the underlying significance of teasing tone, he looked up. "Oh, and what might that toll be?"

"This." She leaned over and kissed him gently and then with greater ardor.

Deciding the report could wait a few moments, he responded to the kiss. The telephone rang and, much as he wanted to just let the caller talk to the answering machine, he knew he had to answer the summons. Victoria pretended to pout as he picked up the receiver. It was the dispatcher from the Brookesmith County Sheriff's Office.

"Chief MacKinnon? Sheriff Jarboe says he'd like you to come out to Wyndham Road."

MacKinnon visualized the location. Wyndham Road was a dirt lane in the woods about a half-mile south of the Talmine city limits. "That's off Addison Farm Road, right? What does he need?"

"He says he's found that Pontiac you were looking for."

"I'm on my way."

As he hung up the phone, Victoria said, "They found the car?"

"Yeah, gotta go."

"Wake me up when you get home."

Going into the upstairs master bedroom, MacKinnon quickly changed into his dark-blue police uniform, pinned the silver badge over his left breast, and strapped on his leather gun belt. From the top dresser drawer, he withdrew the large Smith & Wesson .45 caliber "Long Colt" revolver and snapped it into his vintage spring-loaded clamshell holster. His gun was a relic in an era when modern cops usually carried sophisticated, seventeen-round auto-pistols, but he knew that if he shot a suspect with the heavy hollow-point bullet, the victim would not be getting up.

Victoria met him at the front door and gave him a tight hug. "Love you, honey, and be careful."

"Love you, too. Be back in a little while."

Getting into this patrol car, he called police dispatch on the radio and advised he was en route to meet with the sheriff. He drove east along York Avenue through downtown, and stopped at the police station to retrieve the camera and forensic equipment. Returning to the car, he continued east on York and turned right onto Addison Farm Road. Before long, he was out of town and passing through woodland, interrupted with the occasional small field. In the darkness, he nearly missed the unmarked, narrow dirt track that was Wyndham Road. Turning west, he saw headlights about a hundred yards ahead.

There were two bronze-colored Brookesmith County Sheriff squad cars parked in the clearing, and both had their spotlights shining on the Pontiac Bonneville, which was partially hidden behind a ramshackle wooden shed. A deputy sheriff stood by the wanted car, filling in the blanks of a vehicle impound form. Sheriff Tom Jarboe approached as MacKinnon got out of his car. The sheriff was tall and lanky, with a receding hairline, and wore a tan uniform shirt and brown trousers.

"Howdy, Mac," said Jarboe. "Deputy Young found it and called me. Got a tow on the way."

"Thanks, Tom, and thanks again for the use of your deputies earlier today. It would have been a real mess without them."

"Glad we could help. Hey, I hear Jean Dumfries is thoroughly pissed at you."

"Does anything stay a secret in this town for longer than forty-eight hours?"

Jarboe chuckled. "Nope. Besides, from what I hear, Jean the Queen ain't trying to keep her 'concerns'—that's the word she's using—a secret. Mac, have you ever wondered why I didn't apply to be the chief? After all, I grew up here, and your job pays better than my sheriff's salary."

"Let me take a wild guess. Could it be your esteem for Mayor Dumfries?" asked MacKinnon. Suddenly, Jarboe's utter lack of interest in becoming the police chief of his hometown was less a mystery.

"I was wondering when you were going to figure that out. Ever since high school, Jean Dumfries has been like the Burger King customer from hell; she wants things her way."

"Yeah, I learned that after we pitted her girlfriend for DUI." MacKinnon hooked a thumb at the Pontiac. "You find anything worthwhile?"

"Forced entry on the driver's side and it's been hot-wired. But we didn't search the vehicle. Figured you'd want to get photos and prints before you started messing with it."

Jarboe may look like an archetypal rustic lawman, MacKinnon thought, *but he is a skilled cop.*

"Let me get some pictures, and then we'll take a look," MacKinnon said.

He loaded the camera and took a series of orientation photographs of the Pontiac. Then he saw a flash of yellowish light on the western horizon. A few seconds later, he heard the distant rumble of thunder.

"Looks like we've got some weather coming. Heard on the news there's a line of thunderstorms heading in this direction," said Jarboe, glancing skyward.

"Then we'll have to hurry."

MacKinnon walked around to the driver's side of the Pontiac and noticed that the triangular rear window had been broken out; one of the more common ways that crooks broke into cars. Turning his flashlight on, he saw safety glass scattered on the back seat, but there was no sign of what had been used to shatter the window. He shifted the flashlight beam downward along the side of the car, hoping to see some indication of latent fingerprints in the oblique lighting. There were no signs of prints, but something on the ground caught his eye.

MacKinnon muttered, "What's wrong with this picture?"

"What do you mean?" asked Jarboe.

"We've got broken safety glass on the ground, which means the window was broken here," MacKinnon replied.

Jarboe crouched low to take a better look. "You mean the suspect got into the car some other way, stole it, and then broke the window when he got here? Why would he do that?"

"My best guess is that he wanted to make us think it was a routine auto theft."

MacKinnon shifted the flashlight's beam to the steering wheel. Whoever had stolen the car was a pro. He or she had attacked the ignition system through the left side of the steering column. It was more than likely a screwdriver had been used to turn the ignition, but it was gone now. Then MacKinnon noticed something else. There was a slight yellowish sheen on the driver's door handle.

"That doesn't look good," he muttered.

He shot several photos of the Pontiac and then returned to his patrol car, got the evidence box, and opened it. Taking a cotton swab, he collected a sample of the residue from the door handle. Jarboe shined his flashlight on the swab as MacKinnon held it up to take a closer look.

"What is it?" asked Jarboe.

"Some kind of motor oil, which means the suspect wiped this thing down to destroy latent prints." MacKinnon tilted the flashlight to examine the driver's side mirror and grunted. "Whoever did this was very good. Your garden-variety crook doesn't usually remember to wipe down the mirrors. And I'll bet we'll find oil all over the interior too."

"Maybe a professional car thief?"

"If that were the case, this thing would already be loaded on a container ship bound for parts unknown."

Jarboe rubbed his balding head. "So, why run the risk of

being caught stealing a car, only to drive it a short distance and abandon it?"

The answer suddenly struck MacKinnon. "It only makes sense if the only reason he stole it was to take it someplace isolated like this to clean it for prints. But he couldn't take it too far, because he had to walk back to town."

"You think our killer is a local?" Jarboe's disbelief was obvious.

"It's a remote possibility, but not likely. I tend to think the suspect dumped the car and then went back to get his own."

"Makes sense. But why even mess with the car?"

"The only reason I can think of is that our suspect has his fingerprints in some sort of database. He knew that if we recovered any latents, we'd submit them for computer analysis."

There was another flash of lightning, this time closer, followed by a roll of thunder that reminded MacKinnon of the sound of a chipped bowling ball slowly tumbling along a wooden lane. Tree branches began to rustle as the wind rose. The storm was almost upon them. From Addison Road a fresh set of headlights appeared. It was the tow truck. MacKinnon quickly completed his photographs and then collected sample fragments of the broken glass as the rain began to fall. After the Pontiac was hooked to the tow truck, he instructed the driver to follow him to the police department's single-bay garage. It was the only place where the stolen car would be safe from the elements until he could properly process it for evidence.

"Well, good luck," shouted Jarboe as he buttoned his raincoat. "And remember one thing, Mac."

"What's that?" MacKinnon flinched as a jagged tracery of lightning arced across the sky. The rain was falling in earnest now.

"If Jean the Queen really decides to fire you, I can always use a good deputy," Jarboe said. His tone was light, but the message was not intended as a joke.

"That's good to know, Tom, and thanks for everything."

On the journey back to the police station, MacKinnon called dispatch and cancelled the BOLO for the Pontiac. Kathy Sayers acknowledged the communication and smugly advised that the mayor had just called. Jean Dumfries wanted him to come to her house for a chat as soon as he was finished. MacKinnon instructed the dispatcher to call the mayor back and tell her that he would be there in about twenty minutes.

After securing the Pontiac in the cramped police garage, MacKinnon went upstairs to the evidence room and retrieved the victim's car keys. He didn't expect to find any evidence in the trunk of the Pontiac, but needed to make certain before calling it a night. His diligence was spurred by the memory of isolated instances back in California when lazy cops had impounded a car, overlooked checking the trunk, and vital evidence or contraband remained hidden for weeks. Or even worse, a dead body within remained undiscovered, until the smell made its presence nauseatingly apparent. But as MacKinnon suspected, the trunk was empty.

He returned the keys to the evidence room and grabbed his raincoat from his office while upbraiding himself for not having the garment in his patrol car's trunk. By now he should have known that here in Virginia, unlike Southern California, you needed your raingear for more than three weeks out of the year. *What's more, when it rains here, it really rains,* thought MacKinnon, as he splashed across the parking lot to his car. The weather had driven everyone indoors, and downtown was quiet with only a few cars parked in front of the Sandbar. While driving west along River View Drive, he saw a blue-white spear of lightning strike Nail Keg Hill, followed by a geyser of sparks.

There goes the cable TV connection, thought MacKinnon, wondering whether that was a bad or good thing.

Jean Dumfries lived in the western section of town, just a few blocks from MacKinnon's home. In keeping with her status as the most successful realtor in the region, Dumfries lived in a large, modern three-level house on a low bluff overlooking the Potomac. Yet for all the money spent on the home, it was utterly lacking in charm—a Frank Lloyd Wright mutation on anabolic steroids. *Everything is too large, too sharply angular, and far too reminiscent of steak house architecture from the 1970s,* thought MacKinnon.

He drove up the inlaid-brick circular driveway, parked the car near the huge, rosewood front doors, got out, and rang the bell. A small dog began to bark wildly as the mayor's husband, Arthur Dumfries, opened the door while simultaneously attempting to keep the frantic Pomeranian from attacking MacKinnon's shin.

"Art! Don't you dare kick Duchess!" Mayor Dumfries' voice echoed shrilly from the living room.

"I'm not kicking her, darling. I'm just trying to keep her from biting the chief," her husband patiently replied. Art was an affable nonentity who worked as a realtor at Jean's office and had never quite reconciled his glory days as Talmine High School's star athlete with his current role as his wife's major-domo.

"Nonsense. Duchess wouldn't bite anybody."

"Yes, dear." Art closed his eyes and shook his head. "Come on in, Chief."

"Thanks, Art. Hey, are we going to see you Thursday?" asked MacKinnon. On Thursday nights, he and Victoria played on a slow-pitch softball team and Art was their power-hitting third baseman.

"Uh, we'll see," said Art noncommittally, which, translated, meant: that depends on whether or not Jean lets me, but probably not.

MacKinnon was ushered into the living room and Art excused himself. Although it was nearly 10:00 p.m., Jean Dumfries was still dressed for business. She wore a floral-print silk blouse over a beige skirt. She was seated in an armchair and her pose was deliberately, almost absurdly, regal. Indeed, MacKinnon wondered if he suddenly knelt before her whether the mayor wouldn't serenely extend her left hand, Cardinal-like, so that he could kiss her ring. It was pathetically funny how so many local politicians were compelled to behave as if they were members of the nobility.

"Chief, we need to talk," began Dumfries. "This has not been a good day."

"Worse for some folks than others."

Dumfries sighed. "I'm not insensitive to the fact we've had a murder. But it's my duty to look at the bigger picture. The merchants and Chamber of Commerce took a colossal hit today. This hasn't been a good summer season, and they were counting on the profits and publicity from Civil War Days. Wasn't there some recourse other than shutting down the reenactment?"

"No, ma'am, there really wasn't," said MacKinnon, resisting the urge to add something acerbic to the answer. Like most people, the mayor had no concept of the strict evidentiary requirements of a murder prosecution, so it was unreasonable to expect that she would understand his actions. He tried to explain. "Mayor, you only get one shot, just one, at processing a homicide scene, and if you mess it up, there's no going back to redo the work because everything is tainted. That means that even if you identify the killer, he'll likely never be convicted since the evidence is flawed. I don't think you want that sort of work from your police department, do you?"

"No, of course not. But I do have some questions about why you didn't call the State Police in to investigate." Dumfries tapped the wooden armrest of the chair with metallic-gray fingernails to emphasize her annoyance. "In the past, we've ceded authority to them."

"In the past, you didn't have anybody in the department who'd investigated major felonies. But now you do. And it was my understanding at the time I was hired that you and the council wanted me to make this force self-sufficient. Well, that's what I'm doing."

"Are you even close to solving the murder?"

"It's early yet, and we've got a few leads."

"What sort of leads?"

"Some physical evidence collected from the scene. Also, we've recovered the victim's car, and I'm hopeful that after I finish with the autopsy tomorrow, I'll be able to identify the woman." He tried to sound optimistic. "I'll be making a speed run up to BWI to collect some paperwork on the car."

"Fine. But I want you to remember something, Chief." Her tone was frigid. "You serve at the pleasure of the town council, and at this moment I'm not happy. Not at all."

"I won't forget, Mayor," MacKinnon said.

And you don't have to be a member of Mensa to know what that means, he thought as he left the home and stepped out into the pouring rain.

Five:

Body of Evidence

The following morning, Victoria and MacKinnon enjoyed their weekly ritual of reading the Sunday newspaper over coffee in the living room. Both still wore their nightshirts and were in their appointed spots: Victoria on the sofa with Noel, and MacKinnon in his recliner with Chairman Meow on his lap. Outside, the sky was clear, the sun bright, and it looked as if the day would be another scorcher.

"The comics are pathetic. In fact, they have been ever since 'Calvin and Hobbes' went away. Right, Chairman Meow?" said MacKinnon. Then he answered his own question in the low, sassy voice he attributed to the cat, "Yeah, the comics suck like a goddamn Hoover."

"Chairman Meow! Who in the world taught you that expression?" Victoria tried to sound indignant while giggling. Her memories of how grim MacKinnon had been during the early days of their courtship were difficult to reconcile with the cheerful man who now created goofy dialogue for his pets.

MacKinnon continued in the silly voice, "It was your husband."

"Well, he should be ashamed of himself for corrupting a sweet cat like you."

MacKinnon tossed the funnies on the coffee table and leafed through the paper until he found the sports section. When he spoke again, it was in his normal tone. "Thanks for diming me off, Chairman Meow. Now, let's see if this thing went to press before the West Coast scores were in. Padres and San Francisco, late. I guess we'll have to check the Internet to see how badly they were beaten."

"There's a story here that the Santa Ana winds are blowing back . . ." Victoria caught herself before she said "home." She'd lived her entire life in Southern California, and it was sometimes difficult to remember that they now lived on the opposite side of the continent.

"Kind of early in the year for that. Any brushfires?" MacKinnon asked. Blowing off the desert, the furnace-like Santa Ana winds often spawned huge blazes. As a San Diego cop, he'd evacuated residents and directed traffic at fire scenes, and he didn't envy anyone assigned that duty.

"A big one near Lake Elsinore." Victoria took a sip of coffee. "That's one thing I definitely don't miss about California."

"God, remember how mad you used to get when you came home and found your baskets of hanging flowers all scorched?"

Victoria grimaced. "And how it got so dry that you'd get static electricity shocks from touching the cats?"

"Well, that was fun in a sick sort of way," said MacKinnon, reaching out to scratch Chairman Meow behind the ear. The orange and white tomcat rolled onto his back. "And do you remember that time the ash coated everything, and it looked as if we were living downwind from Mount Saint Helens?"

"Kind of puts a thunderstorm into perspective." Victoria put the paper down. "So, you're going up to Baltimore after the autopsy?"

"Yeah. It's the only way I'm going to find out who rented that Pontiac."

"You said they might want a search warrant."

MacKinnon took a sip of coffee. "Well, I think I may have

found a way around that. Maryland State Police work the airport, and I'm going to use the auto theft angle to get them to seize the papers for me until I can get the proper mother-may-I paperwork."

Victoria smiled. "In the meantime, you'll have the information. Clever."

"No, just realistic. You know as well as I do that you've got to be a masochist to try and find the on-call judge to issue a search warrant on a Sunday afternoon. And while I'm at the autopsy, you're going to swing by Harmon's later and pick up the first batch of pictures?"

"Uh-huh. When he called last night, I told him that you were out and I didn't know when you'd be back. And I sure wasn't going out in that weather. Eeyore wanted me to make sure you understood that although he's usually closed on Sundays, he was going to be back in the shop after church."

"When you go in, be nice and thank him for me." MacKinnon nudged the cat onto the floor and got up from the chair. He checked Victoria's coffee cup. "You ready for a refill yet?"

"Nope. I want something else." Victoria reached up to tug on the bottom of his nightshirt. She said half-accusingly, "You didn't wake me up last night."

He settled next to her on the couch and removed his wife's reading glasses. "Sorry. It was late and I had a lot on my mind."

"The mayor?" Victoria undid the top button of his nightshirt and began to play with the hairs on his chest.

"Yeah. She made it absolutely clear that I'm on thin ice."

"Honey, if you had yesterday to do all over again, would you change anything you did?" Victoria rested her head against his arm and looked up into her husband's eyes.

MacKinnon thought before answering. "No."

"Then there's no point in worrying yourself sick over what Jean Dumfries thinks. You're dealing with a politician, Steve, the lowest form of life on the planet. Today you may be on thin ice, but when you solve this case, she'll be back to trumpeting you as her personal choice for chief and you'll be the greatest thing since sliced bread."

"I guess you're right."

Victoria smiled. "And as long as we're talking about the mayor, have you ever wondered about Jean and Art?"

"How do you mean?"

"Do you think she'd ever do this with him on their couch?" Victoria asked coyly.

MacKinnon gasped. "No. She'd be way too worried about ruining the upholstery."

"Poor girl. She doesn't know what she's missing."

Afterwards, MacKinnon showered, shaved, and put on his uniform. Kissing Victoria goodbye, he drove to the County Administration Building. Most people still went to church in Talmine, so the streets were nearly empty, with the exception of a brightly-colored flock of long-distance bicyclists drinking overpriced lattes outside the Coffee Emporium. MacKinnon stopped briefly to warn the group that the stop signs applied to bicyclists too, and that he had no great desire to see one of them converted into an impromptu vehicle hood ornament. Five minutes later, he descended the cement stairs into the basement of the County Administration Building and found the door to the Coroner's Office open. Dr. Morris was already present.

"Morning, Steve. Doughnut?" Morris motioned toward a cardboard box of the sweet, fried delicacies known colloquially among police officers as "gut bombs."

"No, thanks."

"I thought all cops liked doughnuts."

"I love doughnuts. But as a former fat-boy, I also love being able to bend over to tie my shoes, without panting for breath."

"One doughnut won't hurt."

"Al, I've never eaten just one doughnut in my life," MacKinnon confessed. He looked into the box. "Get thee behind me, cinnamon roll."

"Suit yourself. Are we any closer to having a name on the victim?" Morris popped the final piece of the custard-filled, chocolate-covered goody into his mouth.

"Not really, but I might have something for you later this afternoon. I'm going up to BWI to check on that paperwork."

Morris picked up a pair of fingerprint exemplar cards and handed them to MacKinnon. "If you come up dry, you can enter her prints into the system. Rolled them just a little bit ago. Ready to get started?"

They entered the small, adjoining examination room and MacKinnon's nose wrinkled. A stainless steel examination table stood in the center of the room and on it was the victim. MacKinnon could see that the woman was very thin and there was a tiny tattoo of a rose on her left hip. Near her head was a metal tray containing the tools of Morris' trade. Stepping up to the body, Morris spoke into a hanging microphone as he described the victim and her injury. Meanwhile, MacKinnon took a fresh series of photographs of the gunshot wound.

Then he retrieved a gunshot residue kit from his evidence box and applied the adhesive pads to the woman's hands. He had no doubt the subsequent examination by the State Police's scanning electron microscope would reveal some black gunpowder particles on the pads, for everybody attending the smoky reenactment in Brookesmith Park would have been coated with at least a little gunpowder residue. But if there wasn't a significant amount of the material on her hands, he could safely discard the feeble theory that the victim had shot herself and that the gun had been subsequently removed.

Yet the woman's hands and lower arms yielded an unforeseen and strange bit of information unconnected with gunpowder. The flesh was pockmarked with clusters of small sores and scabs. *They look like speed bumps,* thought MacKinnon with a start. Since leaving San Diego, he thankfully hadn't encountered many speed-freaks, but he'd dealt with so many crystal addicts over the years that there was no way he could be mistaken about these scabs. Long-term methamphetamine users almost invariably developed skin eruptions that often became infected because the hype couldn't resist scratching the wound. MacKinnon turned the woman's left arm to look at the inside portion of the elbow. Sure enough, there were both old and fresh injection sites.

"Better living through chemistry," MacKinnon grunted.

"I was wondering when you were going to find those," Morris said serenely. "She's got drug tracks on the other arm too."

"You mean you don't think she donated blood recently? I'll offer you three to one odds that when the drug tox comes back, it'll show meth in her system."

"Really? I would have guessed heroin."

"Nope, it's crank. Those lovely sores are a dead giveaway," said MacKinnon. "The stuff is so damn toxic; it causes skin eruptions that never heal, because the speed-freak is always picking at the scabs. Later on, the stuff begins to strip the enamel from their teeth, and they start looking like they live at Chernobyl."

After photographing the injection sites, MacKinnon took a fresh gunshot residue kit and applied several pads to the flesh around the wound, collecting samples of both partially-burnt and unburned powder. When he was finished, Morris took a scalpel and made an incision across the victim's forehead, just above the brow line, and peeled the flesh backward, revealing the top of the skull. The sound was like masking tape being slowly pulled from a box. Morris picked up the rotary power saw, and MacKinnon backed away to avoid being struck by flying debris as the coroner cut through the skull. Soon the air was filled with the smell of pulverized bone. When the cutting was complete, Morris took the hammer and chisel and popped the skullcap off with a single, deft blow. Now the victim's brain was visible, and there was obvious trauma to the left hemisphere.

With speedy efficiency, Morris removed the brain, placed it on a metal tray, and went to work with the scalpel. After tissue samples were collected for toxicological analysis, the coroner began searching for the projectile. When he found the bullet, he emitted a low whistle.

"Pay dirt?" asked MacKinnon.

Using forceps, Morris held up a round metal ball about the size of a quarter. "You were right about the weapon probably being black powder. Jesus Christ! Is this thing a musket ball or a softball?"

"Yeah, but it's too big and the wrong shape to have been fired from most of the reenactors' rifles, which are .58 caliber. Put it down and let me do a quick measurement."

After taking a photograph of the bloody musket ball as it lay on a tray, MacKinnon took a ruler from his evidence kit. The round, metal projectile measured slightly more than five-eighths of an inch, which meant that it could have been fired from an old .69 caliber smoothbore, a replica rifle carried by reenactors portraying units from early in the Civil War. Another distant possibility was that the ball had been fired from a handgun. But MacKinnon could only think of one revolver large enough to discharge such a huge bullet: the LeMat, an exotic, two-barreled hand cannon that featured a nine-shot cylinder of .42 caliber bullets that revolved around a central .65 caliber barrel. Developed in the Confederacy, LeMats were popular with Southern reenactors. MacKinnon used a pair of forceps to place the lead ball on a paper towel, so that the blood could dry before it was placed into an evidence envelope.

Dr. Morris resumed the autopsy and began examining the area above the victim's left eye. His conclusion, based on the scorching to the skin around the wounds, was that the weapon had only been a few feet from the woman when it was fired, but wasn't close enough to have created the distinctive stellar-shaped, ripping injuries of a contact wound. Then, although there weren't any obvious injuries to the torso, MacKinnon remained to photograph the rest of the procedure.

It was just past 11:45 a.m. when they finished the examination and retired to the coroner's office. Morris opened a locked closet, removed two bulging paper shopping bags, and placed them on the desk. The bags contained the woman's uniform, underwear, shoes, and false beard. MacKinnon pulled the gray uniform coat from one of the bags and inspected the garment. It was a late-model Richmond Depot shell jacket with six brass buttons. Inside the coat he found what he was looking for—the manufacturer's label. A business called the Northern Shenandoah Quartermaster, in Front Royal, Virginia, had produced the woolen coat. MacKinnon folded the gray jacket and put it back into the bag.

"Looks like you've got a real puzzle on your hands," said Morris.

"Yeah, like something from one of those brain-candy mystery novels by what's her name—Rita Mae Brown?—that Victoria loves. Maybe I'll put my cats to work on the case. That always seems to work in her books."

"Oh yeah, as if that could happen in real life. The only thing my cat does is eat, sleep, and crap in the flowerbeds," Morris said scornfully. Then he added half-wistfully, "Not that I don't sometimes envy the little bastard. It looks like a pretty good life." Before going home, MacKinnon stopped at the police station to drop off the new evidence. Walking through the rear parking lot, he stopped in his tracks. The locking hasp to the police garage door had been jimmied off, and the twisted metal hinge and attached padlock lay on the pavement near the door. As he approached the building to investigate further, he heard a rattle and then something striking the garage floor. Someone was still inside.

MacKinnon jerked the revolver from his holster and threw the wooden door open. It was dark inside the small building, but he could see the inky silhouette of a large man swiftly moving to conceal himself in front of the open driver's door of the Pontiac. MacKinnon only got a split-second look at the figure, but it was enough time to see something silvery and metallic in the burglar's right hand.

Shifting to a position of cover beside the wall, MacKinnon aimed his gun at the intruder and said, "Okay, pal, drop the gun or you're a dead man."

There was a pause and then a frightened, bleary, and confused man said, "I don't have a gun, sir."

MacKinnon recognized the voice and slowly allowed himself to relax. "Is that you, Lee?"

"Yes, sir."

"Come on out."

Like a toddler just awakened from a nap, Lee Hanford tottered from the garage and blinked painfully in the bright sunlight. At six-foot-three and 280 pounds, he was a bear of a man and had a beer gut large enough to be used as a helipad. In Hanford's right hand was a twelve-ounce silver can of Coors Lite, the item MacKinnon had mistaken for a gun. Hanford was the closest thing Talmine had to a town drunk, and his notion of civic duty was to voluntarily spend most evenings in the police department's holding cell rather than try to drive home.

Holstering his gun, MacKinnon asked, "Lee, what the hell were you doing in there?"

"When the Sandbar closed, I tried to find Officer Plummer to let me in." Hanford nodded in the direction of the police station and the detention cell that was his nightly home. "It was raining—raining real hard—and I couldn't find him."

"So you broke into the garage?"

"No, sir, I didn't break in." Hanford sounded slightly offended. "I may drink a little too much, but I'm not a burglar. The door was open, and so I thought I'd wait there until Officer Plummer came back to the station. Guess I fell asleep."

Glancing into the garage, MacKinnon now noticed that the Pontiac's trunk was ajar and all the car doors were open. He went inside to investigate further. The rear bench cushion was on the cement floor near the vehicle, and inside the car the seats had been slashed with a sharp instrument. He was certain the motive wasn't simple vandalism. No, this was a very thorough and destructive search. Furthermore, the fact that the perpetrator had been willing to accept the risk of breaking into the police garage indicated the item sought was something of great importance.

Coming back outside, MacKinnon asked, "Was the car like that when you went inside the garage?"

"Yes, sir. It was all tore up, but I didn't touch anything."

"Did you see anybody else here last night?"

"No, sir."

Calling dispatch on the radio, MacKinnon requested Sergeant Sayers come to the station immediately. A few minutes later, Sayers pulled into the parking lot, got out of his patrol car, and blinked in surprise at Lee Hanford and then the damaged Pontiac.

MacKinnon glared at the sergeant. "Ron, I'm a very unhappy fellow this morning. When a crook can break into our stationhouse and we don't even notice the forced entry until hours afterwards, I'm inclined to scorch some asses."

"When did this happen?" Sayers bent over to examine the twisted hasp.

"Being that you've been here since seven, I was hoping you could answer that. When I left here last night, it was locked up tight." MacKinnon folded his arms. "I take it Plummer didn't mention this when he went EOS this morning?"

"No, sir."

"And you didn't notice it?" MacKinnon's tone was angrily cool and deliberate.

Sayers swallowed nervously. "I guess I didn't. But I was only back here for a second. Is Lee . . ."

"No, Lee didn't break in. He found the door open sometime after the Sandbar closed, and spent the night inside," said MacKinnon. He gritted his teeth and resisted adding: *And I, for one, am proud—very proud—to know that the town drunk discovered that our police station was burglarized before we did.*

He took a deep breath and struggled to control his temper. It wasn't really fair to vent his ire on the sergeant. Talmine's small police station wasn't like the fortified law enforcement facilities in the big cities for two excellent reasons: the crime rate was low and his officers weren't a de facto occupying army. Furthermore, even MacKinnon hadn't anticipated the break-in, but he silently acknowledged that he wouldn't be so unvigilant in the future.

Then another disturbing thought intruded. Last night he'd automatically assumed the woman's killer had stolen the Pontiac, but now MacKinnon wasn't so certain. It didn't make sense for the auto thief to have spent the time and effort to carefully erase his fingerprints, only to later force entry into the police station and search the car. After all, the Bonneville had likely been parked on Wyndham Road for several hours before being discovered by the cops, more than enough time for the suspect to thoroughly search the car. Yet last night MacKinnon had seen nothing to indicate the thief had been interested in the vehicle's contents.

His temper recovered, MacKinnon began ticking off instructions: "Ron, I'm sorry for jumping down your throat. There was no call for it. Now, the first thing I want you to do is go to Plummer's house and wake him up. I want to know if he saw anything last night. Then, when you finish with Plummer, come back and photograph this mess and dust everything for latents."

"And I'll buy a new hasp." Sayers peered at the slashed seats. "What do you suppose he was looking for?"

"It turns out our victim was a hardcore hype, so dope is a possibility," MacKinnon replied. "And that gives me an idea. When you get the chance, call the State Police and see if they'll bring one of their drug dogs over to search the car. Maybe they'll find a hidden compartment or something."

"Yes, sir."

"But if it wasn't dope, and if this dude was willing to break into our garage, what's to stop him from hitting our evidence locker tomorrow night?" MacKinnon pondered aloud. "From now until we get this thing solved, all the station doors stay locked, including the lobby, and I want you to take the homicide evidence over to the Sheriff's Department and store it there. I'll call Sheriff Jarboe and make the arrangements."

"Are you still going up to Baltimore?" asked Sayers.

"Yeah, I'll be leaving in about half an hour, so you'll be in charge until I get back," MacKinnon replied. "But you can call me if anything important comes up."

"And what about Lee?"

MacKinnon turned to the drunk. "Lee, you want a ride home or to the Sandbar?"

Hanford squinted at the sun and, apparently deciding it was late enough in the day to resume drinking, replied, "The Sandbar, please."

"Get in my car."

A few minutes later, as he stopped to drop Hanford off at the tavern, MacKinnon spotted a familiar face emerging from Pelham's Antique Shop. It was Joseph Carnes, today conventionally attired in slacks and a sport shirt, and carrying several bags of merchandise. MacKinnon pulled over to the curb and got out of the car to speak with the imperious witness.

"Hi, Mr. Carnes. I'd have thought you'd be back up in New York by now."

Carnes looked up and showed a wary smile. "Chief, I was just going to drop by the police station and see if you were in."

"What can I do for you?"

Carnes inhaled deeply. "I wanted to apologize for my poor behavior yesterday. It was hot, I was upset, and I'm afraid I overreacted. A little later I realized that you were only doing your job."

"No apology necessary, Mr. Carnes, but thank you."

"Are you any closer to finding out who killed that woman?"

"A little," MacKinnon replied. "So, what kept you in town?"

"Treasure hunting. You've got some nice shops here." Carnes held up the bags. "Anyway, after the episode with the dead girl, I wasn't in the mood to shop. I went back to the motel, had a swim, and basically hibernated for the rest of the day. But I wasn't going home empty-handed."

"Looks like you've done well."

"I'm pleased. In fact, I just found a very nice *carte de visite* of a Union officer at that shop." Carnes pointed across the street to Berkeley's Antiques.

MacKinnon tried to suppress a groan. For several weeks he'd had his eye on that tintype calling card. "I hope you aren't talking about that one of the cavalryman striking the Napoleon pose."

"You've seen it."

"Yes, and coveted it, but one hundred and seventy-five was a little too rich for me."

"Then I suppose you'll be a little upset when I tell you that I only paid one twenty-five," Carnes announced proudly.

"How'd you manage that?"

Carnes looked smug. "It's simple. I just decided in advance what I was going to pay for it and wouldn't budge from that figure. Call it a contest of wills between Mrs. Berkeley and myself that I won."

"I had no idea that the antique business was so warlike."

"Not just the antique business, Chief," Carnes said gravely. "At the risk of sounding like a cruel Social Darwinist, it's the model for life. Whether we like it or not, the human race is composed of winners and losers, and the only thing that separates them is their resolve to succeed. I don't allow myself to lose."

"Some folks would call that the Law of the Tooth."

Carnes locked eyes with MacKinnon. "Only the losers. And I think if you were candid, you'd agree with me, since it's obvious that you're accustomed to having your own way."

"There might be some truth to that," MacKinnon admitted. "So, as one tyrant to another, a question: What happens when you come up against someone with a superior will?"

"That hasn't happened yet." The conversation came to an uncomfortable pause. Finally, Carnes extended his hand and said, "Thanks for being so understanding, Chief. And remember that if you really want to sell that Clauberg, give me a call."

"I've got your card," MacKinnon replied, shaking hands with Carnes. "Now, I've got to get back to work."

As he pulled away from the curb, MacKinnon studied Carnes in the rearview mirror. The antique dealer was on his way into Keeley's Antique Junction. *Carnes would likely find no joy there,* thought MacKinnon. Kevin Keeley's idea of antiques was Billy Carter memorabilia, Flintstone-decorated jelly jars, *Star Wars* toy figures, and *The Man From U.N.C.L.E.* lunchboxes—plastic and pressed metal schlock from the 1960s and 1970s that, amazingly, commanded enormous prices.

When MacKinnon got home, he found Victoria in her sewing room examining the first set of reenactment photographs with a large magnifying glass. There were stacks of photographs carefully arranged on the table and, set to the side, were four pictures that Victoria had separated from the mass of images. Also on the table, curled up and napping in the cardboard box that had contained the photographs, was Mother Superior, a small calico cat.

Kissing his wife on the top of her head, MacKinnon said, "We had a visitor at the station last night."

Victoria looked up from the photographs. "How do you mean?"

"Someone broke into the garage and thoroughly tossed the victim's car." MacKinnon sat down. "I'd already checked it and it was empty, so I'm guessing he didn't get what he was looking for."

"If the killer stole the car yesterday, why did he wait until it was in the police garage to search it? That doesn't make any sense . . . unless we're dealing with two different crooks."

"Great minds think alike," said MacKinnon.

"Any idea of what he was after?"

MacKinnon shook his head. "Who knows? Since it turns out our victim was a crystal freak, my first guess would be drugs or money. But the longer I think about it, the less I think that dope has anything to do with it."

"And, whoever it was, isn't it a little strange he knew exactly where to look for the car?"

"Yeah, it either means that someone was watching the station or we're dealing with a cop who knows the procedure for securing evidence. It makes me wonder if Detective Benham actually went back to Maryland yesterday." MacKinnon hooked a thumb at the photographs. "How's it coming?"

"Slowly. So far I've come up dry on the male/female team—"

"If they ever even existed," MacKinnon muttered.

"But I think I've found one picture of our victim, a couple of a Confederate general, and one of Benham."

"Really? Let's see."

She handed him the small collection of pictures. The first had been taken in the sutlers' encampment, and among the dozen or so people in the photograph there was a man wearing a Baltimore Ravens football jersey standing near a tent. His back was turned to the camera, so it was impossible to positively identify the man as Benham; nonetheless, MacKinnon was certain it was the Sharpsburg detective.

"This is kind of strange." MacKinnon tapped the picture with his finger.

"How so?"

"Benham said that prior to the shooting, he was Code Five on a suspect's car," said MacKinnon, slipping into California police argot to describe a stakeout. "In fact, he told me that he was in the parking lot until after the ambulance arrived and the word started to spread that there'd been a shooting."

Victoria looked up. "Maybe it was taken just after the shooting."

"Yeah, but if that's the case, why is he just hanging out, trying to look inconspicuous? I wish there was some way we could know what time that picture was taken."

"There is." Victoria took the photograph. "You see this shadow from the tent? Well, we just have to go back out to the park, set up a pole or something, and wait until the shadow is at about the same angle. It won't be precise, but it will give us a ballpark estimate of when the picture was taken."

MacKinnon began to rub his wife's shoulders. "Brains and she's dynamite in bed. Let's see the picture of the victim."

Victoria held up a photograph and he bent over to examine it. The picture was of a trio of faux Rebel artillerists trying to recreate the stiff poses of the daguerreotype era. Passing behind the men was a small Confederate soldier seen in three-quarter profile, as if she were aware of the camera and trying to turn away from it before the shutter snapped. Even at a distance, the fake beard was a miserable failure at concealing the victim's gender.

"Yeah, that's her and she's wearing the cloth haversack, but there's no way of telling whether she's got anything inside of it," said MacKinnon. "This was taken near the parking lot. Do you think we can compute a time for this picture too?"

Victoria peered at the photograph. "If we use the shadows from those trees." She pointed to some pines in the picture's background.

"Excellent. Now let's see the pictures of Carnes."

"Well, I hope one of them is Carnes. I picked out two that matched your description."

She handed him the photographs. The man in the first picture wasn't the antique dealer, but he was the focus of the second snapshot. Carnes stood, posing uncomfortably with some smiling young children who were clutching the strings of helium-filled balloons. MacKinnon pointed to the frowning Confederate officer. "Him."

"Looks like he's having fun," Victoria said.

"Oh yeah, he's one of the jolliest guys I've met in years, so long as you don't get in his way at an antique store. I saw him downtown a little bit ago and stopped to talk to him. He snagged that *carte de visite* at Berkeley's that I wanted, and it looked like he wasn't going to be happy until he'd pillaged all the shops."

"Damn. That tintype was going to be one of your Christmas presents."

"Don't worry about it. Besides, the only present I want to unwrap on Christmas morning has hair," said MacKinnon, provoking a blush on his wife's cheeks. "Now, are you ready for lunch?"

"In a minute." She picked up another stack of photographs. "I just want to look at a couple more pictures."

But as MacKinnon suspected, Victoria did not come down in a minute and, instead, remained at the table examining the pictures. His wife was a natural if obsessive puzzle-solver, and once she resolved to unravel a secret, she lost all track of time in her single-minded pursuit of a solution. He made a pair of turkey and provolone sandwiches and carried them, along with some sodas, tortilla chips, and salsa, on a tray upstairs to the sewing room.

"Madame, lunch is served," MacKinnon said in his best butler's voice.

Victoria looked up in surprise. "Thanks, baby doll. I guess I got a little sidetracked."

"Did you come up with anything else?"

"Just some pictures of consenting adults." Victoria's eyes rolled upward. "I'd guess whoever took them forgot they were on the first part of the roll. My Lord, he was wearing cavalry boots with spurs and his wife—I hope it's his wife—she was . . . well, never mind."

MacKinnon put his sandwich on the plate and reached for a stack of envelopes containing pictures. "Maybe I'd better take a look to make sure they don't have some sort of evidentiary value."

"Please, Steve," Victoria said half-pleadingly.

He laughed. "Won't they be surprised when they get those photos in the mail."

After lunch, he went to his office and telephoned directory assistance for Front Royal. There was a listing for the Northern Shenandoah Quartermaster and he called the number. As he expected, because it was Sunday he made contact with an answering machine. He left a message identifying who he was and requested that the owners contact him immediately. Replacing the receiver, he considered calling the Front Royal Police and asking them to try and contact the business, but he didn't have the owner's name and the only address was a post office box. It was frustrating, but he would probably have to wait until tomorrow to pursue the lead.

However, as he was brushing his teeth, the telephone rang. Victoria answered it, and a moment later she handed him the portable phone. "Ralph Denton from the quartermaster company in Front Royal," she whispered.

MacKinnon took the phone and thanked Denton for responding so quickly. After the chief had briefly explained the purpose of his inquiry, Denton stated that he did most of his business through telephone mail orders and the Internet, so he almost never met his customers in person. However, the merchant offered to go through his company records and make up a list of all female customers over the past year. MacKinnon thanked Denton and gave him the number to the facsimile machine in his den.

A few minutes later, he hugged and kissed Victoria goodbye.

"You be careful," said Victoria, straightening his shirt's pocket flap. "It's Sunday afternoon and every nut on the East Coast will be on the road trying to get home."

"I will, honey. Depending on the traffic, I ought to be back sometime around seven or eight. And one other thing. I've been thinking that if someone was clever enough to stake out the police station, he's also intelligent enough to find out where we live. So, I'm going to ask you to be careful."

Six:

The Digital Masquerade

MacKinnon crossed over the long, narrow bridge spanning the Potomac River into Maryland and made his way northward along US Route 301. Despite having cut his driving teeth on the overcrowded Los Angeles freeway system—where the on-ramps should have been labeled with the same warning that Dante noted at the gates of Hell: *Abandon hope, all ye who enter*—MacKinnon found the crawling journey to BWI an exercise in smoldering frustration.

The highway was a sluggish stream of red brake lights, periodically dammed by fender-bender accidents. And, rather than do the sensible thing and pull over to the side of the road to exchange insurance information, the drivers unfailingly stopped their cars in the middle of the thoroughfare to argue, and sometimes fight, over who'd caused the collision. Even when the road was relatively clear, the vehicles ahead invariably slowed to well below the speed limit when the apprehensive drivers caught sight of MacKinnon's marked patrol car.

It was all too reminiscent of the perpetual gridlock of Southern California, with the exception that the drivers weren't routinely exchanging gunfire *yet,* MacKinnon added grimly. One of the reasons he and Victoria had moved was to escape this sort of vehicular constipation and its taut atmosphere of barely-constrained violence. In Talmine it was still possible to drive from point-A-to-point-B without inducing homicidal tendencies, but the closer one got to Washington DC, the more unmistakable were the signs of the "Cali-fornication" of the local highways.

At Dorrs Corner, he got on Interstate 97 and began to make slightly better time. It was just after 3:00 p.m. when MacKinnon pulled into a parking garage at BWI. Grabbing his briefcase, he walked out into the harsh sunlight. It was hot, and the air was faintly redolent with the sweetly pungent aroma of jet fuel. Fifteen minutes later, he entered the airport office of the Maryland State Police, introduced himself to the desk sergeant, and explained the purpose for his visit.

"From their attitude over the phone, I have a feeling they might be more willing to give you guys the paperwork than me," he said. "So, is there any chance I can get one of your officers to come with me to the rental agency?"

"Sure, when I get a cop available," said the desk sergeant. "But we're busy right now, so I don't know when that'll be."

"Well, if you can shake a unit free for me, I'd appreciate it. In the meantime, I'll go down and try to sweet-talk them myself."

As he proceeded through the terminal, MacKinnon noted the mass of harried, unhappy travelers and wondered when the romance of air travel had finally become extinct. He could still remember the early 1960s, when international airports were considered glamorous places, but now the facilities were disturbingly reminiscent of downtown bus stations, with one important difference. Buses usually departed on schedule, a claim that couldn't be made for most airlines.

There was a line of customers at the rental car agency desk, and MacKinnon walked to the rear of the queue. Over the years he'd seen far too many cops behave as if the simple rules of courtesy—like waiting for your turn—didn't apply to the police, and it always made him cringe. But from behind the counter a middle-aged woman noticed him and said, "Excuse me, are you the police officer from Virginia who called yesterday afternoon?"

"Yes, ma'am. I'm Chief MacKinnon."

"And I'm Mary Granger, the manager. Why don't you come back to my office, and we'll talk there." The woman opened the low door leading behind the counter.

Granger had done her best to brighten the otherwise-stark office cubicle. One wall was decorated with a framed Anne Geddes poster of a cherubic baby girl sitting among oversized snapdragon petals, and the metal desk's centerpiece was a Boyds teddy bear wearing a plaid woolen coat. MacKinnon recognized the stuffed animal. He'd given the same bear to Victoria for her birthday last year.

"Amanda. That's her name, isn't it?" MacKinnon pointed to the bear. "My wife has her set up in a tea-party tableau on her dresser."

"Amanda Huntington." Granger tugged at the pleat of the bear's long coat. "The very last thing I expected was a police officer to know anything about teddy bears."

"It's just a sad commentary on my deteriorating intellect," MacKinnon said with a laugh. "I'm no longer very good at remembering crooks, but I can identify seventy-five percent of Boyds Bears by name, a fact I find very frightening. I hope my secret is safe with you."

Granger giggled, suddenly looking much younger than her years. "Tell your wife I envy her."

"Thank you, but now I've got to change the subject and talk about something a little less pleasant than teddy bears."

"The murder."

MacKinnon nodded. "Our victim probably rented a car from you folks yesterday morning. We still don't know her name, and I'm hoping that the rental paperwork will give us some clue to her identity. Whoever I spoke with yesterday told me that I was going to need a search warrant, and I'm going to be up-front and tell you I don't have one yet."

Granger sat down behind her desk, removed a rental form from a drawer, and handed the document to MacKinnon. "When I got back from lunch yesterday, Danielle told me you'd called—she's the woman you spoke with—and I want you to know that she wasn't trying to be deliberately uncooperative. It's company policy not to release any information on customers without a court order, and she was simply following our rules."

"I understand."

"But because you said this involved a murder, I thought there might be an exception to the rule," Granger continued. "So, I called around and managed to contact someone from our legal department yesterday afternoon. He suggested we cooperate fully with your investigation."

"I can't tell you how much I appreciate that. And before I do anything else, I want to bring you up to date on the status of your car. It was stolen sometime yesterday afternoon and then recovered later that night. Right now, it's being stored at my police station."

"Stolen? Was it damaged?"

"At the risk of sounding like a bad comedian, I have some good news and some bad news. The good news is that that the damage isn't too bad. The steering column sheath is broken, someone wiped it down with oil, and the upholstery's been slashed, but it's all easily repairable."

"And the bad news?"

"The bad news is that we're going to have to maintain possession of the car until a suspect is caught and the case goes to trial."

Granger blinked and looked at MacKinnon as if he'd suddenly begun speaking an incomprehensible foreign language.

Finally she said, "Do you mind telling me why?"

With a sigh, MacKinnon explained. "If it were up to me, I'd give you the car back now, but if I did that, here's what would happen. Let's say that six months from now we arrest the murderer. When we finally got into court, the first thing the defendant's attorney would do is move to have the charges dismissed, alleging his client can't receive a fair trial because evidence was destroyed."

"But what does that have to do with the car?"

"The Pontiac is evidence," MacKinnon replied. "The crook's lawyer would claim that if he'd only had the chance to have his forensic experts examine the Pontiac, they would have found something to exonerate his client. So that's why we've got to hang onto the car—to protect the killer's right to a fair trial."

"That's crazy," Granger declared.

"You're preaching to the choir, Ms. Granger," said MacKinnon. "But that's how the system works, or doesn't, depending on how you look at it. And after delivering that wonderful news, I have a request. Is it possible for me to interview the employee who rented the car to the victim?"

"Her name is Kanika Truax, and I knew you were going to want to talk to her. I'll get her, provided you solemnly promise you aren't going to hang onto her until the trial is finished."

"Touché, madam." He chuckled. "The interview will only take a few minutes."

While waiting for Truax, he took a seat behind the desk and conducted a cursory examination of the paperwork. The car had been rented the previous day, to an Anita Fesler of Xenia, Ohio, and a VISA card had been used for payment. MacKinnon noted the date of birth, April 23, 1968, and realized there was a problem. The birth date made Fesler thirty-six years old, yet the dead woman appeared to have been in her mid-twenties.

Suddenly suspicious, he scrutinized Fesler's labored signature. Inordinately heavy pressure had been used to produce the handwriting, and the lowercase letters were slanted in different directions. Furthermore, the script was sharply angular, like a barracuda's teeth, and the capital "F" in Fesler bore the classic felon's "claw." MacKinnon was no expert in the art of handwriting analysis, but he'd studied enough graphology to surmise the signature was a forgery.

MacKinnon grimaced. If the signature was indeed fraudulent, it meant he wasn't any closer to identifying the dead woman. Furthermore, it probably signified the victim had stolen Fesler's identity, a popular form of crime among crystal addicts.

A young and anxious-looking woman entered the office. Collecting some background information before proceeding with the interview, MacKinnon learned that when Kanika Truax wasn't working at the airport, she was a student at Baltimore Community College in nearby Catonsville, and hoped to someday pursue a career in accounting.

"I guess you know why I'm here," MacKinnon began.

"Oh, yes. After you called yesterday, Danielle told everyone that the police had phoned about a murder," replied Truax. "Then we checked the computer and—oh, God—it was really weird to find out that I'd rented the car earlier that morning."

"So, I'd imagine you've already had a chance to look at the paperwork. Do you remember the woman?" MacKinnon pulled a notebook from his briefcase.

"Yes, she showed up at the desk just before seven."

"Did she have any luggage?"

"None that I could see, but we were pretty busy, so I wasn't really looking."

"I'd like you to look at a picture, but I've got to warn you in advance that it's a little gory." MacKinnon held out a Polaroid photograph of the victim's face. "Was that the lady who rented the car?"

"Yes, that was her." Truax winced slightly, but did not turn her eyes from the picture.

He put the photograph away. "Can you remember how she was dressed?"

"I think it was blue jeans and an olive green pullover top."

"With as many people as I imagine you deal with in a day, I'm impressed you'd remember that. Any reason why?"

Truax shrugged. "You want to know the truth? I remember her because she looked like a crackhead: all jittery, eyes clicking back and forth, and talking too fast. You notice that right away when you grow up around coke fiends."

"But you rented her the car anyway?" MacKinnon looked up from his notes.

"Look, sir, I don't mean to be a smart-ass, but if I refused to rent a car to anyone who didn't look one-hundred-percent straight, I'd be looking for a new job." She folded her arms across her chest and sat back in the chair. "Besides, she wasn't high; just twitchy, you know? It was like it had been a little while since she'd had any."

"Relax, Ms. Truax. I'm not sitting in judgment of you," MacKinnon said gently. "Now did this woman mention where she'd come in from?"

"As I recall, she said that she'd just gotten in from Cincinnati and needed a car for the day."

"Did you notice if she had airline tickets?"

"Now that you mention it, she didn't." Truax frowned. "It's kind of strange I didn't notice that at the time, because people usually have their ticket envelopes in hand, but she didn't."

"Was anyone with her?"

"Not that I could see."

"And she paid with a . . . VISA card," said MacKinnon, referring to the rental agreement. "I assume you compared the card against her driver's license?"

"That's company procedure."

"And were there any problems with the transaction?"

"I wouldn't have rented her the car if there'd been."

"After you finished the paperwork, where would she have gone?"

Truax pointed toward the terminal. "Since she hadn't reserved a car in advance, we wouldn't have had one for her in the parking structure, so she would have had to take the shuttle out to our satellite lot."

His questions answered, MacKinnon thanked Truax for her cooperation and gave her his business card, asking the woman to call if she remembered anything else. When Mary Granger returned, MacKinnon took out another card and wrote a name and telephone number on the back. Handing it to Granger he said, "Thanks so much for your assistance, and you'll want to pass that number on to your legal department. It's the direct line for Norman Pawling, the Talmine Town Attorney. Let the lawyers haggle over the Pontiac."

"Thanks." Granger put the card down near the telephone. "Is there anything else you need?"

"Actually there is. I want to talk to whoever gave my victim the car at your satellite lot. Is it possible for you to give them a call and tell them I'm on my way?"

"I'll call right now."

"And can I trouble you for directions to the lot?"

Granger smiled. "A man who likes teddy bears and actually asks for directions. Are there any more like you at home, Chief MacKinnon?"

Before leaving the terminal MacKinnon briefly returned to the State Police office. Looking up from his computer screen, the desk sergeant said, "I just got a unit clear. Still need them to respond?"

"Thanks, but no. They were great and I got everything I needed." He held up the paperwork. "But you can do me a big favor. Is there someone here at the airport you can call to confirm whether or not a flight arrived from Cincinnati yesterday?"

"Sure. Airport operations has that info."

MacKinnon handed the rental contract to the desk sergeant. "Oh, and I know this will shock you as much as it did me, but I'm pretty sure my victim—who was a crystal freak, by the way—used bogus ID and a falsely-obtained credit card to get the car. No doubt your auto theft guys are going to want a copy of this paperwork."

The desk sergeant pretended to be stunned. "Credit card fraud here? I refuse to believe it. You want some coffee while I make the copies and check out that information on the flight?"

"Thanks. I could use a cup."

The desk sergeant led MacKinnon to the tiny lounge and began searching the cupboards and drawers. Of course, there were no clean Styrofoam cups; there never were at police stations. Throughout his career, he had visited at least a hundred police departments throughout the United States, and once, on vacation, had even spent the day at New Scotland Yard, chatting with homicide detectives of the London Metropolitan Police. But irrespective of the locale or department, two things could always be depended upon—and this included his own police station, now that he reflected on the matter: the coffee was always old and there were never any cups.

Holding up the coffee carafe for inspection, he swirled the container and squinted suspiciously at the viscous black fluid. Finally, he said, "No offense intended, but on second thought, I think I'll pass on the coffee . . . if that's what this stuff was."

"The secret is to add plenty of sugar."

"Cardiac arrhythmia, anyone? I appreciate your hospitality, but I think I'll stick to something safe, like methamphetamine."

"Just as well. We don't have any cups anyway," said the desk sergeant.

After making copies of the rental paperwork, the desk sergeant called airport operations. When he hung up the phone, he said, "There were only two flights inbound from Cincinnati yesterday. The first arrived at ten-forty-seven a.m. and the second didn't get in until six-eleven p.m."

"And it was around seven a.m. when she told the clerk she'd just arrived from Cincinnati," said MacKinnon as he wrote the information in his notepad.

"Looks like your victim was a liar."

"Oh, 'liar' sounds so harsh and judgmental," MacKinnon said. "As a sensitive New Age guy, I prefer the expression 'ethically challenged.' "

The desk sergeant snorted with bitter amusement. "I'm impressed you could say that without gagging."

"Hey, I was born in California. The talent for wallowing in psychobabble is embedded in my genetic code."

Returning to his car, MacKinnon made the short but confusing drive through the airport. After narrowly avoiding being shuttled onto the freeway to Baltimore, he pulled into the rental car storage facility. Already advised that the chief was on his way, the lot supervisor had sequestered the employee who'd dealt with the woman. Unfortunately, it looked as if there wasn't much to learn from Mykel Duvall.

After looking at the photograph and identifying the victim, he provided a sparse description of the encounter. The woman had gotten off the shuttle bus, produced the rental paperwork, and driven from the lot. There hadn't been any conversation and Duvall hadn't noticed anything suspicious, other than the fact that the woman had no luggage, just a plastic shopping bag and a large manila envelope.

"A shopping bag?" MacKinnon asked quickly.

"Yeah, with some stuff inside."

"Clothing?"

"Could have been," agreed Duvall. "Whatever it was, she wasn't afraid of breaking it, because she tossed it onto the floor on the passenger side."

"Did you notice any sort of logo on the bag?"

Duvall closed his eyes for a moment. "Wal-Mart, I think."

Great. That narrowed her place of origin to just about any city in the United States with a population of over 10,000, thought MacKinnon. Still, the information was valuable because it showed the victim had collected the bag, which probably contained the Confederate uniform, sometime between her visit to the rental car desk and getting on the shuttle bus. Since airport security officers were always on the lookout for unattended bags, it also suggested that someone had held the sack for the victim while she completed the rental paperwork.

"The envelope; did you notice any writing on it? Maybe an address?"

"No."

"How about stamps? Did it look like it'd been mailed?" he pressed.

"It was just a big envelope," said Duvall, sounding annoyed.

"How big?"

"Like for carrying regular papers."

"Do you think there were papers inside?"

"How should I know?" Duvall made no effort to hide his exasperation. "Look, man, my job is to check gas gauges and give people their cars. I don't know what she had in the envelope and, to be honest with you, I don't really care."

There wasn't much point in continuing the interview, so MacKinnon allowed Duvall to return to work and then began his journey back to Talmine. The southbound traffic was a little less balky; still, it was just after 6:30 p.m. when he pulled into his driveway.

Victoria was in the front yard, carefully trimming dead buds from the rose bushes, while chatting with neighbor Judith Landrum. On the lawn, Rob Roy and Noel were running in tight circles, hotly pursued by Blucher, the Landrums' miniature dachshund. However, the game came to an instant halt when the golden retrievers saw that MacKinnon was home, and they ran to his car, barking joyfully. While Victoria and MacKinnon exchanged hugs, Judith said goodbye, scooped up Blucher, and went home.

Holding hands with his wife as they walked inside, MacKinnon said, "It's good to be home."

"I missed you too. So how did it go?"

"Reasonably well, I suppose." MacKinnon unhooked his gun belt and hung it from a kitchen chair. "I have the rental paperwork, but I don't think it's going to be much help."

"She used a false ID?"

"More than likely," MacKinnon said with a sigh. "The name she gave was Anita Fesler, but the signature looks forged and the DOB on her Ohio DL would make her thirty-six years old."

Victoria nodded. "That girl wasn't thirty-six."

"Agreed, so I guess I'll be driving over to Fredericksburg tomorrow morning to submit her fingerprints for analysis."

"Hungry?"

"Starving."

"We can eat whenever you're ready, but I have a feeling you may want to take a look at one of the videotapes first," said Victoria, removing a pan of Cajun-style chicken breasts from the oven.

"Did you come up with something?"

"I think I may have found the male/female team that Carnes claimed he saw." Victoria's voice was mildly triumphant. "You can only see them from the rear, but they're walking toward Crumper's Woods. I've got it cued up on the VCR, if you want to take a look."

MacKinnon briefly forgot about dinner and entered the living room. Turning on the TV and VCR, he reviewed the videotape twice. The jerky footage revealed a Confederate artillery crew loading a brass cannon, while in the background a man and woman—both wearing the clothes described by Carnes—walked into the woods. At one point the woman pointed toward the trees. However, with their backs turned to the video camera, it was impossible to identify the pair.

"Well, what do you know?" MacKinnon said in quiet wonderment. "The arrogant son-of-a-bitch was telling the truth."

Later, as they ate, Victoria relayed a series of messages she'd received throughout the day. Sergeant Sayers had called, advising that he'd had no luck recovering any fingerprints from the Pontiac, and the search by the narcotics dog had met with negative results. Then Officer Plummer called to apologize for not discovering the burglary and report that he hadn't noticed anything suspicious during his shift. Finally, Mayor Dumfries had telephoned twice, requesting an update on the investigation.

"Oh, and after I went to Harmon's to collect a fresh batch of pictures, I dropped by the station to run background checks on Carnes and Benham," said Victoria. "The print-outs are on your desk."

"Anything worthwhile?"

"Nope. No record for either of them."

"Too bad, but I guess it was unrealistic to hope we'd find that one of them was a member of the Medellín Cartel."

His dinner finished, MacKinnon played with the dogs for a few minutes and then retired to his office to telephone Jean Dumfries. After receiving a brief synopsis of his investigation, the mayor expressed icy displeasure with his lack of progress.

"So, you still don't even know the dead girl's name?" she said.

"No, but then she went out of her way to conceal her identity," MacKinnon replied, hoping this didn't sound like a feeble rationalization for his lack of success. "I'm pretty certain that the computer analysis of her fingerprints will give us her name by tomorrow afternoon."

"I'm also told that someone broke into the police garage last night." Dumfries sounded maliciously amused.

"I was going to call, but then I figured there was no need, because my resident snitch, Kathy Sayers, wouldn't waste any time passing that news on to you," said MacKinnon, suddenly incapable of tact. It had been a long and fruitless day, and he wasn't in the mood for Dumfries' needling.

There was a sharp intake of breath from the receiver and, when Dumfries spoke, her voice was choleric. "Maybe you'd better remember who you're talking to."

"I'm talking to you, Mayor. Just for once, let's stop bullshitting each other and speak plainly." MacKinnon realized there was no point in apologizing; he'd already gone past the point of no return. He continued in an equitable tone, "You don't like me because I'm a dumb cop who doesn't realize that collecting a few shekels for the town treasury is more important than catching a killer. You also don't like me because I won't genuflect to my social superiors. As a consequence, you're in the process of cobbling together a package to have me fired."

"Who do you think you—"

"Wait, I'm not finished. I don't like you because you're a small-town ward-heeler with unwarranted delusions of grandeur. I like you even less because you tampered with the judges to screw my wife out of the first-place ribbon for her cheesecake at the county fair. And I despise you because you talk to my wife as if she were a retarded child. We don't like each other, but so long as I'm the chief of police, I'm going to run the department my way. So, if you don't care for that state of affairs, find a new chief."

"And don't think I won't," Dumfries said icily.

"Hey, if you've got the votes in council to give me my walking papers, go for it," he casually replied. "This problem isn't going to go away, and the sooner we get it resolved, the better. Now, I'd love to stay and chat, but I've got to get back to work. Good night."

Hanging up the phone, he took a deep breath and thought: *Guess I'd better give Tom Jarboe a call tomorrow about a new job.* It wasn't the most diplomatic moment of his professional career, but he regretted nothing he'd said and was glad to have the conflict out in the open. If he was going to fight Mayor Dumfries to keep his job, he preferred an above-board war to a sneaky guerilla campaign.

"Good for you. It's about time you read that chick the riot act."

He looked up and saw Victoria standing in the doorway. "Kind of put my foot into it, didn't I? How much of that did you hear?"

"Enough to thank you for defending the honor of my cheesecake."

He chuckled. "Well, brace yourself for the fallout. We're about to become untouchables."

Victoria came over and sat on the corner of his desk. "Do you think she has the votes to fire you?"

"Could be. The loyal toadies, Windsor and Adams, will support her majesty and, just to be obstinate, Kelleher and Jacobs will vote against her. That leaves Thatcham and McGilvery to decide my fate," said MacKinnon, calling the roster of town council members. "I'm pretty certain McGilvery will vote to keep me, and Sylvia Thatcham has always been friendly, but . . ."

"But she's like a pillow." Victoria finished the sentence for him. "Whoever sits on her last leaves the biggest impression. Knowing her, she'll abstain."

"So I can count on three votes. Do me a favor, sweetheart, and get the want ads out of the recycling bin," said MacKinnon, trying to sound lighthearted.

She leaned over to kiss him on the forehead. "Steve, I know what you're thinking, and I want you to stop worrying. This is our home now, and nobody—I mean nobody, including that dictator in a skirt—is going to drive us out. Besides, once you have a suspect in custody for the murder, Dumfries will have to withdraw the motion to terminate your contract; otherwise, she'll just look stupid."

"Which means I'd better get back to work." He gave his wife's hand a squeeze. "Thanks for the pep talk, Vic."

"My pleasure. Now I've got to go and make the bread pudding for breakfast."

"No raisins on my side. They're like eating bugs."

Victoria feigned indignation. "How would you know? You've never eaten a bug."

"Well, it's what I imagine a bug would taste like."

Her eyes rolled upward. "All right. I'll do my best to keep the raisins on my side of the bread pudding."

After she had gone downstairs, he called the telephone number for Anita Fesler listed on the rental document. As he expected, the number was invalid, and indeed, when he checked the phone book, he found the area code was incorrect for that portion of Ohio. His bad luck continued when he tried long-distance directory assistance and found there was no listing for Fesler in the Xenia phone book. Out of options, he telephoned the Xenia Police Department and spoke with the watch commander. After explaining he was investigating a homicide, he requested an officer be sent to Fesler's address to see if anyone was home and, if so, to have the resident call him collect in Virginia. It was a quiet night in town, said the watch commander, and he would dispatch an officer to the Fesler home shortly.

About forty-five minutes later, MacKinnon's telephone rang. It was the operator, announcing that she had a long-distance collect call from Anita Fesler. MacKinnon accepted the call, and a second later Fesler was on the line. Curiously, she didn't sound surprised to be hearing from the police.

"So you're with the police in Virginia," she said wearily. "Goody. What am I supposed to have done this time?"

"I take it that someone has been using your name," said MacKinnon.

"My entire identity," Fesler corrected him.

"So I guess it's safe to say that you didn't rent a car at Baltimore-Washington International Airport yesterday morning."

"Nope."

"And you weren't murdered here in Talmine yesterday either," MacKinnon dryly observed.

"No, I'm very much alive. But if you're telling me that the woman who has been pretending to be me is dead, that's the best news I've had in a long time." There was a pause and, when Fesler spoke again, the grim jubilation in her voice was gone, replaced by half-hearted contrition. "Jeez, I know that must make me sound cold, but that bitch just about destroyed my life."

MacKinnon asked Fesler to explain how her identity had come to be co-opted.

"One weekend last October, a girlfriend and I drove down to Hagerstown, in Maryland, for the quilt festival. We got there on Friday night and checked into a motel on Route 40."

"Do you remember the name?"

"The Carrollton Lodge. Anyway, the next morning we woke up and went to get some breakfast. Nancy, that's my friend, told me she'd pay, so I did something really stupid and left my purse in the room."

"And it was missing when you came back," said MacKinnon.

"We were gone less than a half-hour, but I still should have known better. Anyway, we told the manager, and right away he cops this what-do-you-want-me-to-do-about-it attitude, so we called the police. I told the officer I was certain that one of the motel maids had done it because the room hadn't been broken into. Whoever came in had a key," Fesler forcefully declared. "But the cop told me that if I didn't have any witnesses, there wasn't much he could do."

The ritual kiss-off line of a lazy cop, thought MacKinnon.

The least he could have done was to have checked the maids' office and sought permission to look in the motel employees' cars. But in most places, the notion of actually investigating a burglary, instead of writing a meaningless report, was as extinct as the passenger pigeon. Finally, he said, "Did the officer at least write a report?"

"Yeah, for all the good it did."

"Do you know the case number for the report?"

"He gave me a business card with the number written on it. Give me a sec, and I'll go get it," said Fesler. A moment later, MacKinnon could hear the sounds of drawers being opened and shut. Then Fesler was back. "Found it. Got a pen handy?"

"Go ahead."

"The number is H03-282-011."

MacKinnon wrote the number in his notepad. "Got it. So what happened next?"

"I got on the phone and tried to start canceling the credit cards, but do you know how hard that is if you don't have the eight-hundred numbers? It took me about a week to remember all the cards I'd had in my purse and call everyone, but I finally got them all canceled."

"And then?"

"Then, in January, I got a notice in the mail from the Hagerstown Court, saying that they had a warrant for my arrest because I hadn't gone to court for a shoplifting charge. I didn't know what they were talking about, so I called right away and found out that back in November some woman had used my driver's license as ID when she was caught ripping off a drugstore. She even signed my name to the summons." There was frustration in Fesler's voice as she continued. "I asked them to withdraw the warrant, but the clerk told me I would have to come all the way back there, and be fingerprinted, and take care of it in person. But who has the time to do that, and did I really want to take another chance in one of their motels? Besides which, I hadn't done anything wrong."

"And what did they say?"

"Quote, 'Suit yourself, lady,' end quote. She was a real smart-ass."

"Somehow I have a feeling that isn't the end of the story," MacKinnon said, his voice sympathetic.

Fesler took a deep breath. "Oh, no. It was only the beginning. Then came the letters from Shepherdstown, West Virginia and Hagerstown again, saying that now I had traffic warrants for my arrest. I called both places and got the same old story. 'Sorry, nothing we can do about it, unless you come here and sort it out.' Then I called the Hagerstown Police and asked them to try and find the woman using my ID, and the guy said he'd write a report. As if that would do any more good than the first report."

MacKinnon quickly shifted the receiver to his other ear. "So what happened next?"

Fesler's angry tone was replaced by one of listless fatigue. "Last month I wanted to buy a new car, but my credit application was rejected. That's when I discovered that whoever took my ID had applied for fresh credit cards and ran up over eleven-thousand dollars in debt. I finally had to hire a lawyer, and he's still trying to sort out the mess. I hope that explains why I'm not exactly torn up over her having been murdered. In fact, I wish it had happened months ago."

"I understand completely. Unfortunately, I don't have the right to ignore a homicide, even if the world is a much better place because the victim is dead."

"I know."

"Well, I'm going to let you get back to your evening," said MacKinnon. "You have my number and, if your lawyer thinks it will help, you can have him call me. Although I can't promise I'll have more success than you did, I'll talk to the Hagerstown Police about having the warrants recalled."

Later that evening, as MacKinnon sat typing his report, the facsimile machine whined into life.

The document was from Ralph Denton of the Northern Shenandoah Quartermaster, and it contained a roster of all female purchasers of military apparel over the past year. MacKinnon rapidly scanned the sheet, and it came as no surprise when he found Anita Fesler's name on the list. The imposter had ordered a pair of uniform trousers, a shell jacket, and haversack back in late July, and paid with the same VISA card used to rent the Pontiac. However, the merchandise hadn't been shipped to Ohio but to an address on Radford Lane in Boonsboro, Maryland.

MacKinnon accessed the map software and conducted a search for Boonsboro. A second later, the chart appeared and MacKinnon leaned closer to the monitor screen. A small town at the junction of US Highway 40 and Maryland State Route 34, Boonsboro was about ten miles southeast of Hagerstown, where Fesler's wallet had been stolen, and about an equal distance northeast of Sharpsburg, where Detective David Benham worked.

Lighting his pipe, MacKinnon realized that the following morning he would be making another trip to Maryland.

Seven:

The Minotaur

The telephone rang and MacKinnon was instantly awake. Reaching over to pick up the receiver, he glanced at the digital alarm clock. The glowing numerals read 3:12 a.m. *Well, it's either a crash or someone's hurt,* thought MacKinnon. It was never good news at this hour of the morning. Clearing his throat, he said, "MacKinnon here."

It was Dispatcher Wendy Schurz and she sounded worried. "Chief, we need you on a cover call."

"Where?" Rolling out of bed, he nearly tripped over Rob Roy. The dog grumbled and pushed himself farther under the bed.

"The Blackburn Gallery, two-nineteen Old Tavern Road. Plummer responded to an alarm activation, and he thinks he's got a suspect inside."

"Where should I meet him?"

There was a pause as Schurz conferred with Plummer over the police radio. Then she was back on the line. "He's at the rear door."

"I'm on my way." MacKinnon hung up the phone.

"Honey, what is it?" asked Victoria, her voice groggy.

"Watch your eyes," he warned as he turned on the lamp on his side of the bed. "We've got a burglar, there now, at Blackburn's Antiques."

Victoria rubbed her eyes and then sat up to watch her husband throw on a pair of jeans, his ballistic vest, some tennis shoes, and a uniform shirt. Grabbing his gun belt, he strapped it around his waist as he hurried into his office to retrieve his flashlight from the charger. She met him in the hallway and gave him a quick, strong hug. "Sweetheart, I love you. Please be careful."

He kissed his wife on the temple. "Count on it. Be back in a little bit."

After the coolness of the air-conditioned house, he found the atmosphere outside unpleasantly reminiscent of a sauna. The streets of Talmine were dark and deserted at this hour of the morning, and it took less than a minute to drive to the scene. About a block from Blackburn's Antique Gallery, he extinguished his headlights and coasted to a stop just around the corner from the business.

Getting out of the car, he took special care to close the door quietly, so as not to advertise his arrival, and then crept into the alley, his revolver in hand. Plummer flashed his light once very briefly to mark his location, and a second later MacKinnon joined the officer at the slightly-open back door. Inside, MacKinnon could hear items being moved. Plummer pointed to the door handle with his pistol. The hardware had been jimmied.

Leaning close to Plummer, MacKinnon whispered, "You go around the front, just in case he tries to go out through the window. When you're in place, click your radio transmit button twice, and I'll give the announcement."

"Yes, sir," rasped Plummer, and disappeared around the corner.

A few seconds later, MacKinnon's portable radio buzzed twice. He took a deep breath and shouted in through the open door, "This is the Talmine Police Department! We know you're in there! Put your hands up and come on out the back door!"

There was the sound of glass shattering on the floor and

then silence. MacKinnon waited a moment, and yelled again, "Hey, we can do this the easy way or the hard way and, to help you with this decision, let me enlighten you on an ancient law-enforcement tradition. Burglars who don't surrender are almost always injured, when they fall down trying to escape! Catch my drift?"

Still there was no response. MacKinnon lifted his portable radio and whispered, "See anything, Greg?"

"Negative. Thought I saw a flashlight for a second when I got here, but nothing now."

"Copy. Hold your position. Tango One to Control, is there any chance of getting some backup from the SO?"

"Negative." Schurz's voice sounded tinny over the radio speaker. "He can't break from an injury TC."

MacKinnon exhaled sharply. He wanted to wait for backup, but the longer they tarried, the greater the chance the suspect might make for the second floor and then the roof to escape. He pressed the radio transmit button. "Okay. Greg, I'm going to give him one last chance and then make entry. You stay there, in case he rabbits in that direction."

"Ten-four."

MacKinnon cautiously pushed the door open and shouted, "Last opportunity, pal! Come out now with your hands in the air!" There was still no response. Calling on the radio, he murmured, "Negative results. I'm going in."

"Ten-four."

The doorway opened into a narrow corridor, with two doors on the left and one on the right. Louvered, wooden saloon doors marked the end of the hallway, and beyond that was the sales area. Holding his gun close to his body at breast level, MacKinnon slowly pushed the first door on the left open and illuminated the interior with his flashlight. It was a restroom and there was no one inside. The door on the opposite side of the hallway led to a claustrophobic office, and the flashlight beam revealed the filing cabinet and desk drawers had been ransacked. But there was no one inside. Moving on to the third door, MacKinnon discovered it opened into a tiny workshop. Again, the room was vacant.

He crept forward, peered over the top of the saloon doors, and instantly raised his revolver. There was a motionless human figure in the far corner of the room near the large window. But as MacKinnon studied the form, he realized it was a mannequin attired in an old-fashioned diving suit. Scanning the room, he saw several other mannequins. *Or what I hope are mannequins,* he thought anxiously. Holding his flashlight away from his body, he momentarily illuminated the front part of the shop. He didn't see anyone, but that really didn't mean anything. The sales floor was a disorganized labyrinth of wood and glass display cases; large pieces of furniture like roll-top desks and upright pianos; hat racks hung with archaic clothing and crowned with old headwear; and several tall, free-standing mirrors. Not good. There were at least a hundred places where a suspect intent on ambush could hide.

Hoping to flush the crook out into the open, MacKinnon pushed one of the saloon doors open and then let it shut noisily, trying to create the impression he'd entered the sales area. Nothing happened. He then dropped to his hands and knees and crawled under the doors to a position of cover behind a loveseat. Now he could see the entire room, but the back part of the store was as dark and murky as the Maryland State Police coffee at BWI. Slowly standing up, he paused to again scan the room and then moved toward the sales counter to begin his search.

The silence was broken by the sound of a car approaching, and then a pair of headlights illuminated the interior of the shop. Plummer shouted for the driver to turn his fucking headlights off, and suddenly there was a horizontal geyser of yellowish flame from MacKinnon's left, near the stairway. Simultaneously, an invisible sledgehammer slammed the left side of his stomach. Thrown backwards into a glass display case and onto the floor, he was deafened by the roar of the gun being discharged. An instant later, the display window exploded inward and Plummer began to empty his 9mm pistol at the hidden gunman.

Blocking out the intense pain, MacKinnon crawled for a position of cover behind the oak sales counter. *You are not going to die in a glorified thrift shop,* he roughly commanded himself. From the radio on his hip he could hear Wendy Schurz's panicked voice asking their status. The gunfire stopped for a moment as Plummer reloaded and, from the back of the store, MacKinnon detected the sound of ceramic debris being stepped on. Forcing himself to his knees, he leveled his revolver at a shadowy figure and was blinded by another font of saffron fire as his attacker now took a shot at Plummer. Glass shattered and there was a shriek of agony from outside. MacKinnon knew Plummer had been hit.

There was the hollow patter of running footsteps and the saloon doors being thrown open. His night vision still ruined from the enormous muzzle-flash, MacKinnon fired twice at the shadowy figure and knew he'd missed. His natural instinct was to pursue the suspect, yet, rationally, he knew that neither he nor Plummer was in any condition to chase anyone. He heard Plummer's frightened voice erupt into his portable radio, "Tango Three! Shots fired! Shots fired! Tango One is down and I'm hit! Get me paramedics, code three!"

"Where are you hit?" cried Schurz, and the voice MacKinnon heard wasn't that of a professional police dispatcher, but a woman terrified over the fate of her beloved. An incongruous thought intruded: *the stories of the blossoming midnight shift romance are true.*

"My head! My hands!" Plummer said in a despairing voice.

Holding on to the counter, MacKinnon pulled himself to his feet and used the flashlight to examine his own injuries. There was a large, circular hole in his uniform shirt about three inches above his belt. MacKinnon touched the wound experimentally and discovered there was no blood. The ballistic vest had stopped the bullet, but it felt as if the entire cast of *Riverdance* had just used his abdomen as a stage. Then, in the distance, he heard a car engine roar, followed by the squeal of tires. From the sound of it, the vehicle was headed southbound on Old Tavern Road.

"Tango One! Tango One! Your status?" Schurz yelled over the radio.

"He's down!" Plummer shouted.

In the background another man's voice wailed, "What should I do?"

Lifting his portable radio, MacKinnon said in a slightly quavering voice, "Tango One to Control, I'm hit, but I think I'm okay. Suspect vehicle departed southbound on Old Tavern. No suspect description. No vehicle description."

"Tango Three's status?" Schurz was crying.

"I'm going out to check right now, Wendy." MacKinnon secured his revolver in the clamshell holster. "Calm down. It's going to be all right."

"Copy." There was the tiniest sliver of resolve in Schurz's tone. "Rescue squad en route."

"Good. Start a full department recall and call the sheriff."

"Yes, sir."

Carefully climbing out through the shattered window, MacKinnon saw that the moaning Plummer was slumped on the pavement with his back against the building. Blood covered his face, shoulders, and hands. It didn't look good, but MacKinnon reminded himself that head wounds always produced huge amounts of blood. Clutched in Plummer's left hand was a full magazine of 9mm shells, while he blindly slid his right hand over the pavement. Crouched beside the fallen officer was Leonard Blackburn, the owner of the antique shop. Somewhere to the south, a siren began to yelp.

MacKinnon knelt down and took Plummer's hand. "You're going to be fine, Greg. Just hang on."

"Can't see. Where's my gun?" demanded the wounded officer in a confused, querulous voice.

The Beretta 92F was on the sidewalk near the wall. Releasing Plummer's hand for a moment, MacKinnon picked the pistol up, ensured it was unloaded, and tucked it into the back of his gun belt. He put his hand on Plummer's shoulder. "Got it."

"Thanks. Couldn't find it." Plummer sounded a little calmer. "Fucker had to have had a shotgun. Saw you go down, and I tried to get him."

"I know. You did fine. Saved my life. Now you've got to be strong for Wendy. She's scared to death."

Plummer struggled to control his rapid breathing. "I'll try."

"By the way, you two weren't using the sofa in my office for the wild thing, were you?" joked MacKinnon, trying to think of something, anything, to divert the wounded officer's attention from his injuries.

"No," Plummer replied weakly, but there was the flicker of an embarrassed smile on his face.

"Liar," teased MacKinnon.

"Well, only once."

"I thought that stain looked suspicious."

Plummer grinned. *Good,* thought MacKinnon.

Blackburn was stunned. In a frantic voice, he said, "Oh, God, I'm so sorry. The alarm company called and told me there was an activation at the shop. I drove up, and it was too late to turn my headlights off."

"It's not your fault, Mr. Blackburn. Now, I need you to move your car so the paramedics have room," said MacKinnon. Actually, there was enough parking space on the deserted street for every emergency vehicle in town, but, as with Plummer, Blackburn needed distraction from the tragedy.

"I'll take care of it right away." Blackburn looked baffled and frightened, as if he'd awakened from a bad dream only to discover the nightmare was still in progress.

There were more sirens now. However, the first vehicle to skid to a stop in front of the business was a forest green Ford Explorer. MacKinnon recognized the SUV because it normally sat in his driveway. No doubt having heard the frantic broadcasts over the police radio in his office, Victoria had thrown her clothes on and broken a land-speed record getting to the scene. Like a lioness intent on the kill, she leapt from the Explorer and MacKinnon realized she had his Sig-Sauer .45 automatic in her hand. It was abundantly clear that Victoria hadn't come to lament, but to fight, and he'd never been more proud of his wife.

"Code four, sweetheart," he said. "Put the iron away."

"Are you all right?" Victoria slipped the pistol inside the waistband of her jeans and knelt down beside him.

"Bruised. The vest stopped the round."

"How you doing, Greg?"

"He's fine," replied MacKinnon, but when his eyes met Victoria's, a different message was conveyed: *Looks bad.* "Honey, I need you to do me a big favor. It seems that Greg and Wendy . . ."

Victoria understood. "And she's alone in dispatch. I'll get over there, right now."

"Thanks. From the sound of it, she's about to have a nervous breakdown."

"Can't blame her. I'm postponing mine until you get home," Victoria said, her voice suddenly husky. "Are you sure you're all right?"

"I'm fine. Sore and scared shitless, but otherwise fine."

As Victoria departed, a Brookesmith County Sheriff's car appeared on Old Tavern Road, its light bar flashing and siren howling. The cruiser slued to a halt and a deputy jumped out, shotgun in hand.

"Bring me your first aid kit!" shouted MacKinnon.

The deputy tossed the shotgun back inside the car and grabbed the first aid gear from the trunk. A moment later MacKinnon was gently pressing a mound of gauze against Plummer's left eye and temple. Then the fire department and paramedics arrived and began to prepare Plummer for transportation to Talmine Community Hospital.

"Okay, Greg, these guys are gonna take good care of you," MacKinnon said. "And once we get someone to take over the radio, my wife is going to drive Wendy over to the hospital."

"Thanks, Chief. Sorry about the couch." Plummer showed a feeble smile.

"You can use it on your honeymoon."

Moving out of the way of the busy paramedics, MacKinnon leaned against the wall and felt his knees quiver and hands shake with adrenaline palsy. He took a deep breath and winced. His side was really beginning to hurt. Then he noticed the deputy—his last name was Dawes, so naturally everybody called him Deputy Dawg—standing nearby. "Did you see anything as you came into town?" MacKinnon asked.

"Nothing. Not a goddamn thing." Dawes looked from the

smashed store window to Plummer being loaded into the ambulance and growled, "Fuck!"

"What?"

"It's just that I'd have been here, if it weren't for that bogus fucking call."

"Wait a minute! They told us you were out on a traffic crash."

"There was no traffic crash. Our dispatch got a call on the non-emergency line from an anonymous RP saying a vehicle had gone off the road and into Wert Creek."

"Almost all the way out to the county line."

"Right. Anyway, I got out there and started looking around and didn't see shit. And then all hell breaks loose here in town . . ." Dawes paused. "I was decoyed."

Gritting his teeth, MacKinnon said, "We all were."

Over the next few minutes, several more patrol cars pulled up and a handful of half-dressed residents began to gather on the sidewalk across the street. They wore perplexed and anxious expressions, unable to believe that something so irrational and violent had happened in their safe little town. Then Sergeant Sayers arrived and reported his wife had taken over dispatch duties and that Victoria had driven Wendy to the hospital.

"Good. Now let's see about trying to make some sense out of this crime scene," said MacKinnon.

Sayers pointed to the hole in MacKinnon's shirt. "Chief, we can handle it. You'd better get yourself over to the hospital and have them take a look at that. Wouldn't be surprised if you didn't have some broken ribs."

"I'll go over in a little bit. But first we've got to—"

"Chief, you're hurt. Why don't you go to the hospital and find out how bad?"

Of course, Sayers was right, thought MacKinnon. Indeed, if one of his officers had sustained any sort of gunshot impact to his ballistic vest, MacKinnon would have ordered him to the hospital for an examination; no ifs, ands, or buts. Grunting with pain, he placed a hand on Sayers' shoulder. "Okay, Ron, I'll go. But you're going to need to know how it all went down before you begin processing the scene."

Sayers shook his head. "No rush. We aren't going to touch anything for a while. I'll send a cop over with a tape recorder, and you can dictate it while you're waiting to be looked at."

"Fine, but do me a favor in the meantime."

"What's that?"

"Send someone over to the Regal Inn right now and see if Joseph Carnes is still there. If so, have them check his car to see if the engine is warm."

Sayers frowned. "You think this is connected with the murder in the park?"

"Ron, we don't get much major crime in this town, but in the space of less than forty-eight hours we've had one woman killed, a car stolen, and now two cops shot. I believe in a lot of strange things, but not that volume of coincidence."

"And if it looks like he's been out driving in the last hour?"

"Call me. In the meantime, sit on his room, but don't try to make contact. We're not going to have any more cops shot today." MacKinnon retrieved Plummer's pistol from the back of his gun belt and handed the weapon to Sayers. "Oh, and you'll want to log this in as evidence. Now I'm going to go to the hospital and try to talk the nurse out of making me wear one of those goofy smocks. I'll call you the moment I get some word on Greg."

A minute later, MacKinnon discovered that his side was beginning to hurt so much that he almost couldn't twist his body enough to get into the patrol car. By the time he settled in behind the steering wheel, he was panting like the valedictorian of a Lamaze birthing class. Now that the crisis was past, his body was allowing itself to feel the full breadth and scope of the pain. This was something that films and television misrepresented about the so-called bulletproof vest. In Hollywood, the hero could be struck a dozen times in the chest by high-velocity bullets and be unaffected. However, real life was a little different. While it was true that the ballistic vest would stop most handgun bullets, there was no way to defend against the kinetic shock of something hitting you at over 1,200 feet per second. That kind of force could break bones and cause trauma to vital organs.

Before starting the car, he cautiously touched the left side of his abdomen and wondered which of his internal parts was beneath the hole. He was reasonably certain his liver was on the right side, but he thought his kidneys were in there someplace. *I guess that'll be answered if my urine comes out looking like vintage port wine when I use the restroom,* he thought.

Talmine Community Hospital was a small, brick facility on York Avenue, just around the corner and about a block east of the police station. The tiny parking lot was full, so MacKinnon parked his car on the street and hobbled up to the emergency room entrance. Electric automatic doors opened with a hiss, and he stepped into an environment of controlled pandemonium.

Behind the reception desk, a woman was arguing with someone over the phone, while writing information on a medical form. Down the corridor, nurses and technicians were scurrying in and out of the treatment room, where an unseen doctor was issuing a series of instructions. An orderly rushed past MacKinnon, pushing a portable X-ray camera; then the paramedics emerged from the treatment room, one of them pulling bloody latex gloves from his hands. The surreal theme music for the unfolding tragedy was a gloomy and thoroughly insipid orchestral version of "Hey, Hey, We're the Monkees," oozing from the hospital's public address system.

Approaching the intake counter, MacKinnon overheard the receptionist snarl, "I'm going to say this for the third time: no, we aren't going to airlift him to Fredericksburg. No, I don't know why. I guess it's a doctor secret or something. Now stop arguing with me and get over here now!" She slammed the receiver down and fixed MacKinnon with a steely glare. "I'll brief you on his condition when I know something, so there's no point in hanging around the desk."

"Where can I find his girlfriend? She's with my wife."

"They were in the waiting room a second ago," the receptionist said. Her eyes flicked downward to the dried blood on MacKinnon's hands and the hole in his shirt. "Are you the other one who got shot?"

"It's not my blood, so there's no rush getting to me."

"Like hell." The receptionist called to a passing nurse, "Nancy, our second patient has arrived."

"Treatment Room One!" shouted the nurse, not pausing. She disappeared into the room where Plummer was being prepared for surgery.

The receptionist stepped from behind the counter and pointed to a doorway. "In there and take your clothes off. There's a gown on the table."

MacKinnon quietly groaned. "I really don't think I'm hurt all that badly. Can we skip the gown?"

"Do I come to the police station and tell you how to do things?" The receptionist made no effort to conceal her irritation.

"No."

"Then don't tell me my job. Reality check: you were shot. We've already got one medical crisis this morning, and we don't need another because you want to play John Wayne or something."

MacKinnon raised his palms in supplication. "Okay, okay, I'll go in and get undressed right after I speak to my wife and Wendy. Be back in a second."

"You've got two minutes. Don't make me come looking for you."

He peered at the woman's nametag. "Understood, Myra. Two minutes."

Realizing the last thing Wendy needed to see was Plummer's dried blood on his hands, MacKinnon ducked into the restroom to wash. Afterwards, he used the toilet and was enormously relieved to discover that everything came out both properly and in the appropriate color. Washing his hands a second time, he scrutinized his unshaven, pale face in the mirror. "Pal," he told himself, "you look like a very bad embalming job."

He found his wife and Wendy sitting on a frayed couch in the waiting room. Victoria was holding the dispatcher's hand and was speaking quietly to Wendy, whose eyes were red and puffy and cheeks stained with brown rivulets of mascara. Both women looked up anxiously when MacKinnon came into the room.

"No news yet. They're getting ready to do surgery."

"How bad is it?" asked Wendy, obviously fearing the answer.

Two decades earlier as a rookie cop, one of the first skills MacKinnon had learned was how to lie convincingly. "I'm no doctor, but I think he'll be fine. They'll brief you the minute they have something to report."

Wendy nodded and looked imploringly at Victoria. "Do you ever get used to this, Mrs. MacKinnon?"

"I'll let you know the next time it happens." Victoria gripped the dispatcher's hand.

Stifling a moan, MacKinnon bent over to kiss his wife. "I'd love to stay, but Myra—she's the former Marine drill sergeant at the reception desk—is going to beat me like a baby harp seal at fur harvest time, if I don't get into the treatment room."

Victoria squinted at her husband. She hadn't missed his painful exhalation. "Do you need help getting undressed?"

"I'll be fine, and thanks for being here, sweetheart."

"As if you could keep me away."

Myra glanced up from her paperwork and gave him a stern nod as he walked into the treatment room. Inside, he drew the curtains closed and cautiously took off his gun belt and uniform shirt. In a metal basket at the foot of the examination table, he found a large plastic bag and put the shirt inside it for evidence processing. Next, he removed the ballistic vest and peeked under the tee shirt. The flesh beneath where the bullet had struck the vest was already beginning to turn magenta.

Across the hall, MacKinnon could hear low voices and the electronic beeps of medical monitoring equipment. The surgeon had apparently arrived and they'd begun to work on trying to save Plummer. Although MacKinnon wasn't particularly religious, he dispatched a prayer for the officer's recovery and was instantly ashamed at his capacity for hypocrisy. Ordinarily, he didn't devote much thought to God; over the years, he'd seen far too much human wickedness and violent death to imagine the Cosmic Big Fella paid very close attention to the human race. When things went bad, he remembered to pray, but he was honest enough to admit that his appeals were really nothing more than an ethereal version of on-line shopping. You ordered a happy outcome from *supremebeing.com*, hoping the miracle was in stock and that you hadn't gone over the limit on your spiritual credit card.

Okay, so I'm a fraud, but if You're there, You already know my moral shortcomings and don't have any right to be shocked. What's more, if You don't come through and save Greg Plummer, this will be the last time I visit this Website . . . until I need another favor. Amen.

Taking off his jeans and tee shirt, MacKinnon put on the pale-blue gown and sat down on the examination table. But he quickly found himself incapable of sitting around doing nothing, so he began exploring the drawers of the treatment room until he found some scissors. He cut an irregular rectangle from the fabric of the ballistic vest surrounding the spot where the bullet was lodged, and gently manipulated the piece of ceramic fabric until he could pluck the gray projectile from the cavity with his fingers.

He placed the flattened bullet on the countertop and found a small ruler. The round was about three-eighths of an inch across, and there was no evidence of the copper jacketing seen on most modern ammunition. It was an old-fashioned lead slug. Looking in the drawers, he located a small prescription envelope and put the bullet into it for safekeeping.

The curtains parted and a woman wearing a wrinkled white smock entered the treatment room, a metal clipboard in hand. Her nametag read "Rose" and, from the tousled condition of her hair and lack of makeup, it was obvious to MacKinnon that she'd just been awakened and called into work.

"And just what do you think you're doing?" she asked.

"You know, I'll bet you're not a morning person."

"Not at four a.m. Up on the table, Chief. And lose the boxers."

MacKinnon complied and, after having his temperature taken and blood pressure checked, Rose asked him to describe what happened and then began to examine his abdomen while he clutched at the gown to cover his nether regions.

"No skin breakage," Rose muttered to herself. Then she pressed on the bruise. "On a scale of one to five, rate the pain."

MacKinnon grunted. "Three."

Her hand slid slightly upwards to the lower portion of his ribcage. "And there?"

"Two, I guess."

She withdrew her hand and made a note on MacKinnon's medical intake form. Finally, she said, "Obviously you have a large hematoma and probably a fractured rib or two. We'll send you over for X-rays to make sure. Then, tomorrow, I'm certain the doctor is going to want you to go to Fredericksburg for an MRI."

"How's it going next door?" MacKinnon motioned with his head toward where the surgery was proceeding.

"You'll have to ask the doctor."

"Come on, Rose. The guy saved my life."

She peeked around the curtains to make certain they were alone. "It looks like he has birdshot in his head, upper body, and left hand. He's not going to die, but he's probably going to lose his left eye. But you didn't hear that from me."

"Shit," said MacKinnon in a voice composed of equal measure of nausea and rage. He knew Plummer's injuries were serious, but somehow having the information confirmed was an ugly shock. His hands curled into tight fists and he suddenly wished he felt well enough to smash everything in the treatment room. Another terrible thought intruded: *Just how was he going to go back into that waiting room and tell Wendy that her sweetheart was maimed for life?*

"You asked," Rose said defensively.

"I know and thanks for being honest." MacKinnon

sighed. "When will we know for certain?"

"We've got a specialist en route from Richmond, so I wouldn't say anything to anyone until he has a chance to take a look. Now, let's get you over to X-ray."

Although MacKinnon wanted to walk to the radiology lab, Rose insisted that an orderly transport him there on a gurney. Along the way, he heard the rapid clatter of footfalls as someone attempted to overtake the gurney and then the voice of the very last person on earth he wanted to chat with this awful morning.

"Chief MacKinnon? Hold it there a second, you. Chief MacKinnon, we need to talk."

He could see that Jean Dumfries had taken the time to apply makeup before leaving home. Like most politicians, she viewed any occurrence of public tragedy (so long as it wasn't her own) as a photo op, so it was vital to look good for the cameras, should any journalists appear.

"Mayor, can this wait? This really isn't the place to talk," MacKinnon said wearily.

"This will only take a second. I just want you to know that I hold you personally responsible for this insanity."

"What the hell are you talking about?"

"I'm talking about how you handled that call this morning. Because of your utter incompetence, an officer was shot and the person who did it escaped. You can spare yourself and the town a lot of unpleasantness if you just submit your resignation later today."

"You know, Mayor, it takes a truly despicable person to try and turn a political advantage from a cop being shot." MacKinnon sat up on the gurney. "Jesus, how do you look at yourself in the mirror without vomiting?"

"Hey! What part of 'You can't go back there' didn't you understand?" Summoned by the orderly, Myra appeared from around the corner. "Jean Dumfries, you get your liposuctioned butt out of here right now, or I'll throw you out myself!"

"You wouldn't dare." Dumfries turned to face the swiftly-approaching receptionist.

"Honey, that's about the silliest thing I've ever heard. You have *no* idea of what I'd dare." Myra's face was now within inches of the mayor's and a fierce light shone from the receptionist's eyes. "You may think you're the queen of northern Virginia, but you don't mess with the patients in *my* hospital. Now git, before I forget I'm a Christian woman and smack you so hard that everybody in your family tree bleeds."

"You know, Mayor, I do believe she means it," said MacKinnon.

"You hush up," snapped Myra, slapping the gurney's metal railing for emphasis. But her eyes never left those of Dumfries. "I don't need anyone's help dealing with this sneaky little copperhead. Git, sister, or you're gonna take a tumble on these new-waxed floors, and the only witnesses to the accident will be me and the chief."

Dumfries slowly backed down the hall, but fired a parting shot. "It's your choice, MacKinnon. You've got until four o'clock this afternoon to quit. After that, the gloves come off."

"You know, I've just thought of one really good thing about these short hospital gowns. They're perfectly designed for you to kiss my ass." When the mayor had disappeared, he said, "Thanks, Myra."

"No need," she replied, her expression grim. "I've had that woman in my crosshairs ever since the council condemned my mama's house to make room for the new shopping center. Funny thing; her highness owned the other two adjoining parcels. They called it 'eminent domain,' but I call it thievery, pure and simple."

Twenty minutes later, the orderly pushed MacKinnon's gurney back into the treatment room, where Sheriff Jarboe sat perched on a stool.

"Hey, Mac. How you doin'?"

"I've had better days, Tom."

"And Plummer?"

"Too early to tell." MacKinnon tried to lie, but the truth came spilling out. "Actually, that's complete bullshit. A nurse told me that even if he pulls through, he's going to lose an eye. Dammit, Tom, I feel so bad. I went down and he . . ."

And without warning he could no longer speak. Hot tears filled his eyes and it was only with the greatest of effort that he managed to refrain from sobbing. He was ashamed of being unable to suppress his emotions, and the sheriff's hand on his shoulder made him feel even more vulnerable.

"It's all right, Mac. Let it out," Jarboe said gently.

MacKinnon took a deep breath, roughly wiped at his eyes with the gown sleeve, and was in control again. He said sternly, "No, it's not all right. Blubbering about it isn't going to fix anything. What's happening out at the scene?"

Jarboe nodded and showed a melancholy smile. "It's under control. Ron wanted me to pass on some information. First, that guy is not at the motel."

"Carnes?"

"Right. The manager said he checked out yesterday afternoon at one. And Ron knew you were going to ask this, so I'm supposed to tell you that he's already checked all the other motels in town for the guy. Negative results. Ron got the guy's vehicle information and wants to know if you want a BOLO issued."

"Not yet. I don't have anything even resembling probable cause."

"So why do you think it's him?"

"Hand me my shorts and I'll explain." A moment later, MacKinnon climbed from the gurney and removed the bullet from the envelope. He dropped the slug into the sheriff's hand. "Now I can't prove it's him, but something occurred to me as I was being X-rayed. Take a look at this."

"Soft lead. Looks like maybe a wad cutter for a .41 Magnum." Jarboe said, not quite understanding the point MacKinnon was trying to make.

"I was shot with this, and Plummer was hit with a shotgun blast. On Saturday, my murder victim was shot in the head with about a .65 caliber musket ball."

"Which means?"

"If the shootings are connected, either three different guns were used, or just one."

Jarboe looked puzzled. "One?"

"Believe it or not, one. It's called a LeMat, and it was a goddamned deadly and amazing weapon, a real hog-leg. It had a nine-shot, .42 caliber cylinder revolving around a central .65 caliber barrel that could fire either a ball or a shotgun round. It was manufactured during the Civil War for the Confederacy, but you can buy a fully-operable replica now from a couple of different gun companies."

"Okay, but what does that have to do with Carnes? Sayers told me this guy was an antique dealer. Why would he come to town and start shooting people with a hand cannon?"

"He's an antique dealer who likes to masquerade as a Confederate general. Or, for that matter, he might be nuts and think he's a real Rebel officer. I know it's a real stretch at this point, but he's our killer; I'd bet the farm on it."

"And his motive?"

MacKinnon slowly exhaled. "I don't know, Tom. But I'd really like to find out before we end up with another dead body."

Eight:

The Harvest of Error

It was shortly past 6:00 a.m. when MacKinnon signed the documents clearing him for release from the hospital. Myra handed him a prescription form for painkilling pills, a sheaf of after-treatment instructions for his fractured rib, and a preprinted map to the medical center in Fredericksburg. The MRI was scheduled for 1:30 that afternoon and, although MacKinnon said nothing, he already knew he was going to miss the appointment.

"Chief, you'd best not blow this off," said Myra, noting the distant look in his eyes. "If you've got internal injuries, take my word, you want to find out now, rather than later."

"I'll be there."

"For an old cop you're a bad liar." Myra pointed to a telephone number on the bottom of the map. "At least do them the courtesy of calling to reschedule, because I already know you aren't going to be there."

"I'm heartsick that you'd think I'd be anything less than one hundred percent truthful with you, Myra," MacKinnon deadpanned.

"Yeah, I'll bet." When she spoke again, her tone was belligerently encouraging. "And Chief, don't you even think of giving in to Dumfries. There are lots of people here in town that like how you run the police department. So hang tough for us."

"Thanks, Myra."

As Myra left the treatment room, she held the door open

for Victoria and Wendy. Both women looked exhausted. The surgery on Plummer was still underway but, with the arrival of the specialist from Richmond, there were some cautious signs of optimism among the medical staff. This was a good thing, because Wendy had crumbled anew when the medical staff had advised her of her boyfriend's grave condition. It was likely that several more hours would pass before the surgery was completed, so Victoria insisted that Wendy come home with them to get some rest.

"You can have a little breakfast and then take a nap in our spare bedroom," said Victoria. "I'll wake you up the minute they call."

"I couldn't," Wendy said in a shy and uncertain voice.

"Wendy, you'd have better luck trying to argue with an earthquake than with my darling wife once she's decided on something," said MacKinnon, as his hand found Victoria's. "You might as well say yes now and spare yourself a debate you're going to lose."

"If you say so."

"Good." He kissed Victoria and added, "I'll see you at home in about forty-five minutes. I've got a couple of errands to do."

She pulled on his hand. "Steve, the doctor said you were supposed to rest."

"I promise this will only take a couple of minutes."

"I'm going to hold you to that." She raised her left wrist to the level of MacKinnon's eyes and tapped the face of her watch with her right index finger. "It's six-thirteen now and, if you aren't home by seven, I'm going to come find you."

"See what I mean about arguing with her, Wendy?" MacKinnon joked, but he saw that Victoria wasn't smiling. "Honey, you have my word that I'll be home by seven. Then I'm done for the day."

He waited until the women left the treatment room, before opening the cupboard to retrieve two large plastic bags. One contained his shirt, ballistic vest, and the expended bullet, while the other held Plummer's bloodstained uniform, gun belt, and equipment.

It was a beautiful morning outside, but seeing a cardinal dart skyward from a nearby tree, MacKinnon was reminded of blood.

Leaving the hospital parking lot, he drove to the police station, where the two bags and his revolver were secured in the evidence closet. It was standard procedure after a police shooting for the officer's weapon to be minutely inspected to determine whether it was operating properly, and if he was carrying authorized ammunition. This meant that until he got his gun back, he would be forced to use a loaner. Unlocking the department armory, he ignored the modern 9mm pistols and selected a vintage Smith & Wesson Model 27, .357 Magnum revolver from the pistol rack. He loaded the hefty pistol with hollow-point ammunition and stuck it into a discarded holster he found in the cupboard. Next, he searched the drawers and eventually located a pair of speed loaders for his spare ammunition, with their leather case, for his belt. A few minutes later, the new armaments were attached to his gun belt and he walked downstairs.

Pausing in the dispatch room, he checked with Kathy Sayers for any new developments. For the first time in recent memory, the dispatcher didn't offer him an oily grin as she reported the city was quiet. Indeed, the conversation was almost companionable as he brought her up to date on Plummer's condition. It was really too bad that it took a life-threatening emergency for Kathy to temporarily bury the hatchet. *But don't even think for a minute that she's forgotten where she buried the hatchet,* he reminded himself. After confirming that Kathy was going to be relieved at 9:00 by Julie Crozier, he said goodbye and returned to his car.

His next stop was Blackburn's Antiques, where the cops were still processing the scene. Ron Sayers and Sheriff Jarboe stood near the front door while a TV news team shot video of them against the backdrop of the shop's shattered window. Slipping under the crime scene barrier tape, MacKinnon noticed that someone had placed a bunch of flowers on the sidewalk near Plummer's drying puddles of blood. Neither Sayers nor Jarboe seemed particularly surprised to see the chief.

Checking his watch, Sayers said to Jarboe, "I win."

"Me and Ron had a little wager as to when you'd get back here," Jarboe explained. Sort of an over-and-under bet. Ron thought you'd be back before seven, and I thought that it would at least take until nine before you talked Victoria into letting you go."

MacKinnon pretended his dignity was affronted. "Tom, I'll have you know that I'm the supreme lord and master of my home. Benevolent tyrants don't ask permission of their wives."

"Oh yeah, just like me," snorted Jarboe. "How much time did she give you?"

"Until seven," MacKinnon admitted sheepishly. He turned to Sayers. "Why don't you gather everybody together for a moment, and I'll give them an update on Greg." A few moments later, the officers formed a loose semicircle around the chief. "Guys, Greg is still in surgery, but from what they told me, I guess it's looking better for him. They've got a specialist in from Richmond, but it's going to take some time before we know anything for certain, so please stop calling the hospital every fifteen minutes. I know you're worried, but they won't have anything to report for at least a couple of hours. Questions?"

"Are they going to need blood donations?" asked Officer Booth.

"Not right now, Keith. Our account was in pretty good shape after the last blood drive." He pointed to Deshawn Williams, who had raised his hand.

"Chief, this guy Carnes. The rumor is he's our shooter. Is that true?" Williams' face was grim.

"I didn't get a look at the suspect. I do want to talk with Carnes, but I also want to stress that there is no PC for his arrest. At the same time, I want you to exercise maximum officer safety if you contact him."

"Do we have any pictures of this guy?" asked Sayers.

"Not yet, but once this meeting is concluded, I want you to call the New York State Police and see if they'll rush us a driver's license picture. Have them e-mail us a good copy and send us an original via overnight mail."

"If we do find him, what do you want us to do?" asked Officer Venard.

"I don't think we're going to see him around town but, if you do, get some backup and call me. Officially, right now I only want to talk to him, but if he's CCW, hook him up."

"What's he driving?" asked Booth.

MacKinnon glanced at Sayers, who opened his notebook and announced, "A two-thousand-four Saab nine-thousand, metallic red in color, with New York vanity plates of CSALGEN."

"See Salgen?" said Venard, trying to make sense of the license plate letters.

"CSA—Confederate States of America—and LGEN for Lieutenant General," explained MacKinnon. "Carnes is a serious Civil War buff, and he's probably carrying a replica Civil War pistol that's a combination revolver and shotgun. So be careful."

There were no more questions, and the officers returned to their posts. Glancing toward the antique shop, MacKinnon said to Sayers, "I know you got the cassette tape of my statement on the shooting, but it will help if I walk you through the scene."

Entering the store, MacKinnon assessed the destruction and knew the department budget was going to take a severe hit when the check was written to make good the damage to the antiques. *Of course, if Dumfries has her way, that isn't going to be my problem,* he reminded himself. His cursory inspection revealed a ruined Tiffany lamp, the broken bottom third of a cut glass brandy decanter, and a framed, limited-edition lithograph of Don Troiani's *Barksdales Charge*, a painting of the Battle of Gettysburg, now ruined because one of the bullets had left a perfect, round hole in the Sherfy farmhouse. *I don't even want to look at the price tag on that,* he thought.

Going to where he'd been shot, he noticed an overturned and shattered glass case and probably a dozen dismembered Hummel figurines scattered on the floor. He'd apparently knocked it over, but he had no recollection of smashing into the display case.

In the rear of the shop, he could see where Sayers had circled the bullet holes from Plummer's 9mm with white chalk. Some were in the wall, while others had struck a tall, rosewood china cabinet, and one had struck dead center on an Elvis in Las Vegas commemorative plate. *Well, at least some good had come from the tragedy,* MacKinnon sardonically reflected. Picking his way through the jagged mosaic of broken, colored glass littering the floor, he inspected the saloon doors to see where the two rounds he'd fired had gone. He found one hole in the doorframe, at about head height, and the other had pierced the louvered slats and come to rest at an oblique angle in the corridor wall beyond.

"We found a flashlight up here, so this is probably where the suspect was, when he opened up on you," called Sayers.

The sergeant stood on the landing, about five feet above the sales floor, where the stairway to the second floor made a 180-degree turn upwards. The wooden stair railing was draped with throw rugs and a large tapestry of an English hunting scene. In the dark, anyone in that position would have been both invisible and in possession of an uninhibited field of fire throughout the shop. MacKinnon knew that he'd been lucky and that by all rights he should be dead.

"Any chance for prints from the flashlight?" he asked.

"It's a matte plastic. Maybe if we get lucky," said Sayers, but he didn't sound confident.

"We'll probably have better luck printing the batteries. Let's not try to mess with fingerprint powder. We'll let the lab superglue it and use their laser."

Sayers nodded. "That's what I figured."

"You notice the ransacking?" Jarboe called from the office.

MacKinnon joined him in the doorway. "Yeah. Pretty thorough."

"Folders all over the floor. Looks like he was after some kind of papers," said Jarboe. "So what do you think the connection is between the dead girl and the antique shop?"

"Beats the hell out of me, unless Carnes thought that whatever he was looking for was here. Maybe Blackburn can tell us."

Leonard Blackburn stood outside the shop, cautiously sipping coffee from a cardboard cup and wincing slightly whenever he heard a fresh tinkle of broken glass from inside.

"I'm sorry about the mess, and I'll be getting back to you with the forms you'll need to make a claim against the city for the damages," said MacKinnon. "But right now I need to pick your brain. Did you have any distinctive customers on Saturday morning?"

"How do you mean? There were a lot of people from out of town, what with Civil War Days."

"Was there anyone who offered to sell you something?"

Blackburn blew on his coffee. "Yes, sir, now that you mention it, we did have a lady come in, and she asked if I was interested in purchasing some Civil War documents."

"What kind of documents?"

"A collection of letters from a Confederate officer and a piece of official correspondence from Lee's Army."

"The Army of Northern Virginia?"

Blackburn nodded. "The order was from some headquarters colonel. I can't recollect his name at this moment, but it wasn't the same guy who wrote the letters. It said that soldiers who didn't have shoes weren't exempted from duty. I looked and it was good quality stuff, so I bought it."

"Would you recognize this woman if you saw her again?"

"Sure."

"Ron, the case file with the victim's picture is in my office. Check around and see if one our guys has a copy of the photo we distributed Saturday." As Sayers went in search of the picture, MacKinnon resumed his questioning. "I don't mean to be intrusive, but how much did you pay for these documents?"

"Nine hundred and fifty dollars."

"And how much are they actually worth?"

"Well, Chief, that's kind of hard to say." Blackburn's tone was both coy and guarded.

"Would it be kind of hard to say that the lady didn't know the true value of the papers?" *And that you took the seller to the cleaners,* MacKinnon wanted to add, but there was no point in unnecessarily antagonizing the witness.

"Umm. No," mumbled Blackburn.

Sayers reappeared with the picture in hand. "Deshawn had a copy."

"Thanks." MacKinnon held out the picture for Blackburn to examine.

The antique dealer swallowed uncomfortably when he saw the huge gunshot wound in the woman's head. "No, that wasn't her. This was a much older lady from North Carolina. I've got her address and phone number in my desk, if you need it."

"When we get done here, I'm going to need that information," said MacKinnon. "So, who knew about this purchase?"

"Just the wife and I. I wanted to have the papers appraised before I put them on the market." There was a pause, then Blackburn added, "But you know, I did mention buying some Civil War documents to that guy who was in here yesterday. He was real interested in anything from that period."

Remembering the previous day's encounter with Carnes, MacKinnon said, "Was this a man carrying bags from the other antique shops and wearing blue slacks and a green shirt with a white checkerboard pattern?"

"You know who I'm talking about?"

"His name is Joseph Carnes and he's an antique dealer from New York. Tell me what happened."

"I just told him that I'd bought an order from the Army of Northern Virginia from a lady, but that it wasn't for sale until I could have it valued. He wasn't happy about that one bit. Then he got a little pissy and finally left the shop in a huff."

"Mr. Blackburn, could you check and see if those papers are still in your shop and get the information on the lady you bought them from?"

"Oh, the documents aren't in the shop. They're in my safe

at home. But I'll get you the receipt with the lady's address." Blackburn led the cops into the shop and back to the office. He peered unhappily at the papers scattered all over the floor. "It was on the desk. Is it all right if I go through this stuff?"

MacKinnon shot a questioning glance at Sayers, who said, "Photos and prints are finished in here. I don't think there's a problem."

Blackburn knelt down and sifted through the paperwork. At length he held up a slip of yellow paper. "Here it is."

"Thanks, and I'll get this back to you as soon as I can." MacKinnon took the receipt and examined the information at the top of the sheet. Blackburn had purchased the documents from a Ruth O'Connor of Gum Corner, North Carolina. Then MacKinnon looked at his watch. "Guys, I've got exactly four minutes to get home or I'm going to be grounded. Call me if you come up with anything else, and I'll try to sneak out later."

He pulled into the driveway at 6:59 a.m. and was met at the door by Victoria, who was holding both dogs by their muzzles to prevent them from barking. She whispered, "Honey, you need to be quiet. Wendy went in to take a nap about twenty minutes ago."

"Good. Any word from the hospital yet?"

"Nothing."

"Well, I just found out something interesting," MacKinnon said in a low voice as he followed the delicious aroma of hot coffee and breakfast into the kitchen.

"Be good. No jump on Daddy. No bark." Victoria spoke in pidgin to the golden retrievers, then released her grip on their jaws.

"I didn't know our dogs talked like Tarzan," said MacKinnon.

But there was no answering smile from Victoria. Instead,

her lower lip began to tremble, tears filled her eyes, and she rushed into his arms. His side hurt, but somehow that wasn't very important. For about a half-minute, she cried quietly into his chest and gripped his shirt with tight fists. Finally there was a huge sob and Victoria tried to speak.

"I heard you say you were going in, and then I heard popping sounds from downtown and, oh God—"

MacKinnon stroked her hair. "It's all right."

"Then Plummer said you were down and I was so frightened, Steve, and I didn't know what I'd do if you were dead."

"So you got the gun from my office and came to help," he said in quiet admiration. "You were willing to risk your life for me, darling, and it's a little terrifying to know how much you love me."

They held each other, and he murmured words of comfort until his wife had no more tears to shed. Then she released him, wiped her eyes with the back of her hand, and said with a sniffle, "Sorry. I got your shirt all wet."

He kissed her forehead. "That's okay."

"Hungry?"

"I could eat."

Opening the oven, she removed some sausage patties that had been warming. "So, what did you find out that was interesting?"

"It seems that on Saturday, Blackburn bilked some old lady from North Carolina out of some Civil War era documents, and on Sunday, he mentioned that fact to Carnes." MacKinnon poured himself a cup of coffee. "Blackburn told me Carnes flamed out when he was told that the papers weren't for sale."

"Which means you think Carnes was the shooter tonight?"

"Yep."

"And you think he was after those papers?"

MacKinnon slowly settled into a kitchen chair. "Well, with the way he searched the dead girl, we know he was looking for something."

"But what's the link between the murder victim and this lady from North Carolina who was cheated?" Victoria cracked two eggs over the frying pan.

"I'm going to call her after breakfast and see." As he sipped his coffee, a thought struck him. "Try this one on. Maybe the two women aren't connected, but Carnes thinks they are."

Victoria looked up from the frying pan. "Go on."

"Let's assume that Carnes met with our murder victim to buy some sort of document from her. But being a cagey hype that lives in the wonderful world of dope rip-offs, she doesn't bring the merchandise to the meet. Carnes gets mad and gives her a .65 caliber lobotomy—"

"But she doesn't tell him where the goods are, so he starts looking around town." Victoria finished the thought.

"Which explains why I saw him on Antique Row yesterday. Maybe he figured she tried to sell the papers there. So the next day, when Carnes gets to Blackburn's, Blackburn refuses to let him see the papers and, less than eighteen hours later, we've got the burglary and shooting."

"And?" Victoria put the plate of food down in front of him.

"What if there are two entirely different and unconnected sets of documents? What if it was just a horrible coincidence that some gullible fossil from Gum Corner came to town to sell some Civil War papers on the same day our victim and Carnes were set to deal?" MacKinnon speared a piece of sausage with his fork.

Victoria opened the refrigerator and retrieved a glass

pitcher of orange juice. "But what sort of papers would be worth killing someone over?"

"I don't know, but maybe if we get the victim identified we'll find out." MacKinnon kept his eyes on his plate.

"Steve, you aren't going to Hagerstown today," said Victoria. She'd instantly recognized his last statement as a preamble to the announcement that he'd be leaving for Maryland after breakfast.

"Saw right through me, huh?"

She nodded.

"Well, I can't just sit here and do nothing," he said plaintively.

"Why not?"

"Because the clock is ticking. The longer those papers are missing, the greater the chance Carnes is going to blast somebody else. And if that wacky son-of-a-bitch is willing to shoot it out with two cops, there's no telling what else he might do. So, after breakfast I'm going to Fredericksburg to drop the victim's prints off at the lab and then I'm heading up to Maryland."

Victoria frowned. "And what happens if you start to bleed internally?"

"That's not going to happen."

"But what if it does?"

"Then I'll go to a hospital."

She shook her head. "Steven Matthew MacKinnon, you are the most frustrating man I've ever known."

"But you understand why I've got to go."

"Yes. But that doesn't mean I have to like it."

After breakfast, MacKinnon telephoned Ruth O'Connor in North Carolina. When the lady answered the phone, her voice only barely won out over that of the saleswoman boosting genuine cubic zirconium pendants on a TV shopping channel in the background. Once O'Connor had turned down the volume of her TV, MacKinnon explained the purpose of his call and said, "I've just got a couple of questions, ma'am. You were in Talmine on Saturday, right?"

"Yes. My daughter and her husband drove me up. She'd heard about your festival from a neighbor, and we thought it might be the place to sell some family heirlooms."

"And that would be the Civil War papers. If you don't mind me asking, where did they come from?"

"Oh, I reckon they've been in a box in my attic ever since my Great Grandpa Josiah passed on. He fought in the war. Josiah was an officer in the Forty-seventh North Carolina. Lost a leg at Gettysburg."

"Johnson Pettigrew's brigade," MacKinnon said, unable to resist the brief conversational detour into his favorite topic: the Battle of Gettysburg. "They fought well on the first day."

O'Connor sniffed indignantly. "Young man, I can tell you my Great Grandma Mary didn't care a damn, forgive my language, if they fought well or not. Her husband was a cripple; stumped around on a wooden peg to the end of his days. Down here there are still some folks who are unreconstructed Rebels, but I'm not one of them. Neither was my Great Grandpa. Whenever the family used to gather, some numbskull cousin would ask him to talk about the war, and all he would say was, 'Rich man's war, poor man's fight.' "

"I'm sorry if my interest seemed insensitive," MacKinnon said. "It's just that I've always been a real student of the Civil War."

"Well, at least you aren't like those tubby old fools I saw in your town, all gussied up in uniform and pretending they're fighting the war. They need to grow up, that's what I think."

Ouch, thought MacKinnon. He said, "Can I ask a few more questions?"

"Of course."

"While you were in Talmine on Saturday, did you happen to meet a young woman who was also trying to sell some Civil War papers?"

"No."

"Or talk with a gentleman dressed as a Confederate general?"

"Certainly not," O'Connor said disdainfully. "I've got better things to do than encourage that sort of silly behavior."

Concluding the call, MacKinnon went downstairs to the kitchen and provided Victoria with a short summary of his conversation with O'Connor.

"So you were right, there's no connection with our victim." Victoria looked up from the sink, where she was washing the breakfast dishes.

He retrieved a dishtowel and began to dry a plate. "Yeah, but it doesn't get us any closer to knowing what Carnes was really after. While I'm gone, can you do something for me?"

"What's that?"

"Can you give the cops in Saugerties, New York, a call and do some discreet checking on Carnes? I know he's clean in the system, but that doesn't mean the local cops don't know him."

"And can tell us whether he's fifty-one fifty," she said, using the California police expression for a mentally disturbed person.

"Precisely."

She glanced at the kitchen clock. "I guess you're going to want to get on the road soon."

"Thought I might shave and brush my teeth first."

MacKinnon squinted at his reflection in the dish. "I look like an utter rummy."

"You look like you were hustled out of bed in the middle of the night and shot. And I just finished looking at that paperwork you brought home. You didn't say anything about an MRI."

"Guess I forgot."

"Guess you decided to be sneaky and not tell me."

"I'll call them and reschedule for tomorrow."

She stuck out her tongue and gave him a raspberry, wanting him to understand that although he'd won the battle over his journey to Maryland, he hadn't won the war.

Ten minutes later, he kissed her goodbye and drove to the police station to fill his patrol car with gasoline. His next stop was Blackburn's Antiques, where he informed Sayers of his mission in Maryland and requested the sergeant call him on the wireless phone when he received any word on Plummer's condition. The drive into Fredericksburg took about forty minutes and, once he arrived at the State Police facility, MacKinnon spoke with the fingerprint examination section supervisor.

"Got a favor to ask," entreated MacKinnon.

"Don't tell me. It's a real rush job," replied the balding man, not looking up from his computer monitor.

"As a matter of fact, it is."

"Aren't they all?" The evidence supervisor glanced at the shoulder patch on MacKinnon's sleeve. "Talmine. Hey, didn't they say something on the radio about an officer-involved shooting in your town last night?"

MacKinnon glanced at his watch. "Actually, it happened about five hours ago, and I'm pretty certain our suspect last night, who's still outstanding, killed the woman who owns these prints. That's why I need them done ASAP."

The supervisor double-clicked his computer mouse and stood up. "Give them to me. I'll see to it personally."

"I need these checked through CHARLI," said MacKinnon, using the imperfect and slightly silly acronym for Virginia's Criminal History/Automated Fingerprint Identification System/Remote Live Interface. He handed the man the manila envelope. "My victim is a crystal freak and probably from Maryland so . . ."

"So if we come up dry in our data base, we'll fax a set to Maryland and run these through the FBI files. Not a problem. You can hang loose, but it's probably going to be at least an hour. I'll enter the prints into the system, but even if we come up with a possible, we'll have to wait for whoever has the prints on file to fax us a copy for comparison."

MacKinnon took out a business card and wrote his wireless phone number on the back. "I wish I could stay, but I've got to head up to Maryland to follow up another lead. Can you call me?"

"As soon as I have something to tell you."

Returning to the parking lot, MacKinnon glanced toward Marye's Heights. These days the ridge was covered with buildings, but back in December of 1862 the Union Army had repeatedly marched up the slope, only to smash itself uselessly against Lee's entrenched troops. Thousands had been butchered to no good cause and, recalling how he'd tried to staunch Plummer's wounds, MacKinnon suddenly knew precisely how the Yankee troops had felt after the battle.

Nine:

Jane Doe Redeemed

Before leaving Fredericksburg, MacKinnon decided against subjecting himself to the motorized insanity of Interstate 95 on a Monday morning and instead resolved to make his way north on secondary roads. He pulled into a supermarket parking lot and examined the road map. After a few moments he put the map away, knowing he would not need it again since the route was now firmly fixed in his mind's eye. Some of his friends thought this was a peculiar and innate talent, but he knew otherwise. If he had a good memory, it was because he'd deliberately honed his powers of recall. Indeed, he was convinced that anyone could develop his or her capacity for remembering; it was simply a matter of disciplined effort. But with personal computers, instant xerographic copies, and other recording devices now common elements of American life, there was little impetus for people to have good memories.

Yet cops didn't always have the luxury of relying on artificial memory, and the best officers understood the capacity for recall was the most valuable tool and weapon they possessed. MacKinnon knew if you remembered the way to an obscure address, you might shave seconds off your response time and stop a crime in progress. If you remembered a vehicle or license plate, you might bag a bank robber. If you remembered the face of a dangerous felon, you might save your own life.

Before starting the car, he packed his pipe with shag and lit the tobacco. Then he made his way northward on US Route

1, crossed over the Rappahannock River and, arriving at the junction with Old Warrenton Road, turned west. Soon he'd left the city behind and was making his way through woods and farmland, but he noticed that the spaces between towns was narrowing and he wondered how much of this pastoral landscape would be left in another fifty years.

At Warrenton, he turned northeast and took the highway to Leesburg. He was getting progressively closer to the ever-expanding Washington suburbs now and traffic grew heavier. Looping around the outskirts of Leesburg, he continued north, crossing the Potomac on a narrow bridge at Point of Rocks.

He was in Maryland now and, arriving at the small town of Braddock, he turned west onto US Route 40, the Old National Road. Begun in 1811, the Old National Road was the original interstate highway, running from Maryland to the frontier in Illinois. But with the modern obsession for speed, most motorists opted for the nearby Interstate 70 freeway rather than the older road, which was just fine with MacKinnon. If he never drove on another crowded freeway again, it would be too soon.

His digital telephone rang and he pulled over to the side of the road. From the first day he'd owned a wireless phone, he'd implemented a hard and fast rule: never talk and drive at the same time. One of his pet peeves was that people paid more attention to their telephone conversations than the fact they were guiding a two-ton vehicle down a roadway. Answering the phone he said, "MacKinnon here."

"Hi, sweetheart, it's me." Victoria's voice was cheerful.

"With good news, I hope."

"Very good news. I'm at the hospital with Wendy, and they just told us it looks like Greg is going to be all right. The surgeon said he thinks Greg may have some slight vision impairment and might need glasses, but that he should be able to come back to work in a couple of months."

"That is great news. When you get the chance to talk to him, tell him how happy I am. And tell him that he and Wendy can have my couch. He'll know what I mean."

"I know what that means, and I'm certainly not going to tell him that," Victoria said primly. "So, where are you?"

"I just crossed over into Maryland."

"And how are you feeling?"

"Oh, a little achy, I suppose."

"A lot achy, I'll bet."

"Hey, I'm a tough guy. I can take it," MacKinnon joked. However, the truth was that his side had been throbbing for the past hour.

Victoria sighed. "You should be home in bed."

"I promise I'll rest when I get home later tonight."

"You'd better."

"Love you, Vic."

"Love you too, honey. Be careful."

Pulling back onto the road, he began to ascend the green ramparts of South Mountain through Turner's Gap. The appellation of "mountain" always struck him as slightly ridiculous. Compared to the Sierra Nevada Mountains or even the San Gabriel range near Los Angeles, South Mountain was nothing more than a glorified line of gentle foothills. MacKinnon saw a sign for the South Mountain Battlefield Park. In September 1862, the Federal Iron Brigade won fame for their intrepid assault on the Confederate forces in Turner's Gap. *Few people remember that now,* he thought sadly. In fact, it seemed as if most modern Americans knew more about the scatological plot of "South Park" than the war that irrevocably changed the United States.

Passing through Boonsboro, MacKinnon resisted the impulse to go directly to the address where the Rebel uniform had been mailed. Before doing so, he wanted to collect background information from the Hagerstown Police and the motel where Anita Fesler's purse had been stolen.

Less than a half-hour later, he entered Hagerstown Police Headquarters and collected a copy of the crime report. He scanned the document and saw that it contained no suspect information and, as a consequence, the crime had never been assigned for follow-up investigation. *It's the way of modern police work,* he thought glumly. Unless the suspect was foolish enough to leave his name, photograph, forwarding address, and a notarized written confession, petty crimes were seldom investigated. However, the report did confirm what Fesler had said the previous evening: it was pretty clear that the theft had occurred at the motel and had probably been committed by an employee.

MacKinnon drove back the way he'd come along US Route 40 to the Carrollton Lodge. The well-maintained building was an archetypal motel from the early 1960s, and the neon sign above the office proudly announced that the rooms were equipped with color television. *Unfortunately, you're old enough to remember when that statement constituted a genuine brag,* he thought. There was a tiny swimming pool in the central courtyard where a woman sat beside a sunbonnet-clad toddler splashing on the top step. With the heat and dressed in his police uniform, MacKinnon envied the child.

Parking his patrol car in the lot, he entered the lobby, handed his business card to the clerk, and asked to speak with the manager. A moment later, Shastri Patel emerged from a back office. He was a gray-haired and slightly plump man, wearing a short-sleeved white shirt and a gold medallion of the Indian God, Ganesha, on a chain around his neck.

"Good morning, Chief MacKinnon," said Patel, with a

precise and slightly lilting British-Indian accent. He studied the business card. "My clerk tells me that you've come all the way from Virginia. How might I help you?"

"I'm investigating a murder that may be connected with the theft of a purse that occurred here last October. You may remember the lady who lost the purse. Her name was Anita Fesler, and she thought one of your employees might have been responsible."

"Fesler?" Patel asked innocently.

With his side aching, MacKinnon was not in the mood for unconvincing pantomimes. "Yes, Fesler. Unless your guests are routinely the victims of burglary, she ought to be very easy to remember."

"Oh, yes. Miss Fesler. I do remember her. From Ohio, as I recall. She was quite unhappy."

"Well, in light of the fact her purse was stolen, I guess she had a good reason."

MacKinnon could already understand why Fesler had been angry with the motel manager. Although he was scrupulously polite, and sounded as if he genuinely wanted to be forthcoming, Patel was a master of passive resistance. It made MacKinnon wonder if the manager had benefited from the thefts or had cultivated a deliberate ignorance of how his employees were supplementing their incomes.

"Of course," Patel replied smoothly. "But what does this stolen purse have to do with a murder?"

"It's a possibility that the dead woman is one of your employees. I'm hoping you can perhaps look at a photograph and see if you can identify her."

"I'll be happy to try," Patel said doubtfully.

MacKinnon opened his briefcase, withdrew the picture of the victim, and handed it to the motel manager. Patel looked at the picture, licked his lips, and for an instant indecision flickered in his eyes. MacKinnon recognized the look. The motel manager obviously knew the woman in the photograph but was trying to weigh the consequences of admitting that fact.

"What's her name, Mr. Patel? And please don't tell me that you don't know, because you aren't nearly as good an actor as you think."

Several seconds passed, and then Patel spoke in a voice that was sad but not surprised. "It is Christine."

"Last name?"

"Norland. She worked here until last month."

"Did she quit or was she fired?"

Patel handed the picture back. "I suggested that she might want to find some other employment."

"Because she was stealing everything that wasn't nailed down?"

The manager refused to rise to the bait. He replied mildly, "There were . . . irregularities and complaints from the occasional guest. Nothing that could be proven, you understand."

"Did you know she was a drug addict?"

"No, of course not."

"Did she have any friends here among the other employees?"

"I couldn't really say."

MacKinnon locked eyes with the motel manager. "But you wouldn't mind if I spoke with your staff to find out, would you?"

Patel nodded. "I'll help in whatever way I can."

"That's awfully good to hear, and I promise not to interfere too much with their work," said MacKinnon, laying on the artificial courtesy with a trowel. "In the meantime, could I please look at Christine's employment application?"

"I'll go and get it now." Patel walked toward the office and returned a moment later with a nine-by-twelve-inch sheet of paper.

MacKinnon took the employment application and reviewed the sloppy, handwritten answers on the form. If the information was accurate—and there was no way at present of being certain of that—the woman's name was Christine Dorothy Norland and she had been twenty-three years old. MacKinnon didn't need to compare the address on the application with that on the list of customers from the Northern Shenandoah Quartermaster, it was the same: Radford Lane in Boonsboro.

The next item of interest was that Norland had earned an AA degree in history from Hagerstown Community College. His gaze then moved down the page to the employment history listings. There was only one entry: a nine-month stint as an entry-level document retrieval technician—which MacKinnon supposed actually meant she was a clerk—at the Library of Congress. The reason for leaving that job was given as "career advancement." *Oh yeah, what college history major wouldn't trade a job at the Library of Congress for cleaning motel toilets and changing other people's dirty sheets?* No doubt Norland had been forced to quit, and probably for the same reasons Patel had discharged her.

His digital phone rang and MacKinnon pulled the device from his belt. "MacKinnon."

"Chief, this is Herb King, the guy you talked to at the crime lab. I just finished comparing the prints and have a name for your victim."

"Why am I not surprised to learn she had an arrest record?"

"Because you're a cynical, mean-spirited cop, that's why. You have no faith in the goodness of people," the crime lab supervisor said. "Anyway, we had to run the prints through

Maryland, but we did get an ID. Got a pen handy?"

"I'm clear to copy."

"Her name is Christine Dorothy Norland, AKA Chris North, Kathy Norland, Dorothy Land. There are another six versions of the name, but I'll spare you the rest. Anyway, I took the liberty of running her Maryland rap for you. It's mostly petty stuff, but in oh-one she had a felony conviction for possession of dangerous drugs. Doesn't look like she did any time. Oh, and she also had a felony warrant out of Washington County, Maryland."

"What was the charge?"

"One count of elder fiduciary abuse. Swindling old people. Your murder victim was a real class act. I'll fax this stuff over to your office and I hope it helps."

"Thanks, Herb, and I owe you one."

Disconnecting from the call, MacKinnon telephoned Allen Morris, but got the County Coroner's answering machine. He left a message providing the victim's name, and promised to call if he discovered any information on Norland's next-of-kin so that Morris could make the death notification. The second call completed, MacKinnon handed the employment application back to the motel manager. "Mr. Patel, you're going to want to make a copy of this for your files, because I'd like to keep the original for now."

"You're welcome to keep it. I already have a copy." Patel returned the sheet to MacKinnon.

"Thanks, and now I'm going to wander over and chat with your employees."

The maids' office was in a hot and noisy room on the opposite side of the motel. A hip-hop chant extolling the virtues of murdering Korean shopkeepers was blaring from the radio, washing machines were churning noisily, and the exhaust from the two rumbling electric dryers filled the room with humid air. A soiled playpen stood in the corner of the room, and in it a two-year old girl, with the most beautiful auburn hair MacKinnon had ever seen, sat playing with a nude and headless Barbie. Beside the child was a box of Cheez-Its, and the bottom of the playpen was covered with broken crackers.

There were three maids on duty, and none of them looked very pleased to see a cop in their work area. MacKinnon introduced himself and learned that one of the women had been hired to replace Norland and didn't know her, but Guadalupe Rosas and Samantha White had worked with the victim. MacKinnon glanced from White to the girl in the playpen and knew she was the child's mother.

Deciding to interview Rosas first, MacKinnon led her outside so they wouldn't be disturbed. It didn't take psychic powers to perceive the young woman's tense demeanor, and it was clear to MacKinnon that Rosas would rather bungee-jump from the top of the Washington Monument than talk to him. It was a look MacKinnon recognized; he'd seen it countless times as a cop back in San Diego when dealing with undocumented Mexican immigrants who were fearful that their contact with the police would result in a free bus ride back to Tijuana.

"I'd just like to ask a few questions about Christine, the girl who used to work here," began MacKinnon.

"No habla Englais, senor." Rosas pulled nervously at a hand towel.

"That's all right, I speak a little Spanish," MacKinnon said, switching languages. "Tell me about Christine."

"She doesn't work here anymore, sir."

"I know. In fact, she was murdered Saturday," said MacKinnon.

"Mother of God," whispered Rosas. She made the sign of

the cross and kissed her thumb.

"Were you friends with her?"

"No, sir."

"Did you ever talk with her?"

"No, sir."

MacKinnon pursed his lips. Compared with Rosas, Patel had been a font of information. He decided to start again. "Senora Rosas, I'm not with the *Migra,* I don't care if you have a green card, and I'm not going to call Immigration when I leave. I'm just looking for a little help in trying to find out why Christine was killed."

Rosas relaxed slightly. "But I don't know anything, sir."

"Did she have any friends here?"

"There was Samantha, and sometimes a man came to see her at lunch. Sometimes they used the empty rooms to . . . you know," replied Rosas with an embarrassed smile.

"This man, do you know his name?" MacKinnon asked.

"She called him David, sir."

"And what did he look like?"

"About as tall as you, sir. But heavier."

"Anglo?"

"Yes, sir."

MacKinnon pulled his sunglasses out of his pocket. "And he wore these all the time, right?"

Rosas's mouth fell open, showing gold dental work. "Yes, sir. How did you know?"

"I think I met him on Saturday."

Thanking Rosas for her cooperation, MacKinnon next interviewed Samantha White. He began by collecting some basic personal information, and learned that despite her haggard and worn appearance, the maid was only twenty-four years old. Indeed, the coarse expression, "used hard and put away wet," might have been coined with White in mind. And before even a few seconds had passed, MacKinnon also knew why White had been a friend of Christine Norland. With her constricted pupils, staccato speech, and jittery mien, it was obvious the thin woman had either smoked or injected some crystal earlier that morning. *Methamphetamine: the breakfast of champions,* thought MacKinnon, yet he decided against immediately confronting White with the fact he knew she was high. If the woman proved uncooperative, he would employ the information as a lever.

MacKinnon said, "Tell me about Christine Norland."

"Is she like in trouble?" White asked, but it was clear from the wary tone that her only concern was whether her acquaintance with Norland signified that she was in trouble.

"No, she's dead."

White's eyes reflected both relief and fear. "That's too bad, but, well, you know, I like, hardly knew her. She quit last month."

"That's strange. I heard you guys were pretty good friends."

"Well, we, like, said hello and that, but I didn't really know her," White said nervously. She began to pick furiously at a blouse button. Then, noticing MacKinnon was watching the mindlessly busy hand, she jammed it into her pocket. Finally she said, "Hey, am I under arrest?"

"No."

"Then, like, is there any reason I gotta talk to you?" White asked a little defiantly. "I already told you I don't know anything, and I've got work to do."

"You know, Samantha, I'm a big fan of the 'carrot and stick' school of behavior modification. Ever heard of it?" MacKinnon smiled, but the look in his eyes was as cold as frozen oxygen.

"No."

"Well, it's the way you train an unruly donkey. The carrot is a reward and, in this instance, that means if you tell me the truth, I'll get out of your life." MacKinnon knew his serene voice accentuated the menace of his words. "However, if you persist in lying to me, I'll be forced to use the metaphorical stick. That means I call the Hagerstown cops and have them arrest you for being under the influence of crystal, and your little girl goes into a foster home until you get out of jail. And even then, you may not get her back if the local child protective agency decides you're an unfit parent. So, let's try again. Tell me about Christine."

"You bastard." White looked as if she'd just been slapped and couldn't decide whether she wanted to fight back or cry.

"I had hoped you wouldn't be a stubborn donkey." He removed the digital phone from his belt.

Tears were glistening in White's eyes. "I'll tell you what I know."

"Go on," he said, his finger poised above the phone's keypad.

"Chris came to work here after being fired from a job in DC."

"I know. Did she say why she was terminated?"

White glanced toward the maid's office. "Because, like, some old lady walked into the bathroom and caught her shooting up."

"Fortunately for you and Chris, Mr. Patel doesn't check the bathrooms here. Next question: I'm pretty sure she came to my town to sell something to an antique dealer and, the way I figure it, he decided Chris was trying to shit backwards on him, so he blew her brains out. Did she ever talk to you about this deal?"

"Not exactly."

"But you have some idea of what she was selling?"

"The only thing I know is that she said she had some papers she'd, like, lifted from the library."

"What kind of papers?"

"Swear to God, I don't know," White said in a fearful voice. "She just said it was some papers that could be worth a lot, if she could find a buyer."

The panic was genuine and he knew she was telling the truth. "Okay. Now tell me about the cop she was screwing, David Benham."

"You know about him?"

MacKinnon cocked his head and arched his eyebrows. He said nothing and waited for an answer.

"Chris met him back in, I don't know, like April or May. He stopped her and cut her some slack when he found out she was holding." White reached into her pocket and pulled out a package of cigarettes. "Can I smoke?"

"Go ahead. Was Benham supplying her with crystal?"

White lit a cigarette and took a long drag. "No, I don't think so."

"So what was the attraction?"

"This'll sound stupid, but I think he really liked her." White sounded almost envious. "She told me that he used to talk about getting her into treatment to get off the crystal, but he was getting totally shit-faced on booze every night."

It is a familiar scenario, thought MacKinnon. He'd known tormented and emotionally crippled cops who'd embraced the role of rescuers, because trying to solve other people's problems was easier than addressing their own personal demons. "And how did she feel about him?"

"She thought he was a total loser, but Chris figured if she gave him a little head and the occasional fuck, he'd keep her from being busted. She used to laugh about how he thought they were going to have a normal life. Her favorite thing was to call herself June Cleaver and say that Ward, Benham, you know, was a little tough on the Beaver."

"Sounds like a charming girl."

White removed the cigarette from her mouth and blew a jet of smoke skyward. "Look, I guess I'm sorry she's dead, but I'm not gonna miss Chris. She'd use anyone to get what she wanted."

"So why were you so set on protecting her sainted memory by not talking to me?"

"I was afraid of getting busted," White answered sullenly.

"Because she wasn't the only one stealing from the guests?"

"Yeah, I guess."

MacKinnon put the digital phone back on his belt. "You've earned the carrot, Samantha. But before I go, can I offer you a piece of advice? Back away from the crystal."

"As if you really care."

"You're right. I don't care about you. But I do care about that little girl of yours. You'd like to pretend you adore her, but if you really loved her, you'd stop pumping that toxic waste into your body and become a real mother. Just think about it. End of sermon. Okay, you can go back to work."

Leaving the motel, MacKinnon drove back down US Highway 40 to Boonsboro. However, before going to Norland's residence, he made a stop at the town hall to announce his presence to the local police. The visit wasn't simply a matter of professional courtesy. As he knew from past experience, there was a huge and unnecessary potential for tragedy when you pursued a case in another jurisdiction without letting the hometown cops know you were operating in their bailiwick.

However, the town hall receptionist informed MacKinnon that Boonsboro didn't have a police department. The law consisted of a single resident deputy from the Washington County Sheriff's Department by the name of Gary Shafer. She telephoned Shafer at home, and a few minutes later a white patrol car pulled up in front of the town hall. The blonde-haired and gray-uniformed deputy reminded MacKinnon of a fire hydrant: he was short and solidly built.

After MacKinnon provided some background on his investigation and explained the purpose of his visit, Shafer said, "Norland, huh?"

"You knew her?"

"Oh, yeah. I popped her for possession of crack. That girl had a real talent for blowing smoke," replied Shafer with a weary shake of his head.

"How do you mean?"

"All the way to CJ she sweet-talked me about how she wanted to get straight and how she was glad she finally had been arrested because she could get into drug diversion. Oh, she cried and thanked me, and cried some more. It was a real three-hankie performance and, stupid me, I bought it. Meanwhile, she slipped the handcuffs and bailed when I opened the car door to take her into booking. I had to chase her for a block, and when I caught her she tried to bite me, so I pepper-sprayed her."

"And then the tears were real."

"You betcha," Shafer cheerfully agreed.

"So, do you know anything about a relationship between Christine and Detective David Benham from Sharpsburg PD?"

Shafer's jaw dropped in surprise. "Detective? Benham has never been anything more than a beat cop, and a piss-poor one at that. Who told you he was a detective?"

"He did, when I spoke with him on Saturday."

"Yeah, well he's full of shit. The only thing Benham's

good at detecting is free drinks and a place to coop on midnight shift. But back to your original question. When I had the chance, I used to keep an eye on the traffic going to and from Norland's apartment, and his license plate came up. What's a cop doing hanging around with some skank crystal freak, I asked myself."

"Did you brace him about it?"

"Yeah, when I saw him at court. He got all defensive and told me she was a CI."

"But you didn't think she was a confidential informant?"

"No way."

"So what did you do?"

"I talked to my lieutenant and he dropped a dime to Sharpsburg's chief. I never saw Benham back at the apartment, so I figured they'd handled the problem. But, obviously, if his name has come up in your investigation, he just stopped meeting Norland here." After a short pause, he added in a dumbfounded and grim voice, "Jesus H. Christ! Is he your suspect?"

"No. I don't think Benham killed her, but he was up to something so shady that when he saw Christine's body, he denied knowing her. I'm going to go take a look at Norland's apartment. Interested in joining me?"

Shafer nodded. "Wouldn't miss it for the world. Hop in your car and follow me over. The street's unmarked and it's easy to miss, unless you know where you're going."

Five minutes later, the two patrol cars rolled into Radford Lane, a narrow cul-de-sac off St. Paul Street on the northern outskirts of town. The street was Boonsboro's version of a junk drawer in an otherwise tidy kitchen, hidden and messy. Norland's address was the last in a series of three small and unkempt cottages that fronted the road. Several cars were parked in the gravel lot behind the buildings, and Shafer pointed to a rusting Toyota Celica with District of Columbia license plates. MacKinnon parked his squad car next to the Toyota.

"Welcome to White Trash heaven," said Shafer. "That's her car."

The Celica was unlocked and MacKinnon conducted a quick but thorough search of the interior, which reeked of stale cigarette smoke. *It's an archetypal tweaker-mobile,* he thought, wishing he'd thought to put on some latex gloves before exploring the mess. The floor and seats were littered with fast food wrappers, empty plastic soda bottles, and about a half-dozen tiny zip-seal plastic bags that had once contained methamphetamine. In the glove compartment, he found a traffic ticket from the Hagerstown Police, in Anita Fesler's name.

MacKinnon handed the citation to Shafer and said, "Can you do me a big favor? Norland stole this lady's identity and now Fesler has arrest warrants in the system. She tried to call the court, but they weren't very helpful. Maybe you could cut a report and have the warrant for this ticket withdrawn?"

"Our public servants unresponsive to the community? Say it ain't so," replied the deputy with mock astonishment. He folded the citation and stuck it into his breast pocket. "I'll knock out a report this afternoon."

Turning toward the cottages, MacKinnon briefly glimpsed a woman looking at them from the middle residence. Then the face disappeared behind the curtains and a moment later he thought he heard the sound of a toilet being flushed. Shafer had also seen the face and smiled wickedly. He walked over to the window, tapped on the glass, and merrily called out, "False alarm, Leslie! Hope you didn't flush your entire stash on our account."

"Fuck you, Shafer!" she shouted from inside the house.

"Not on my worst day, honey." Shafer grinned at MacKinnon. "God, I love this job!"

The two cops walked around to the front of Norland's cottage and MacKinnon noticed the door was slightly ajar. Slowly pushing the door open, he saw that a human tornado had swept through the residence. Drawers had been emptied and tossed aside, the mattress was pulled from the bed, and clothing had been pulled from the tiny closet and lay scattered across the floor and sofa. The bookshelves had also been swept clean and dozens of books littered the floor. MacKinnon took note of the titles.

Christine Norland may have been a predatory, lying, and thieving crystal freak, but she was also a serious student of the Civil War. He saw Harry Pfanz's *Gettysburg: The Second Day*, William Frassanito's *Grant and Lee*, and all five, heavy volumes of *The Photographic History of the Civil War.* There were other works, probably a century old, leather-covered with gold-embossed pages, and MacKinnon's heart ached to see the way that the antiquated books had been carelessly hurled to the floor.

"Looks like your killer paid a visit," observed Shafer.

"I don't think so. The guy we're looking at may be a murderer, but he wouldn't have done this to antique books. My guess is that Benham was here looking for something."

"Well, how about I go next door and ask Miss Leslie if Benham was here?"

"Thanks. I'd appreciate that."

"Yeah, well I know she won't," said the deputy with a nasty chuckle.

Shafer departed, and MacKinnon continued his inspection of the home. Benham had utterly trashed the cottage, but it was clear that the place hadn't been any too spruce to begin with. The carpet, which he guessed might have been beige when first installed, was now the same color as an inner city sidewalk and with a similar number of unidentifiable stains. Moreover, the cheap furniture was so filthy that MacKinnon suspected he'd stick to the upholstery if he were reckless enough to sit down. Although he ran the risk of destroying fingerprints, he slid the two living room windows open, for the miasmic aroma of cigarettes, decaying food, and urine was almost overwhelming.

He entered the kitchenette and caught a glimpse of something he hoped was a mouse, and not a leviathan roach, scurry beneath the grimy stove. The cupboards had been emptied—*not that there had been much inside in the first place,* he thought—and the refrigerator stood open. Food and dishes had been tossed haphazardly onto the counters and into the sink. If it had been Benham, he'd been thorough, not particularly neat.

MacKinnon returned to the living room and heard a plaintive "meow" from the corner of the room where the stained mattress and other household debris had been thrown. Sifting through the junk, he found an orange, tiger-striped kitten with absurdly large front paws cowering beneath a lean-to of books and sofa cushions. The kitten arched its back and hissed at his approach. Realizing the animal had probably not eaten since Saturday, MacKinnon went back into the kitchen and reemerged with a bowl of water and box of cat food. He set the bowl on the floor near the kitten and poured out a small pile of cat food.

"C'mon, little one," said MacKinnon. "I'm not going to hurt you."

The cat was wary, but hunger swiftly drove it to approach the bowl and it began to frantically gobble the dry food. After it had eaten its fill and lapped up a little water, it darted back into its trashy asylum.

A moment later, Shafer returned looking pleased. "Success. Leslie says that Benham was here late Saturday night."

"She was certain it was Benham?"

"Oh, yeah. She knows him."

"Well, I suppose the time has come to have a chat with one of Sharpsburg's finest," said MacKinnon. "Will you do a burglary report on this and mail me a copy?"

"Sure. I'll take some crime scene photos too."

"Thanks, and what will happen if I leave the kitten here?" He pointed at the animal. It was a needless question. He already knew the answer.

"I'll take it to the county animal shelter . . ." Shafer said uncomfortably.

"Where it will be put to sleep if someone doesn't claim it after three days," MacKinnon finished. "Hell, I've already got five cats, but I can't stand the idea of this little guy or girl—I don't know which it is, because I haven't checked the plumbing—being put down because Norland was a flake. Help me find a box."

Ten minutes, three scratches, and a small bite on his hand later, MacKinnon was driving back into Hagerstown with the wailing kitten penned inside a large cardboard boot box. During the chase and struggle to trap the terrified cat, he'd discovered the animal was a male that hadn't been neutered. *But we'll soon fix that,* MacKinnon silently told the feline.

Arriving in Hagerstown, he stopped for a quick, late lunch and then, returning to his car, telephoned Sharpsburg PD. The dispatcher told him Benham didn't go on duty until 11:00 p.m., but agreed to try and call the officer at home and leave a message for him to call MacKinnon on his wireless phone. There was nothing to do now but wait. MacKinnon knew that if Benham was working the graveyard shift, he was probably still asleep, so there was no way of telling when, or if, he would call. This meant he might have to spend the night in Hagerstown, and he didn't relish the idea of trying to explain that to Victoria, on top of the news that they had acquired a new cat.

"A new cat with his own Ringling Brothers, Barnum and Bailey flea circus." He saw a tiny black insect jump onto his trousers. He tried to pinch it, but it got away.

He drove to the Washington County Sheriff's Department headquarters and, leaving the wailing cat in the car, went inside to the records section to request a copy of Christine Norland's arrest warrant. The records clerk was helpful and conducted a computer check to see which law enforcement agency had requested the arrest warrant. As it turned out, the elder fiduciary abuse had occurred in the small town of Williamsport, which was part of the sheriff's jurisdiction. The crime report and follow-up investigation were on file there in the records department, and the clerk offered to make him copies of those documents also.

A few minutes later, the clerk reappeared and handed him photocopies of the warrant and crime report. MacKinnon thanked the woman, tucked the paperwork into his folder, and returned to his car. Midway across the parking lot, his wireless phone rang.

"This is Chief MacKinnon."

There was a pause and then David Benham made a pathetic effort to sound nonchalant. "Uh, hi Chief. I just checked my messages and there was one saying you wanted to talk to me."

"Yeah, *Detective* Benham, we need to talk in person and if you really want to piss me off, pretend you don't know what I want to chat with you about."

Benham sighed. "I know. When do you want to see me?"

"Tonight. I'm here in Hagerstown."

"I can't. I'm going in early to work some OT. Our night watch officer is sick."

"Tomorrow morning after work then." He made it clear this was a command and not a suggestion. "Let's meet someplace where we can talk freely. Any suggestions?"

"No," Benham said bleakly.

"Then I'll choose. Meet me in the Antietam Battlefield Park at a place called the Sunken Road. Think you can find it?"

"I'll be there about seven-thirty."

"You'd better be, Benham. Because if you FTA, I guarantee that you won't like what happens if you make me come looking for you."

With some time to waste, MacKinnon found a pet supply store and bought a plastic pet carrier, a flea collar, a litter pan and bag of litter, and some cans of cat food.

The town looked to be full of vacationers and, fearing that he might not be able to get a motel room if he delayed much longer, he went in search of lodgings. The Carrollton Lodge was definitely out of the question, but there were vacancies at the nearby Hampton Inn. He saw a cautionary note on the registration card that read "No Pets," but was certain the prohibition didn't apply to cats on official police business.

Once inside the motel room, MacKinnon pulled the howling, flailing kitten from the box and, after a brief struggle, secured the flea collar around its scrawny neck. Then he released the cat, which instantly disappeared beneath the bed. MacKinnon's side was really beginning to throb and he knew he should lie down and rest, but first he had to call his wife.

Bracing himself for Victoria's displeasure over the fact that he wouldn't be home as promised, he cautiously began, "Hi, sweetheart. Bet you can't guess where I am?"

Like her namesake, Victoria Regina, his wife was not amused. "You're staying the night in Hagerstown, right?"

"Let me explain why before you get mad. We got an ID on our victim. Her name is Christine Norland and I visited her apartment a little while ago. It was four-five-nined and I'm pretty certain it was Benham who did it. I just got off the phone with him, and we're scheduled to meet early tomorrow morning in Sharpsburg, so I have to stay the night."

The cat began to wail and Victoria said, "Sweetheart, what is that?"

"A kitten. I found him at Norland's place and, well, I couldn't let him go to cat prison."

"Honey, are you telling me we have another cat?"

"He's a pain in the butt, but cute."

"The same thing might be said about you." She sounded a little less annoyed. "How's your side?"

"Sore but manageable. I just took some aspirin and thought I'd lie down for a while."

"Well, before you do, I've got two interesting bits of information for you," she said. "First, I called Saugerties PD and chatted with one of their detectives. He wasn't very surprised to hear that Carnes was in trouble."

"Why is that?"

"Apparently he's the most victimized merchant in the entire Hudson Valley. They can't prove Carnes is dirty, but the PD has all sorts of crime reports from him, reporting merchandise shoplifted from his store. On the average he's ripped off every six or seven weeks. The funny thing is that all the items stolen have been there on consignment. Nothing that belongs to Carnes is ever stolen."

"What an amazing coincidence."

"Are you ready for another?" She didn't wait for an answer. "Here's interesting item number two. After looking at the Talmine *Courier* this afternoon, I think I've identified the woman who was seen going into Crumper's Woods. Her picture was there on page one."

"Who is it?"

"Jean Dumfries."

"Honey, I hope this is your idea of an evil practical joke."

"No joke, sweetheart. It's her," insisted Victoria, her voice becoming excited. "The clothing matches both the video and Carnes' description. It also explains why Dumfries didn't want you investigating the murder."

"I don't know what it explains. But it looks like Jean the Queen and I are going to have a heart-to-heart talk when I get home."

Ten:

The Lost Order

There was an alarm clock in the room, but MacKinnon didn't need it. He was awake long before 6:00 a.m. Actually, he'd been awake on and off throughout the night, protracted sleep made impossible by the kitten. When the animal wasn't rocketing around the room as if he were high on the same drugs used by his former mistress, he wailed and howled until MacKinnon thought his ears were going to bleed. By morning, the kitten had a name: *Farshee,* the male counterpart of the Gaelic banshee.

Slowly rolling out of bed, MacKinnon peeked underneath the nightstand and saw the kitten was tucked in a tiny ball and had finally gone to sleep. He briefly considered vengefully poking the cat to awaken it, but discarded the notion when he realized that he'd rather hear anything—including the audio torture of Rush Limbaugh explaining the evils of campaign finance reform—than another session of Farshee's noisy protests.

MacKinnon shuffled into the bathroom, turned the shower on, and winced as he looked at his reflection in the mirror. He looked tired and old, which wasn't really very strange, since he felt tired and old. There was a large, polychromatic bruise on the left side of his abdomen where the vest had stopped the bullet. He felt very stiff, but by the time he had finished showering and shaving, a fresh dose of aspirin had begun to take effect. Then it was time for some bracing morning aerobics as he chased the now-awake Farshee around the motel room, eventually grabbing the kitten by its tail as it darted beneath the nightstand. The cat turned to bite the back of his hand, yet MacKinnon hung on until he got the frightened and enraged feline into the pet carrier.

"You know, Farshee, ordinarily I'm opposed to animals being used for laboratory testing," growled MacKinnon, nursing the bleeding wound. "But in your instance, I think I could make an exception."

After getting a Band-Aid from the first aid kit in his car's trunk, MacKinnon went into the lounge adjoining the reception desk and had the Continental breakfast. The selection of baked goods looked delicious, but he wasn't in the mood for the inevitable stale witticisms from other guests about cops and doughnuts. He settled for a bowl of corn flakes, a banana, and two cups of weak, black coffee.

Leaving the motel, he drove south along the Sharpsburg Pike while, in the cat carrier, Farshee yowled continuously. It looked as if another torrid day was in the cards, but there was still a thin, spectral mist cloaking the fields and woodlands. After about twenty minutes, MacKinnon saw the Potomac River to his distant right and knew he was near the battlefield. He saw a road sign for the National Park, and turned onto the scene of the bloodiest single day in American military history.

On September 17, 1862, the Union Army of the Potomac smashed itself against Lee's Confederate Army of Northern Virginia in one of the pivotal battles of the war. The Rebels had invaded the North, and a Southern victory would have spelled the end of the Civil War, for both Britain and France would surely have recognized the Confederacy and interceded to stop the war. The fighting was savage and, when the day was finished, 23,000 men were dead, wounded, or missing. Although it was a drawn battle, Lee had been forced to retreat back into Virginia, and this small upturn in Union fortunes allowed President Lincoln to later issue the

Emancipation Proclamation.

This wasn't MacKinnon's first visit to Antietam. The previous year, on the anniversary of the battle, he'd led his reenactment group on a field trip across the pastoral battlefield, retracing the route of the Eighth Ohio, the regiment they recreated. But the park had been crowded then, full of tourists shooting video and children climbing on the silent cannons, and MacKinnon had been unable to tap into the elusive yet dreadful magic of the place. However, this morning was very different. Silent and vacant of visitors, there was an eerie and almost spectral quality to the rural landscape. Glancing to his left at the famous Miller Cornfield, he imagined that if he looked long enough, he'd see the serried rows of bayonets visible just above the stalks.

Off to the right was the West Woods and, to the east and beyond the Cornfield, was the East Woods—places with unremarkable names that had been etched in gunpowder, blood, and suffering. Ahead was the whitewashed Dunker Church, which still bore scars from the battle. Passing the still-closed Visitors' Center, MacKinnon turned left on Richardson Avenue and drove the circuitous route to the Sunken Road. The thoroughfare had begun as a shortcut between the Hagerstown and Boonsboro Pikes, and by 1862 the constant passage of wagons had lowered the road below the level of the surrounding terrain. During the battle, the Confederates occupied this natural fortification and stubbornly repelled repeated Union attacks, until at last being overwhelmed by sheer numbers. By the fighting's end, the thoroughfare was littered with corpses and was ever after known as the Bloody Lane.

MacKinnon parked the patrol car and walked down the gentle, grassy slope toward the hollowed-out dirt road. Tall, zigzagging wooden fences lined both sides of the lane, and he paused briefly to examine a white statue of a soldier holding up a flag. It was a memorial to the One-hundred-thirty-second Pennsylvania Infantry Regiment, commemorating the spot where the Union troops had finally breached the Rebel line. Off to the southeast, about two hundreds yards away, was a stone observation tower. He bent to pick up an empty Pepsi can from the ground and tossed it into a nearby trash can. It was so very peaceful and somehow difficult for him to comprehend that this place had once been a slaughterhouse. He filled his pipe with tobacco, lit it, and waited.

Just before 7:30 a.m., he heard the sound of a vehicle engine approaching. Then a white Isuzu Trooper drove into the parking lot and came to a stop next to MacKinnon's squad car. David Benham trudged down the hill a moment later, his face expressionless. He wore jeans and his hands were tucked into the pockets of a blue windbreaker. When he got to the Sunken Road, he glanced at MacKinnon, sighed, and looked at the ground.

MacKinnon allowed the uncomfortable silence to continue for several seconds and then said, "Thank you for coming, David. Tell me about Christine Norland."

"I knew her," Benham glumly replied, and MacKinnon could smell the odor of hard liquor on his breath. Apparently, the cop had fortified himself for the meeting.

"I knew that on Saturday. Tell me more."

"We were . . ." Benham hesitated, uncertain of how best to describe his relationship with the dead woman.

"Lovers?"

Benham nodded. "By now you know that she was a tweaker, and I know exactly what you're thinking. She was a crystal whore who fucked the local cop to stay out of trouble. But Chrissy meant a lot to me. She was smart and pretty, when she wasn't all sketchy, and you know what was really weird for a tweak? She loved books. She was reading all the time, at least when she wasn't strung out. And I'm not talking about the kind of stuff I read, but really hard stuff, like history books."

"And you loved her."

"Yeah."

MacKinnon pulled his pipe tool from his pocket and stirred the burning tobacco. "So, why did you lie about knowing her? That must have been very hard for you."

"I was fucking ashamed. I just wanted to crawl in a hole. But I knew if word got back to my department that I was with Chrissy again, I'd be in deep shit."

"Particularly since you were involved in the caper to help her sell that stolen document."

Benham looked at the ground. "You know about that."

"Yep. What did she steal from the Library of Congress?"

"Before I say anything else, maybe I ought to have a lawyer."

"You want to invoke your rights? Be my guest, but let me give you something to think about before you decide to do that. Two nights ago, we got into a gunfight with the guy who killed Christine, something that probably could have been avoided if you'd been honest with me on Saturday. The crook got away, and one of my cops was shot and nearly blinded. As you can imagine, that didn't make me a very happy fellow, so I'm going to give you one chance, just one, to do the right thing and talk to me. Otherwise, I'm going to crucify you."

"I'm dead already." Benham swallowed hard.

"Yes, you are. When this is finished, you won't have a badge, and I'm not going to try to BS you about that. But you can try to do the right thing by Christine. The man who killed her is free, and I need your information to find him and put him away."

Benham gazed at the ground and slowly exhaled. "The paper was something she called Order One-nine-one. It was from the Civil War. I've never been very interested in history, so I don't really know what it is and, to tell the truth, I didn't really want to know."

"The Army of Northern Virginia's Order One-*ninety*-one?" Even to his own ears, he sounded incredulous.

"I never heard Chrissy mention northern Virginia, but I'm pretty certain those were the numbers."

"Did she ever call it 'the Lost Order'?"

"Yeah. You've heard of it?"

"Oh, yeah," MacKinnon replied, awestruck. He now understood why the rapacious Carnes had killed Christine Norland.

Order 191 was the most celebrated written command ever issued by Confederate General Robert E. Lee. The document wasn't famous so much for its content, but for what had happened to a copy of the order. In early September 1862, the Army of Northern Virginia was scattered and vulnerable to piecemeal destruction. Recognizing the threat, Lee issued written orders to his commanders to gather at Sharpsburg. But one copy of the instructions was somehow lost and later found by Union soldiers. The story of their discovery was one of the most legendary tales of the war: Yankee troops had been foraging through an abandoned Rebel campsite and came across the orders wrapped around a bundle of cigars. Acting on the information, the Federal army also marched to Sharpsburg, and their meeting with the Confederates resulted in the bloody Battle of Antietam.

"Did you ever see the document?" asked MacKinnon.

"Just once, when Chrissy had it out of the envelope to

make a copy. It was just a couple of sheets of old paper with handwriting on them."

"Tell me about the deal to sell it."

Benham leaned against the fence rails. "Back in May, I think, Chrissy went to a Civil War show down in Richmond to see if she could find a buyer. She met this antique dealer from some town in New York who called himself Hill."

"Whose real name is Joseph Carnes."

"I figured it was an alias," said Benham. "Anyway, they talked, he was very interested, and later they started exchanging e-mails about a deal."

"E-mail? From what I could see, Christine didn't have a computer."

Benham tried to feign indifference. "You've been to her house?"

"Yesterday afternoon. You did one hell of a job tearing that place up." MacKinnon noted that Benham didn't deny the accusation. "But let's not get ahead of ourselves. Back to the e-mail . . ."

"Chris used the computer at my place."

"Do you ever print out any of the messages?" MacKinnon asked eagerly. The communications would be powerful evidence linking Carnes to the victim.

"Never. We deleted them."

"But the information might still be on the hard drive. When we get finished here, we'll go to your house and I'll collect your PC as evidence. There's a computer specialist at the crime lab who might be able to retrieve those e-mails."

Benham shrugged. "Sure, if you think it will help."

"It will. Now this exchange of e-mails; at some point you guys finally decided on a price?"

Benham nodded. "After she faxed him a copy of the paper."

"Did he know the merchandise was stolen?"

"Absolutely. Chrissy told me that this guy was totally plugged into the Civil War and knew the document was supposed to be in the Library of Congress. That was part of the reason he was so jazzed at the chance of getting his hands on it."

"So what was the price?"

"Fifteen thousand. Seventy-five hundred at the time of the sale and the other half after the guy had the chance to examine the paper."

MacKinnon snorted with bitter amusement. "Dave, I'm no expert, but that's probably chump change for an historical artifact like the Lost Order."

Benham looked wistful. "Well, it sounded like a lot of money at the time."

"Okay, so you guys had a deal," said MacKinnon. "Why did Chris dress up in the uniform and come to Talmine?"

"Chrissy was all hinked up. Back in June a couple of FBI agents came by the motel to ask her about the paper."

"Funny, Mr. Patel didn't tell me anything about that," MacKinnon said caustically.

"Patel wouldn't tell you the time of day unless you had a twist on him." Benham smiled weakly. "Anyway, from what I could gather, the Feds didn't think she was a suspect. It was just routine questioning, but Chrissy got it into her head that she was under surveillance."

"Crystal paranoia?" One of the consequences of long-term methamphetamine addiction was that the users often developed an obsessive and unfounded belief that they were under constant surveillance by an army of narcs and federal agents.

"Probably, but there was no talking her out of it," Benham said. "Chrissy figured to do the exchange someplace far from here, where she could blend in with the crowds. She found the Civil War festival in your town on the Web and decided she'd dress up like a soldier. The guy liked the arrangement."

"Go on."

"So she ordered the clothes."

"Using a stolen credit card."

"I don't know anything about that."

"Of course you don't. What happened next?"

"Well, on Saturday morning we got ready to leave and found out her car was ten-seven—the alternator was shot. I drove her down to BWI, she rented the car, and I followed her down to Virginia."

"And naturally, you also didn't know she used bogus ID and a bad credit card to get the car."

Benham looked at the ground. "I didn't ask."

"Why the separate cars?"

"Chrissy said that with two cars, I could keep an eye on her without letting the guy know I was there."

"So, what happened when you got to Talmine?"

Benham glanced toward a distant stand of trees. "Once we hit town, we were supposed to meet the guy at that Lord restaurant on your main street."

"The Lord Sutherland Inn?"

"Yeah."

"Why there?"

"Chrissy found a listing for the place on the Web. We'd never been to Talmine and neither had this dude, Carnes, so we set that up as a meet site . . ." Benham paused for a moment and, when he spoke again, his voice was sorrowful. "We even talked about maybe having lunch there after we'd made the exchange."

"So did you meet the guy there?"

"Chrissy did."

"While you watched from a discreet distance to make sure nothing went wrong."

"Yeah."

"What did he look like?"

"White male adult, about thirty-five years and, I don't know, maybe five-ten and one hundred and seventy pounds. He had a moustache and a short beard, and was dressed up like a Civil War soldier." Benham rattled the information with the same amount of emotion he might have employed to describe a shoplifter.

"What color uniform?"

"Gray."

"Could you recognize him if you saw him again?"

"Yeah."

"Was he carrying any weapons?"

"He had a holster on his belt, but I wasn't close enough to tell whether he had a gun inside of it."

"Didn't that worry you?"

"A little."

"But not enough to do anything about it, right? Fifteen thousand dollars is a lot of money." MacKinnon spoke the words unemotionally, which made them sound that much more damning. Benham swallowed nervously, folded his arms across his chest, and didn't answer. MacKinnon tapped his pipe sharply against a wooden fence rail to dislodge the ashes from the bowl, deliberately letting the silence drag. Finally, he said, "So they talked. What happened next?"

"They split up. She walked back to our cars and told me she was ready to do the deal then and there, but that the guy wanted to go someplace else—the woods near where you guys were having that fake battle. He told Chrissy they were going to hide in plain sight." Benham's tone was grim.

"Now, that had to have made you suspicious."

"Yeah . . ."

"But?"

"But Chrissy wanted to go through with the deal. She said she could handle herself. She told me to hang loose in the restaurant parking lot until she came back."

"Dave, I've looked and you don't have the word 'idiot' stenciled on your forehead." MacKinnon was exasperated because he could see the pieces falling into place and was amazed that Benham was being so willfully blind. "So, don't tell me you didn't think that was just a little strange."

"What do you mean?"

MacKinnon cocked his head to the side and laughed humorlessly. "Good God, Dave, maybe you *are* that stupid. Christine had you come all the way down from Maryland to cover her play and then, at the last moment, she asked you to stay away from where the deal was set to go down. The only way that makes any sense is if she had decided to make the sale and then head off into the sunset without you."

For the first time Benham emerged from his melancholy lassitude. In an angry voice he said, "Chrissy wouldn't have done that."

"Oh, yes, she would have, and you know it. I hate to speak ill of the dead, but from what I've learned about her, if she'd been invited to the Last Supper, Jesus would have had to count the silverware when she left. Time to face facts, Dave. She used you just like she used everyone else who had the misfortune to come into contact with her. If the deal had gone down as planned, she was going to climb into her own car, and you'd have never seen her again."

Benham looked up quickly and met MacKinnon's gaze, but the Sharpsburg cop didn't say anything. He didn't have to.

"And you suspected as much yourself," said MacKinnon, "because you didn't stay at the restaurant. You went to the park and started looking for her, right?"

"Yeah."

"Did you find her?"

"Not until I saw you."

"What happened between the time you arrived at the park and when we met in the woods?"

"I sat in the car for a little while and then got out and wandered around the tents. That's when one of your officers walked by, talking on his radio about a shooting victim in the woods."

"Which brings us to Christine's murder," said MacKinnon. "I'm pretty certain I know who killed her, but here's the puzzling part. It doesn't look as if she had the Lost Order when she was shot. Any idea of what happened to it?"

"No."

"And how about her wallet? She had ID when she rented the car, but we couldn't find it on her body."

Benham grimaced. "She left her wallet with me before she drove over to the park."

"Why?"

"She figured that if the cops got involved, she could always give a false name and get away before someone ran her prints through the system to find out who she really was."

"Where's the wallet now?"

"On the way home, I threw it into a trash can near Fredericksburg."

"You're an incurable romantic, Dave." MacKinnon shook his head in disgust. "Why didn't you just leave it in Chrissy's car after you stole it and dumped it out there on that dirt road?"

"How did you know that I took it?"

"The oil. It was pretty clear that whoever took the car did so just to wipe it down for prints, which left you as a natural candidate. As a cop, you knew that your prints would have turned up in a computer inquiry. But what I don't understand is why you even messed with the rental car in the first place. You hadn't ridden in it. So . . . oh, man, *now* I understand." MacKinnon felt his eyes widening in surprise. Up until now he'd been prepared to believe that nothing more than a combination of selfish love and panic had motivated the alcoholic cop to break the law.

Benham winced and looked down at the ground.

"The reason your prints were in Christine's car was because you searched it for the document while she was in the woods. *You* were going to double-cross *her*. That's kind of a mean thing to do to someone you love, wouldn't you say?" MacKinnon didn't give the cop a chance to answer. "She had the keys. I know you didn't break that window to make entry, so just how did you get into the car?"

"I keep a slim-jim in my truck," mumbled Benham, referring to a tool for getting into locked vehicles, commonly employed by tow truck drivers and auto thieves.

"And you broke the car window afterwards, hoping I'd think the Pontiac had been taken by a run-of-the-mill car thief, right?"

"Yeah."

MacKinnon assembled the rest of the tawdry puzzle. "So after you saw that Christine was dead and my officer was finished with you, you hot-wired the Pontiac and took it to wipe down your fingerprints. Okay, now I've got it. You were the first person to break into the car."

"Huh?"

"Carnes, the killer, broke into the Pontiac again after we recovered it. He must have been looking for the Lost Order."

"I just panicked," moaned Benham. "I knew you guys would find the car and process it for prints. I just couldn't take the chance of being connected to Chrissy."

"Which, I suppose, is the same reason you broke into Christine's house on Saturday night," said MacKinnon, heaving a weary sigh. "What were you looking for?"

"Crank, dope paraphernalia, the credit cards, and pretty much anything that could link me to Chrissy," Benham replied, his voice betraying humiliation. "I knew that someone would come looking. I didn't have any choice. I couldn't let anyone find out I was involved with her. It would have ruined me."

It was more self-pity than MacKinnon could stand and he snarled in response, "Oh yeah, you're a real victim of circumstances. You're good for two counts of burglary, receiving stolen property, credit card fraud, criminal conspiracy, auto theft, and impeding a police investigation, but, God forbid, none of it's your fault. I've only got one more question, Dave. At any point during this goddamn crime spree did you ever stop for a single fucking second and remember you were a cop?"

"Things got out of control," whined Benham.

"No, you got out of control," MacKinnon said.

There was a long interval of silence as he loaded his pipe with tobacco.

Finally Benham said, "So what's going to happen now?"

MacKinnon lit his pipe before answering. "We're going to go to your police station and lay this all out for your chief. After he gets finished putting you on administrative leave and collecting your badge and gun, I want you to provide a voluntary written statement on everything you just told me. If you continue to cooperate with me, there won't be any charges filed against you in Virginia."

"And in Maryland?" Benham looked like a whipped puppy.

"I've got no control over what they do to you up here. Let's get going. I'll follow you into town."

They walked back up the slope to the parking lot and both men got into their vehicles. MacKinnon looked over at Benham and saw that he had a black semi-automatic pistol pressed against his right temple. Throwing his car door open, MacKinnon shouted the officer's name. Benham glanced at the chief and his eyes transmitted a brief and reproachful farewell. There was a gunshot and the driver's side window of the Isuzu was spattered with a spray of bright-red blood and bits of brain. Benham's body fell forward onto the steering wheel and the horn began to blare.

"You stupid son-of-a-bitch!" cried MacKinnon as he ran from the squad car to the SUV and jerked the driver's door open. He pulled Benham back from the steering wheel and felt the cop's body quiver once. MacKinnon grabbed the man's wrist to feel for a pulse, but after a couple of seconds he released the lifeless hand. Looking into the dead man's sleepy eyes, MacKinnon sighed.

Eleven:

Dominion and Control

MacKinnon called 911 on his wireless phone, and a few minutes later a National Park Police car appeared with its emergency lights flashing and siren yelping. The car skidded to a stop and the cop got out of the car, his hand poised above his holster. Then he saw MacKinnon's uniform and relaxed slightly. However, when he looked into the Isuzu he recoiled in shock.

"Oh my God! That's Dave Benham," said the park officer. "What the hell happened?"

"I'd just finished interviewing him on a case I'm working, and I guess he couldn't face what he'd done," replied MacKinnon. "You might want to call Sharpsburg's Chief of Police and give him a heads-up."

The officer made the call. A few minutes later, as MacKinnon was briefing the park cop on what had happened, a red Chevy Suburban belonging to the Antietam Volunteer Rescue Squad howled onto the quiet battlefield, followed by a gray police cruiser that had the word "Chief" stenciled above the insignia of the Sharpsburg Police Department. The rescue vehicle skidded to a stop and two EMTs rushed to Benham's car, each carrying medical kits. Meanwhile, a tall and barrel-chested cop with wavy, gray hair unfolded himself from the patrol car and peered at Benham. He watched for a moment as the medics fumbled to unzip the dead man's jacket and attach EKG sensors to his chest and then turned away. He didn't need a diagnostic printout to know that Benham was beyond help.

"That's Chief Hinds," said the park policeman.

Hinds approached and asked, "What the hell happened here, Phil?"

The park policeman inclined his head toward MacKinnon. "He was here when it happened, Chief."

"And you are?" Hinds' hazel eyes fell upon MacKinnon.

"Steve MacKinnon, I'm the Chief of the Talmine Police Department."

"Virginia, right?"

"Yeah. Near Fredericksburg."

"And just what business did you have in my town?"

"I'm working the murder of Christine Norland. You should recognize the name," MacKinnon replied, and saw Hinds nod. "And, up until about thirty minutes ago, your Officer Benham was one of my suspects. You want the entire story here or at your office?"

"He was back with Norland? God-dammit to hell!" snapped Hinds. "Tell me what happened."

MacKinnon quickly related the tale of Christine's murder, Benham's appearance in Talmine, and the subsequent homicide investigation. When he finished, MacKinnon gestured toward the body and said, "We were on our way in to talk to you when he decided to eat his gun."

"That explains why he didn't answer the phone when I called his place this morning. I wanted him to come back to the station," said Chief Hinds, glancing unhappily at the corpse. "I was going to relieve him of duty. It was the first step in termination proceedings."

"The alcohol?"

Hinds turned away from the body. "Yeah. It was an ongoing problem with Dave. About three months ago we tried to get him into a rehab program, but he gaffed us off. Then this morning, when I got into work, the day-watch officer told me Benham was reeking of booze. There were also some complaints on my answering machine from people who'd seen him last night."

"I'm truly sorry," said MacKinnon.

"No, you aren't and, privately, neither am I." Hinds locked eyes with MacKinnon. "I inherited Dave Benham from the last chief. Benham was a bad cop and, if my hands hadn't been tied by all those civil service protections, he'd have been out on his ass months ago. You're a chief. You know how that goes."

"Yeah, I know what you're saying and can sympathize, but I still wish there'd been a better solution to your problem than him blowing his brains out. Benham was the only eyeball witness who could put Christine Norland and the killer together just before the murder."

"Any chance there'll be some evidence at his house?"

"Possibly. He told me he let Norland use his computer to exchange e-mail with the suspect. And it's also a safe bet he was into credit card fraud and identity theft. That doesn't have much to do with my case, but it might be useful information for you."

"We're gonna need a search warrant to get inside."

"I know."

"You can use my office to type up the affidavit. Let's go."

MacKinnon followed Chief Hinds' patrol car westward from the battlefield and into the nearby, drowsy town of Sharpsburg. Unlike Gettysburg—portions of which were a mercantile free-fire zone—MacKinnon was pleased to discover that the streets of Sharpsburg weren't filled with souvenir shops, wax museums, and fast food restaurants. It was simply a farm village that hadn't changed enormously since September 1862. The brick police station, which was only slightly larger than a modern two-car garage, stood on Mechanic Street. Hinds parked his car in front of the building and waved MacKinnon to another slot that was marked with a sign that read: "Police Vehicles Only."

The Sharpsburg Chief blinked in puzzlement as MacKinnon opened the passenger door of his patrol car and removed the cat carrier from the front seat. MacKinnon had no idea of how long he'd be inside the police station, and it was already growing far too warm to leave Farshee in the closed-up car. The cat began to mewl pitifully.

"I've seen police dogs, but never a police cat," Hinds said, sounding very earnest while trying to suppress a grin. "Does he make a good partner?"

"Yeah, I know this looks a little strange—"

"Just a little."

"But I found him at Christine Norland's place. You know what happens to unclaimed pets, so I decided to take him home."

"Didn't you tell me that Benham searched her place on Saturday night?"

"He did."

"And he left that little kitten to starve?"

"Yep."

"That's another reason to be glad he's dead."

Going inside the stationhouse, Hinds called to the dispatcher, who sat behind a window of transparent and badly-scratched plastic, "Yeah, Helen, it was him. Killed himself."

Helen was a plump woman in her fifties with curly auburn hair that glistened with hairspray. Without looking up from her crossword puzzle, she replied in a bored voice, "Gee, that's too bad."

"I take it Helen isn't going to miss Benham," MacKinnon said as they continued down the short hallway to Hinds' office.

"The only people who'll miss him are the local tavern operator and a couple of liquor store owners up in Hagerstown. And the only reason they'll mourn his passing is because Dave died before paying up his debts."

"Before we get started, is there someplace where I can let this little guy out of the box, but where he can't run away?"

"Got a broom closet." Hinds opened a door.

"It'll do. Let me get him some food, water, and his litter box, and I'll be right with you."

Once he'd taken care of Farshee, MacKinnon joined Hinds in his office. The room was decorated with dusty dead animals and hundreds of police shoulder patches that were secured to the walls with stickpins. Mounted high on the wall behind the desk was a large fish with evil-looking teeth. Opposite the desk, the head of Bambi's father hung on the wall, surrounded by a colorful fabric mosaic of police insignias from across the country and even a few from Europe.

"You a collector?" MacKinnon nodded in the direction of the patches.

"Yeah, I've got about a thousand."

"If you want, I could send you a San Diego PD patch."

"I'd like that. Are you originally from there?"

"Yeah, how could you tell?"

"No offense, but with your 'like totally, dude' accent, I knew you weren't from Virginia. How long were you a cop back there?"

"Twenty-one years, most of it spent in homicide."

"You miss California?"

"Like I would a toothache. Hey, do you mind if I make a call? I need to bring my people up to speed on the investigation."

"Go ahead and I'll go get us some coffee. How do you take yours?"

"Same as my soul: black and bitter."

Hinds emitted a mirthless chuckle. "Be back in a minute."

Sitting down in a straight-backed wooden chair, MacKinnon pulled the wireless phone from his gun belt and pressed his home number.

"Good morning, sweetheart. How are you this morning?" Victoria answered on the first ring.

"I've had days that began on a better note."

"Problems with Benham?"

"Not at first. In fact, the interview went pretty well, right up to the point when he killed himself."

Victoria gasped. "Oh my God. You were there? Are you all right?"

"I'm fine. The good news is that before he opted to take the dirt nap, Benham copped to helping our victim sell a Civil War document that she stole from the Library of Congress. And Benham also said that the intended buyer was an antique dealer from New York."

"Carnes."

"Do we have any news on him?"

"I haven't heard anything."

"He's still around. I can feel it in my bones. When I get off the phone with you, I'm going to call Sayers and tell him there's probable cause for Carnes' arrest," said MacKinnon. "What's the word on Greg?"

"No complications, and the doctors were talking about releasing him in a couple of days. Meanwhile, Wendy is camped out in his room."

"Well, that's one bit of good news." MacKinnon massaged the bridge of his nose. "Okay, I'm going to be here for a little while yet. I have to write a statement on the suicide, knock out a search warrant affidavit, and then go find a judge so I can toss Benham's place. I ought to be home some time this evening."

"Promise?"

"Promise. I love you honey, and I'll see you tonight."

MacKinnon hung up and then called the Talmine Police. Sayers was in the office and, after updating the sergeant on the investigation, MacKinnon said, "Has the photo of Carnes arrived yet?"

"We've got a good quality digital," Sayers replied.

"Good. I want you to amend the original BOLO to indicate there's now probable cause to arrest Carnes for suspicion of murder. When you get the picture, make up a bunch of fliers."

"The PC's kind of thin, isn't it? I mean, you don't have a witness or any physical evidence to link him to the murder."

"That's true, Ron, but we do have a strong set of circumstantial facts that point to Carnes, more than enough for an arrest warrant affidavit, that I'll write when I get back." MacKinnon knew that Sayers was concerned over the possibility of being listed as a defendant in a multi-million-dollar civil lawsuit for false arrest, if his chief's conclusions were proven wrong. Irked with the self-serving sergeant, MacKinnon said, "In the meantime, just do what I say and spare me the Perry Mason routine. If you come up with anything, call me. I should be back in town later tonight."

A moment later, Hinds reentered the office with steaming coffee mugs in both hands.

MacKinnon said, "Well, I guess I'd better get to work on that report. I don't mean this to sound patronizing, but you don't have a computer, do you?"

"Of course, we've got a computer." Hinds sounded slightly surprised. "C'mon back to the report-writing room."

MacKinnon followed and discovered that Hinds was technically telling the truth. The Sharpsburg Police did indeed have a computer: an ancient Leading Edge 286 that seemed to take forever to boot up, and its word processing program was a Bronze-Age version of WordPerfect. Yet, once MacKinnon had mastered the command keys, he quickly completed the witness statement on Benham's suicide.

Thirty minutes later, he got into Hinds' patrol car and they drove out to take a look at Benham's home before starting work on the search warrant affidavit. Based on fifty years' worth of inaccurate television programs, the average citizen assumed that cops got a search warrant by simply telling a judge the street address of the building they wanted to search. Yet MacKinnon knew there was far more to it than that. Along with the house numbers, the issuing judge would also want a thorough description of the structure's exterior, including the number of windows and doors, the building's color, its roof composition, and even how the surrounding property was landscaped.

The journey took them south along the Harper's Ferry Road for about a mile, and then Hinds turned right on Miller's Sawmill Road. After traveling another three hundred yards, Hinds turned left and proceeded down a dirt lane that separated two cornfields. Benham had lived in a dingy, ramshackle, singlewide mobile home that stood in a tiny copse of evergreens. All the window shades were drawn, an asthmatic air conditioner hung haphazardly from a plywood-sheathed window, and the rusting skeleton of a Harley-Davidson motorcycle stood in the narrow carport. The cops got out of the car and walked around the trailer. Out in the cornfields, crows were cawing, and off in the distance MacKinnon could hear the sound of farm machinery.

"Be it ever so humble," said MacKinnon as he jotted down the information.

"I can't wait to see the inside," grunted Hinds.

They returned to the police station and MacKinnon began typing the lengthy statement of facts necessary to apply for the search warrant. An hour and a half later, he stood before a judge in the Hagerstown court complex, his right hand raised, and swore that the facts set forth in the document were true to the best of his knowledge. The search warrant was issued, and Hinds and MacKinnon went back to Benham's trailer.

As the pair mounted the wobbly wooden porch steps, Hinds produced a house key. "While you were getting the warrant, I stopped by the coroner's office and picked up Benham's key ring. Didn't feel like breaking in."

"Might as well make sure there's no one else at home." MacKinnon used his nightstick to pound on the door. "Police! Anyone home? Hello? This is the police and we have a search warrant. Open the door, please!"

There was no answer, nor any sound of hurried footfalls going out the back door. Hinds unlocked the cheap aluminum door, pushed it open, and both cops entered. The living room was as dark and chilly as a tomb, but definitely not as tidy. MacKinnon was instantly reminded of a teenage boy's bedroom. A VCR, with digital numbers blinking 00:00, stood atop a small television that, in turn, stood atop a larger and apparently inoperative television. Next to the video pyramid, a stereo system rested on a shelf made from a length of particleboard and cinder blocks.

Dirty clothing lay on the frayed furniture and floor, and the coffee table was littered with Burger King wrappers and a small assortment of science fiction paperbacks and hardcore skin magazines. The room's single item of decoration was a faded poster of a young woman, wearing nothing but a thong bikini bottom, with her hands on a wall and her airbrushed rump thrusting upward.

Hinds shook his head in disgust. "Unbelievable. This place makes me want to put on a biochemical warfare suit."

"I guess it was the maid's day off," said MacKinnon. He walked into the kitchen, where Benham's computer stood on a table. There was unopened mail stacked on the table next to the computer monitor, and MacKinnon briefly examined the collection of bills and grim-looking envelopes from collection agencies. Then he noticed some illustrated papers near the printer: computer-generated road maps of the route from Sharpsburg to Talmine. He collected the sheets and put them in a large evidence envelope.

Hinds searched the living room and bathroom, while MacKinnon sorted through the rest of the paperwork to ensure that there weren't any copies of the e-mail correspondence with Carnes. He didn't find anything else connected with his case, but did locate some numerical sequences written in ink that he suspected were stolen credit card numbers. He handed the sheet to Hinds, who recognized the significance of the information and scowled.

Returning to the kitchen, MacKinnon dumped the overflowing trash can onto the stained floor. He began to sort through the rubbish and learned more about Benham's lifestyle than he really wanted to know. There were empty bottles of bargain-basement bourbon, a half-consumed can of beef stew that looked as if Benham had been eating the cold food straight from the tin, and a small box that had contained male potency pills. Then MacKinnon noticed a damp ball of crumpled paper inside a plastic lunchmeat wrapper. Gingerly removing the paper from the package, MacKinnon unfolded the sheet and saw it contained a printed copy of an e-mail message.

"Bingo," he murmured to himself as he read the brief text.

The communication was from D. H. Hill to Rose Greenhow and said, "Agreed. Meet in Talmine on Saturday at 10:00 a.m." MacKinnon recognized the latter name as belonging to the most celebrated female Confederate spy of the Civil War. It was also a fitting alias for Christine Norland. Hill, of course, was Carnes, and now there was an opportunity to prove it, because there was an e-mail address listed after the general's name. MacKinnon pulled out his wallet and removed the business card Carnes had given him on Saturday. The e-mail addresses were identical.

"Benham, may the good Lord bless you for being such a slob," MacKinnon happily muttered.

Once he'd finished searching the trash, he disassembled the computer system and loaded the tower and printer into his squad car. Then the police chiefs attacked the messy bedroom together. They found another collection of pornographic magazines, a small baggie of marijuana, and a dope pipe, but nothing connected with the murder investigation. MacKinnon left a receipt and inventory form on the table, and Hinds locked up the trailer.

It had begun to get cloudy while they were inside the mobile home. Hinds glanced into the northwestern sky where a cobalt-blue wall of rain clouds was moving in their direction. The atmosphere was still hot and stagnant, but MacKinnon knew that was going to change very shortly and he congratulated himself for having remembered to bring his raincoat along.

As they returned to their patrol cars, Hinds looked at his watch. "Nearly four. You aren't going to be able to return the warrant to the court today."

"I'll bring it back later in the week," MacKinnon said. "If I have the chance, I'll spend a little time out on the battlefield."

"You a Civil War buff?"

"My wife calls me a fanatic."

"Mine too," Hinds chuckled. "Sometimes at lunch I'll go out to the East Woods or over to the Dunker Church and just sit."

MacKinnon understood the peculiar and powerful enchantment of the battlefield. "I envy you."

"Kind of strange when you think about it."

"What's that?"

Hinds looked thoughtful and then almost troubled. "Lee's Lost Order caused the Battle of Antietam, and over a century later that paper is still killing people."

Twelve:

Hot Pursuit

After collecting Farshee from the Sharpsburg Police Station, MacKinnon made his way homeward, managing to stay just in advance of the line of thunderheads. When traffic was light, he gained on the storm front; when he hit patches of sluggish traffic, the storm almost overtook him. The cat howled for much of the journey but finally stopped, which was a good thing because MacKinnon knew that animal abuse was a felony offense in Virginia. The digital clock on the dashboard read 7:36 as he got off Interstate 95 and turned onto State Route 3. A short while later, he'd left Fredericksburg and was making his way eastward along the Northern Neck.

Nearly home, he thought happily. It had been a very long day and he was ready to get out of the sweaty uniform and take a long, hot shower. Afterwards, he'd have a cold beer while he and Victoria sat on the porch and talked about anything but greed and murder. The report-writing could wait until morning.

There was a sudden static-laden transmission from the radio, and MacKinnon glanced at the radio scanner display. It was channel two, the Brookesmith County Sheriff's Department frequency. Although the excited words were unintelligible, MacKinnon heard a siren in the background and knew by this combination there was probably a pursuit in progress. Then the sheriff's broadcast was replaced by Deshawn Williams' voice on the Talmine PD radio channel. Shouting to be heard over his car's siren, he informed dispatch he was assisting the sheriff and that the pursuit was westbound on Kings Highway, passing the village of Lerty. Kings Highway was the alternate name for State Route 3, and MacKinnon realized the chase was coming in his direction. Kathy Sayers acknowledged Williams' transmission.

At the same time, his wireless phone rang. MacKinnon quickly pulled to the side of the road and snatched the phone from his gun belt. "MacKinnon."

"Chief, we're in pursuit of Carnes' Saab," said Kathy Sayers.

"Thanks. I'm just east of Fredericksburg and en route. If you need anything else, get me on the radio." MacKinnon disconnected the call. He leaned across the front seat to make sure the seat belts that girdled the cat carrier were secure and told Farshee, "Hang on, pal. This could get very interesting."

Switching on the car's overhead emergency lights and siren, he slammed the accelerator to the floor and the vehicle slued onto the vacant highway. There was another radio transmission and, although he couldn't be certain, MacKinnon thought that Williams reported the Saab had passed Flat Iron and was now heading toward the hamlet of Potomac Mills. If that were so, Carnes had to be traveling in excess of one hundred miles an hour. Lightning flickered distantly in the western sky, and MacKinnon hoped that the pursuit could be ended before the rain began to fall. Slick roads, speeding cars, fleeing felons, and excited cops were the perfect ingredients for a calamity.

Traffic was relatively light and he made swift progress eastward along the peninsula. Meanwhile, he listened intently as Officer Williams reported on the reckless journey of the Saab as it careened through the small towns of Latanes and Oak Grove. There was a brief interlude of silence and then came the news that the suspect vehicle had just avoided the tire-shredding teeth of a State Police spike strip near the roadside village of Index, and was still racing westward. The State Police officer from the roadblock then joined the pursuit and she broadcast a partial description of the Saab's driver—a white, male adult with a beard.

MacKinnon grabbed the radio microphone and said, "Tango One to Tango Five, I'm about two miles ahead of you. Keep pushing him in this direction."

"Ten-four, Chief."

Flying into the community of Purkins Corner, MacKinnon slammed on the brakes and felt the pedal throb beneath his foot as the anti-lock system engaged. The car skidded to a stop and the cat carrier strained against the seatbelt, while Farshee wailed in fear. A trio of police cars—two from the King George County Sheriff's Department and a State Police cruiser—blocked the highway just west of the intersection with Ridge Road. The state cop had his shotgun held at port arms while one of the deputies had an AR-15, the civilian version of the M-16 military rifle. There was a gas station on the northeast corner of the junction and a small crowd of onlookers had gathered for the impromptu entertainment.

MacKinnon slowly drove up to the roadblock, but didn't get out of his car. He shouted to the cops, "Did they advise you about who they're chasing?"

"Murder suspect, right?" a deputy called back.

"Right! The guy is also the one who shot my officer in Talmine, two nights ago!"

There was a fresh radio broadcast from Williams: "Still westbound Kings Highway, coming up on three-oh-one. The light's red . . . oh, God! Oh, God! Suspect vehicle TC'd another car! He's still westbound. Roll paramedics and fire, code three! We're still in pursuit!"

"That's just down the road," said one of the King George

deputies as he racked a round into the chamber of his rifle.

MacKinnon could now hear the sound of approaching sirens and, a few seconds later, a cluster of headlights and blue flashing emergency lights appeared on Kings Highway, heading toward the roadblock. In an instant, the damaged Saab was upon them. The car braked, skidded to the right, and left the roadway. Bouncing though a shallow drainage trench, the car plowed through a grassy lot and past the roadblock. The suspect vehicle clipped a light pole as it made a squealing turn into the gas station, and the bystanders threw themselves away from the path of the car.

Meanwhile, the three pursuing cop cars were engaged in emergency maneuvers to avoid smashing into the roadblock. The Brookesmith County unit fishtailed and slid backward into one of the parked King George patrol cars. A little farther behind in the pursuit, both Williams and the State Police officer were able to follow the Saab's off-road path into the gas station. At the same time, MacKinnon threw his squad car into reverse and backed up to the intersection with Ridge Road. He saw the bottom of the Saab bounce hard against the pavement while leaving the gas station, shooting copper sparks in its wake. Now MacKinnon was the third vehicle in the speeding and deafening procession of police cars. But before more than a few seconds had passed, the roadblock cops were behind him.

"East on Ridge Road," called Williams over the radio.

MacKinnon snatched the microphone from its holder and said, "Tango One to Control, call the Maryland State Police. We're coming up on three-oh-one again and this guy might make a run for the state line."

"Just got off the phone with them, Tango One," said Kathy Sayers.

Kathy, you may be a miserable, lying, sneaky spy, but you're also a damn fine police dispatcher and there's no denying that, thought MacKinnon.

Ridge Road ran a meandering and almost parallel course to Kings Highway, and now the Saab was heading back in the general direction from which it had come. It crossed US Route 301 again, this time causing no accident, and the suspect vehicle was now on the tree-lined road that led to the town of Colonial Beach. There was one exciting moment as the entire noisy cavalcade careened past a massive, chugging motor home, but then the road was clear. The Colonial Beach cops were monitoring the pursuit radio traffic, and their dispatcher came on the air announcing they were going to put down a spike strip where the road came close to the river and made a sharp right turn.

And let's just hope that Carnes doesn't have a police scanner in his car, thought MacKinnon as he guided the patrol car through a curve. He sniffed and realized that the kitten had both figuratively and literally been scared shitless. MacKinnon murmured, "Sorry, little guy."

From his position, three cars back, MacKinnon couldn't really see anything of the Saab other than taillights, but knew the spike strip had performed as designed when the brake lights of the patrol vehicles lit up almost at once. There was a shout from the radio: "He's off the road! Off the road! He's bailing!"

All four tires shredded, the Saab had shot from the highway and collided with a tree. The car door was open, and the cops' flashlight beams danced erratically in the darkness. Williams was shouting commands for the suspect to halt, while the state trooper yelled that the man was heading for the river. MacKinnon jumped from his car, and ran to turn off the Saab's still-roaring engine. Then the damaged Brookesmith County unit skidded to a stop next to the suspect vehicle. A furious-looking Brookesmith deputy threw open the rear door of his car and released his passenger, a huge German shepherd.

"Smash my goddamn car up, will you? Find him, Taz! Find him!" yelled the deputy, and the tan and black dog shot off into the tall stand of brush.

"Back off! Let the canine find him!" MacKinnon shouted.

Amazingly, despite their excitement, the other cops did back off. There were several seconds of relative quiet and then came a snapping sound followed by a canine squeal of pain. Next came a shrill human scream that didn't stop. As the cops charged and stumbled through the dark terrain, the shrieks grew louder and louder. MacKinnon ducked beneath a low tree branch and stopped short. The scene made him wonder if he hadn't stumbled onto the set of the horror film, *Wolfen.* Taz was imitating his Warner Bros. cartoon namesake and had become a cyclone of slashing teeth.

It took every ounce of strength the dog-handler possessed to pull his snarling animal away from the suspect. MacKinnon shined his flashlight into the man's face and cursed. It wasn't Carnes. Rather it was a bloody young man, dressed in the shredded remnants of jeans and a tee shirt, who looked as if he'd been subjected to the blades of a food processor. Beside him was the woefully inadequate tree branch he'd used to wallop Taz on the head. But the dog had gotten even and the suspect moaned as he cradled his genitals, which Taz had been using as a chew toy.

After calling over the radio for paramedics, MacKinnon asked the suspect, "Who the hell are you?"

"William Dulay," the suspect wailed. "Help me! I think he bit it off! Ohh! Please, help me find it."

MacKinnon bent low and shined his flashlight at the man's crotch. He winced, exhaled sharply, and said, "Yow.

No, Dulay, it's still there, but I'll bet by tomorrow morning you'll wish it wasn't."

"Shit, it is GTA Dulay," said the state police officer. She turned to MacKinnon and added, "Local mope. Lives out near Dickinsons Corner."

MacKinnon knelt beside the injured suspect. "Where'd you get the car?"

"I found it." Dulay sobbed and several of the officers snickered. Apparently, GTA Dulay had never stolen a car in his life, but he had found and borrowed more than a few.

"Where?"

"On the street near the Boardwalk."

The Colonial Beach officer clarified the statement. "In our town."

"How long ago?" MacKinnon asked.

"Yesterday. The key was in the ignition, so I decided to go cruising."

"Did you find anything inside the car?"

"No," Dulay whimpered. "How come you guys chased me so hard?"

"Because you had the extraordinary bad luck to 'borrow' a car from a murderer," MacKinnon replied with a dry laugh. He stood up and said to the Colonial Beach cop, "My guess is Carnes dumped the car in your town because he knew it was hot. That means he had to have come up with some other form of transportation. Have you had any auto thefts reported in the past two days?"

"Not that I remember."

"It's possible he's still in town then. Can you check out your motels?"

The Colonial Beach officer nodded. "I'll get started when we get done here."

"Thanks." MacKinnon turned to the Brookesmith

County deputy. "If you want to book him for auto theft, we'll do the stolen report and recovery."

"If he doesn't go by ambulance, Deshawn will have to transport," said the deputy. "Because I don't think Dulay is going to want to sit in the back seat of my car with Taz."

"No problem," said Williams.

Back on the road, the Colonial Beach Rescue Squad truck arrived, and moments later the medical technicians jogged up, carrying their first aid kits. As the medics attended to Dulay, MacKinnon commended Williams for his good performance during the pursuit and then brought the officer up to date on what he'd learned about the murder. As they talked, MacKinnon could see lightning across the river in Maryland. Thunder boomed like distant battle, and it looked as if the storm was going to pass to the north.

"So you think Carnes is going to stay in the area until he finds the paper?" Williams asked doubtfully. "Seems to me that he'd know we were looking for him and be in the wind."

"The run-of-the-mill crook would think that way, but Carnes is convinced he's a super genius and that he's up against a bunch of boneheads. And, in fairness to him, so far I haven't given him too many reasons to think otherwise. Let's take a look in his car."

MacKinnon checked the front seat, while Williams looked in the back seat and trunk. The glove box was filled with miscellaneous papers, and there was a half-consumed Miller Genuine Draft in the console cup holder, but there didn't seem to be any evidence connected with the murder. Then MacKinnon lifted up the driver's side floor mat and saw something small and metallic beneath the brake pedal.

Shining his flashlight on the spot, he recognized the item as a brass percussion cap from a Civil War-era pistol. *Perhaps the small explosive cap had been jarred from Carnes' pistol during his flight from the Blackburn Gallery,* thought MacKinnon. The bit of brass was too small to hold even a partial fingerprint, so he picked it up and showed it to his officer.

Williams understood the significance of the discovery. "Even if we don't find the gun, we can at least show that Carnes had black-powder shooting equipment."

"Yeah, and I'll bet that when we vacuum the interior of the car and have the contents processed by a scanning electron microscope, we'll find plenty of gunpowder." MacKinnon tucked the percussion cap into his pocket. "Okay, Deshawn, I'm going to head home. Can you stand by for the tow truck?"

Williams closed the trunk lid. "Yeah, and then I'll hang loose in case numb-nuts Dulay needs transport to county jail. Oh, and I'm glad you're back, Chief."

"Thanks."

MacKinnon pulled into his driveway a few minutes before nine o'clock. The dogs began to bark, and Victoria came out onto the porch to greet him. Putting the cat carrier down, MacKinnon hugged his wife. Meanwhile, the golden retrievers peered into the carrier at the hissing Farshee; Rob Roy chuffed and shot MacKinnon a disapproving glance as if to say: *another damn cat?*

"Sweetheart, what is that smell?" inquired Victoria, her nose wrinkling.

"Farshee, that's his name by the way, had a little accident during the pursuit."

"What pursuit?"

"We just finished chasing Carnes' Saab. It crashed near Colonial Beach, but Carnes wasn't driving."

"So, who was?"

"A local crook who got a bargain vasectomy from a police canine. Very messy." He only half-pretended to shiver. "The guy told me that he boosted the car in Colonial Beach. But somehow I don't think our Mr. Carnes is going to make himself available to testify in the court proceedings against the auto thief. Not that I don't think he's not still around."

"You said that on the phone. Why?"

"Because in his mind the document he's after is worth the risk. Look at it from his point of view. Even if he's caught, he'll do what, maybe twelve years max in state prison?"

"If that," Victoria said.

"Right. You and I both know that we'll never get a death penalty filing on this case. The victim isn't the most sympathetic character in the world and we can't prove any special circumstances. So Carnes does his time like a good boy, and the paper is waiting for him when he gets out."

"But why? He can't sell it."

"I'll tell you about it in the house."

Victoria knelt, opened the metal door to the cat carrier, and reached inside. When Farshee hissed, she said, "It's all right, little one. It's all right." She grabbed the kitten by the scruff of its neck and pulled the terrified animal from the container. Farshee was tucked into a tiny ball and his feet and the underside of his body were smudged with brown feces.

"Bath time for you, mister," declared Victoria.

They went into the house and she began running warm water into the bathroom sink. MacKinnon was certain that this was the prelude to a knockdown-drag-'em-out donnybrook, but he was wrong. Farshee allowed himself to be lowered into the soapy water and submitted to Victoria's gentle ministrations. Meanwhile, Chairman Meow and Tagger stood in the doorway, peering upward at the newcomer, their upright tails flicking to-and-fro.

"So, tell me about this document," said Victoria as she squirted pet shampoo into her hand. She began to work the soap into the kitten's fur. "Oh, Steve, this poor thing is covered in fleas."

"Don't I know? I'll bet I have enough flea bites to make a connect-the-dots puzzle." MacKinnon sat down on the edge of the bathtub. "Anyway, the document: Christine Norland stole it from the Library of Congress. It's usually known as the Lost Order and, next to his farewell address to his troops, it's probably the most well-known document by Robert E. Lee."

"Why?" Victoria began to wash the cat's belly.

"Because a misplaced copy of the command was found wrapped around a bundle of cigars by Union troops and that led to the Battle of Antietam. There aren't many documents from the Civil War that are more famous or potentially valuable."

"Which proves my point," said Victoria. "Carnes can't sell it for anything close to what it's worth, because it's too hot."

"Agreed, but I don't think he's the least bit interested in selling the Lost Order. Carnes wants it for himself, and I'll bet he's decided that a decade or so in the joint is a fair trade for one of the most important documents of the Civil War." MacKinnon wore a sudden look of astonishment. "And, hang on. I want to check something."

He walked upstairs to his office and returned a moment later with Stephen Sears' *Landscape Turned Red*, a history of the Antietam campaign. Turning first to the index and then the front part of the volume, MacKinnon found the desired information and said in an exultant tone, "The original order was apparently lost by a member of General D. H. Hill's staff."

Victoria looked up from the soapy kitten. "And Carnes was dressed as a Confederate general."

"Yep, D. H. Hill," said MacKinnon.

"Honey, this is getting really weird. Are you telling me that Carnes is crazy and thinks he's a dead Confederate officer?"

"That'll be his defense when we catch him, but no, I don't believe he's legally insane." MacKinnon rubbed his chin. "Actually, I think he told me he was Hill because he knew that at some point I was going to find out about the Lost Order and realize that he'd dangled a clue in front of me and I never suspected the fact. Carnes wanted me to understand that he was some sort of modern day Professor Moriarty and too clever to be caught. He gets off on demonstrating how brilliant he is."

Victoria began to rinse Farshee. "Well, he's not that brilliant. He didn't get the document."

"That's because Christine Norland recognized Carnes for what he was: a fellow thief. She hid the document before their meeting."

"And Benham couldn't tell you where it was?"

"No. Christine kept him in the dark. In fact, it's pretty clear she'd decided to do the deal and sky out of town without telling him."

Victoria lifted the wet kitten from the sink and wrapped it in a towel. She held Farshee so that the other cats could look at him and said, "I want you to be nice to Farshee. He's had a bad day." Then she glanced at MacKinnon. "By the way, just what does Farshee mean? It's not some sort of obscene acronym, is it?"

"Honey, you cut me to the quick. Would I give one of our cats a foul name?" He saw the amused and knowing expression on his wife's face. "Okay, don't answer that. It's Gaelic for 'cat who is marginally quieter than the Concorde at takeoff.' "

"Wonderful." Victoria dried the kitten. "Did you find

anything at Benham's place?"

"That's the other major news. We lucked out." MacKinnon told her about the discovery of the discarded e-mail from Carnes.

"But we can't prove that Carnes typed the message," said Victoria as she studied her golden mane in the mirror and frowned. "Bad hair day."

"Your hair looks wonderful." MacKinnon tugged at one of her ringlets. "But back to the problem of linking Carnes with Norland, you're right. The e-mail by itself isn't enough."

"Honey, you're sweet, but my hair looks like it was styled with a weed-whacker." Victoria retrieved a hairbrush from the drawer. "You're going to need Carnes' computer too."

"Which likely means a trip to New York. And we'll also have to touch bases with the organizers of that Civil War show in Richmond to see if they still have their registration forms. If we find that Carnes was an attending dealer, that will go a long way toward corroborating Benham's story."

Victoria lowered the brush, peered at her image in the mirror, and sighed. "It's the best I can do. Are you hungry, or do you want to see the picture of Jean Dumfries first?"

MacKinnon tapped his forehead with his finger. "I'd forgotten about that. Let's take a look at the photo. And don't worry about dinner. I had a sandwich on the way home."

"A sandwich isn't dinner. I'll bet you ate nothing but junk while you were gone."

"Not true. French fries are vegetables."

Victoria rolled her eyes and he followed her upstairs into her sewing room. The Talmine *Courier* lay on the table and he studied the headline that blared: "Civil War Days Cancelled: Cops Cite Death." Beneath it, the sub-headline read: "Merchants Rage at Decision; Mayor Demands Answers."

MacKinnon didn't need to read the article; he knew what it would say. Although the newspaper's motto was, "Consecrated to Truth and Liberty," a more appropriate slogan would have been from the old RCA Victor ads that showed the dog with his ear cocked to the gramophone: "His master's voice." The crusading editor of the Talmine *Courier*, Charles Young, was a human remora who, like the parasitic fish that enjoyed a wary symbiotic relationship with the shark, had firmly attached himself to Jean Dumfries' back.

MacKinnon examined the photograph beneath the headline. It showed Mayor Dumfries in the Civil War camp, posing with her husband and Councilman Adams. She wore a blue skirt and white short-sleeve blouse, the same clothing described by Carnes. Then something else caught his eye. "Vic, honey, do you have that magnifying glass?"

She put Farshee on the sewing table and retrieved the magnifying glass from a storage drawer. As the kitten knocked over a spool of thread and began to play, MacKinnon focused the lens over Dumfries' hands in the picture. Then he gave the magnifying glass to his wife. "Here, take a look at her nails."

After a moment's inspection, Victoria announced, "French manicure."

"Like the nail I found underneath Christine Norland."

Victoria wore an uncomfortable and perplexed expression. "Steve, a lot of women have French manicured nails. Besides, why would she have handled the body?"

"I don't know. But Dumfries' nails were a shiny gray when I was at her house on Saturday night. I remember that because she was tapping them on the chair."

"Which means she changed the coloring sometime after the event," said Victoria.

"Correct. Where does Dumfries get her hair done?"

"The same place I do, Shear Delight."

"Who's the manicurist?"

"Jill DiGiovanni."

"I'll be back in a second." MacKinnon headed toward his office.

"I'm going to take Farshee downstairs and give him some food."

A few minutes later MacKinnon walked into the kitchen. "I just talked to Jill on the phone, and she told me that the mayor came in on Saturday afternoon, just before closing. Dumfries didn't have an appointment, but she absolutely insisted on a new manicure and a new nail color. Jill remembers that the left index fingernail was broken off."

"Sounds to me like you're going to have to interview our favorite local politician," said Victoria as she forked some canned cat food into a saucer and lifted Farshee up onto the counter.

"Yeah. Tonight."

"Then do me a favor, sweetheart."

"What's that?"

"If you can prove she was involved in this thing, lock her into a statement and destroy her. She and her toadies have declared war on us, and I'm about ready to go over to her house and punch her lights out."

A little taken aback by his wife's icy vehemence, MacKinnon put his hand on her shoulder. "What happened, Vic?"

The telephone rang and she snatched the receiver up. She listened for a moment and then cooed, "Pal, if you walked into a wall with a hard-on, you'd break your nose first."

"What the hell was that about?" asked a mystified MacKinnon as his wife slammed the receiver back into the cradle.

"That's what happened while you were gone." She hooked a thumb in the direction of the phone. "Just after lunch, I began getting obscene telephone calls from different guys. From what one of the creeps said, I guessed that someone had posted our home phone number on a local Web bulletin board for perverts, so I got on the computer and began checking the Northern Neck BBS's. I found this." She retrieved a piece of paper from the wicker basket next to the phone and handed it to him.

MacKinnon scanned the message and his jaw began to tighten. There was a posting inviting all kinds of perversions, all of it lewd and vicious, and the smutty epistle ended with their telephone number and the hint that Victoria would be amenable to entertaining nighttime callers. MacKinnon slowly crumpled the paper in his fist.

Ordinarily, when he lost his temper he was quick to recover it, but all bets were off when someone tried to harm his wife. When that happened, his temper tended to remain lost until the thing that had provoked his rage was obliterated. Victoria had once told him that his anger reminded her of an old-fashioned water mill: it was coolly mechanical, implacable in operation, and existed for no other reason but to crush things. Feeling his internal grindstone begin to roll, he promised himself that the message's author was going to suffer mightily for this attempt to make his wife the target of a sexual predator.

Taking Victoria's hand, he said, "Honey, I'm so sorry."

"At first I just laughed at them, but some of them kept calling back. I guess they thought it was part of my rape fantasy," she said tiredly. "Then I realized that someone with a reverse phone directory could look up our number and find our address. That's when I got spooked and really mad."

"I wonder which one of Dumfries' toadies posted the message?"

"That was my first thought, so I called Mark Weiss at his office and asked him to check."

"And?"

"And the message was posted earlier today from the public access computer at the County Library. Mark removed the message from the system, but by then the damage had already been done."

"So anybody could have typed it," MacKinnon said with a sigh. Then he brightened. "But the library should have a log of the people who used the computer today."

"How do we get to the records?"

"Like this." He picked up the phone and called the police station. When Kathy Sayers answered the phone, he said, "Ms. Sayers, when Officer Williams is clear, I want him to respond to my house to take a crime report. You want the nature of the offense? How about Section One-fifty-two-point-seven, Personal Trespass by Computer, and Sixty-point-three, Stalking?"

When he hung the telephone up, Victoria said, "Want to bet me if we called Dumfries house right now, the line would be busy?"

"No bet, and for once I'm not the least bit annoyed at our spy's activities. I want Dumfries to know the fat is in the fire when I call her."

"Good. By the way, what's 'Personal Trespass by Computer'?"

"Basically it says that you can't use a computer network with the intent to cause physical injury to someone else. I think that applies here, and it's a felony." The telephone rang and he answered it. "Hello."

The caller inhaled sharply and said nothing. Apparently

he'd expected a female voice. MacKinnon said, "My friend, you've been misled. Nobody wants to hear your pathetic fantasies, and if you call again, I'm going to find you and do some orthopedic adjustments with my Tony Gwynn baseball bat." There was a sudden click as the caller hung up.

Victoria smiled. "You wouldn't actually do that, would you?"

"Of course not. That autographed bat is way too valuable. I'd use a tire iron." He depressed the disconnect button and then called the mayor.

Dumfries answered on the second ring and, learning it was MacKinnon, said, "You're late. I gave you until four o'clock. I hope this call is your formal notice of resignation."

"Sorry to disappoint you, Mayor, but no, I'm not quitting. In fact, I'm still on duty and it's important that we talk tonight in person."

"Do you have any idea of the time?"

"God, you don't know how long I've wanted to use this line: It's far later than you think." MacKinnon's voice was full of cheerful menace. "I have some questions for you."

"About what?"

"It's not something I'm prepared to talk about over the phone."

There was a long pause, and then Dumfries said in an uncertain voice, "Well, why don't you come by my house?"

"I've got a better idea. Why don't you meet me in my office in about twenty minutes?" Not waiting for a reply, he hung the phone up. Then he turned to his wife and gave her a hug. "I'll be back in a few hours. Don't wait up."

Victoria laughed and picked up the kitten. "Did you hear that, Farshee? Your daddy thinks I'm not going to be waiting with bated breath to hear every delicious detail of the defeat of Queen Jean. Isn't he silly?"

Thirteen:

Queen's Evidence

MacKinnon stopped briefly at the County Sheriff's office to pick up a piece of evidence stored there, then drove to the police station. He paused at the front desk to tell Kathy Sayers that the mayor would be arriving soon and to send her up to his office. He pretended not to notice Kathy's satisfied smile as he mounted the stairs. About ten minutes later, he heard a door open downstairs and the footfalls of someone coming up the steps. Dumfries hadn't taken time to dress up; she wore a pair of gray sweatpants, a lime-colored pullover shirt, and white tennis shoes.

He motioned her to a wooden chair facing his desk. "Sit here." The phrase wasn't a suggestion, but a command that was intended to subtly establish that he was in charge. He perched himself on the edge of the desk so that he could look down on her—another interview control technique—and said, "Now before we get to the main topic of our meeting, there's something I want to tell you. Earlier today, someone used the Internet to target my wife for sexual assault. That sort of Web posting is a felony offense. The message originated in this town, and when I find out who wrote it, they're going to wish they'd never joined the Jean Dumfries Fan Club."

"That's awful. I hope you aren't accusing me of having anything to do with that."

"It's too early to make accusations. But I want you to think about the person who wrote that message. Do you honestly believe he or she is going to take the fall and risk a state prison sentence just to protect you?" MacKinnon saw a look of consternation flicker briefly across her face. When she remained quiet, he answered the question for her, "I don't. The fact is, I've learned more about the weaknesses of human nature than I ever want to know, and I can assure you that the person is going to give you up in a heartbeat."

"I knew nothing about it."

"Mayor, there's no way you couldn't have known about it." He sounded genuinely amused. "After all, how can your lick-spittle clones collect their brownie points, unless they tell you what they've been up to?"

"I resent that," snarled Dumfries.

"Yeah, but I notice you didn't deny it. Well, let's move on." He opened the evidence envelope, turned it over, and shook it gently until a plastic bag containing a broken fragment of acrylic nail fell onto the desk. "As you know, I'm investigating a murder, and I think you have some information that can help me."

She looked from the nail to his inquiring gaze, swallowed nervously, then stared at the fragment of acrylic. "Is this supposed to mean something?"

"Mayor, you sound just like a kid who's been confronted with the bad report card she was hiding."

"But, I don't understand."

She was a good liar, but then she was a politician, MacKinnon reminded himself; it was an intrinsic part of her personality. He said, "Think back to Saturday. What sort of fingernail polish were you wearing?"

"What does this have to do with the murder?"

"Let's stick with me asking the questions for now." He gently flicked the plastic bag with his finger. "I found this beneath the victim's body, and at the time I couldn't make any sense of it. But things have changed a lot since then. Now, please answer the question: What color were your nails on Saturday?"

"Are you accusing me of murder?"

"No. I just want to know what color your nails were on Saturday."

"Gray. Metallic gray."

"That was Saturday night. What about during the day?"

"I don't really remember."

He chuckled. "Well, maybe I can refresh your memory. I just finished looking at the Talmine *Courier*. There's a picture of you on the front page, a nice close-up picture, and would you care to guess what sort of nail polish you have on?"

"I told you, I don't remember." There was a vexed tone in Dumfries' voice. She knew she was being toyed with and didn't like it one bit.

"It's a French manicure. And you know what? A little bit ago I got off the phone with Jill, the lady who does your acrylic nails. She told me that you showed up at the beauty shop late Saturday afternoon demanding she redo your nails. It seems you'd broken one on your car earlier in the day. Or at least that's what you told her."

"Yes, now I remember. I broke it on the Mercedes. But surely you can't have called me here to talk about my manicuring habits."

"You're only partially right. We're going to talk about a lot of things before the night is through, but your manicuring habits are rather important, when combined with the fact that you were seen going into the woods right around the time of the murder." MacKinnon let a few seconds of silence go by as he moved to his chair and sat down.

Dumfries' face began to grow pale. But, whatever her personality deficiencies, the mayor was a fighter. "Who says they saw me going into the woods?"

"The killer did, hoping to divert attention from himself. His name is Joseph Carnes, by the way." MacKinnon tilted the chair back and he linked his fingers behind his head. "Thanks to his information, I have two separate videotapes of you and a man going into the woods. You were in contact with that body, and I want you to tell me what happened."

She started to get up. "MacKinnon, I'm not going to sit here and take this."

"Yes, you are, Mayor. Sit down and listen very carefully, because the decision you make now will have an effect on the rest of your life. Here's the deal. You can tell me what you were doing with that dead body, or I'm going to book you tonight for impeding a police investigation."

"You're bluffing."

"Mayor, one of the first things I learned as a rookie cop working in Barrio Logan was to never make threats I wasn't prepared to back up." He unsnapped the pouch on the rear of his gun belt, produced a pair of shiny steel handcuffs, and tossed them onto the desk with a rattling clunk. "So, what'll it be, the truth or a sleepover at the county slammer?"

He knew this interrogation tactic wouldn't have worked with a hardened criminal. Career crooks weren't afraid of jail and looked at incarceration as nothing more than an unavoidable cost of doing business. But the threat of custody did frighten Dumfries, who began to sag like an old birthday party balloon. Finally, she mumbled, "Okay, I was there."

"Sorry, I couldn't hear you."

"I was there!"

"Why?"

"I was meeting a representative from Hartford-Schliemann."

"The developers who built the new shopping center?"

Hartford-Schliemann Incorporated was a large Mid-Atlantic-region construction firm whose idea of cutting-edge architecture was a rectangular strip mall decorated with faux Colonial trim.

Dumfries nodded.

"Why?"

"We were looking at some property."

"In Brookesmith Park? That's town land."

"And it's prime riverside real estate that's going to waste."

"Go on."

"The sale of some of the parkland and the subsequent commercial tax revenues from development would have boosted town income. I had a duty to examine the opportunity."

"A duty?" MacKinnon snorted and slapped his knee. "God, I love the diligent public servant act. You don't happen to own any of the adjoining land parcels, do you?"

Dumfries looked at the desktop and didn't reply.

"I'll take that as a yes." MacKinnon shook his head in disbelief. "Let me get this straight. You were trying to finagle a covert deal with Hartford-Schliemann to develop some sort of gimcrack mall on the parkland?"

"They were considering a marina, a hotel and resort complex, and commercial center," said Dumfries. "It was a first-rate development that would have benefited the entire town."

"And as the neighboring property owner, it would have benefited you in particular."

"I'll admit it was a secondary consideration."

"Oh, I'll bet it was secondary. So who was this guy from HSI?"

"His name is Peter Phillips."

"Why did you arrange to meet on Saturday?"

"I wanted him to be able to see how many tourists were in town."

"And I spoiled everything by shutting down the event. No wonder you were pissed. By the way, when we get finished I'm going to want Phillips' phone number." MacKinnon jotted the developer's name down on his notepad. "Tell me about what happened when you found the body."

Dumfries studied her right thumbnail. "We went into Crumper's Woods so that Peter could take a look at the land. We came along the trail, and then we saw her lying on the ground."

"The woman in the Confederate uniform?"

"Yes."

"What did you do?"

"I just looked at her. I'd never seen anything like that in my life."

"Did you check to see if she was alive?"

"No."

"You just assumed she was dead?"

"Yes."

"Did you think about calling the paramedics?"

"No."

"How about the police?"

"No." With each answer, Dumfries' voice had grown more and more quiet.

"So, what *did* you do?"

"I made what, at the time, I thought was a good decision." Dumfries tried to sound defiant, but only succeeded in whining. "I knew that if we reported the death, you'd probably shut down the rest of the event, something the town had invested a great deal of time and money to bring about. I assumed the death was an accident and decided that your investigation could wait until after Civil War Days was finished."

"So you covered the body of a murder victim with branches and walked away," said MacKinnon, amazed. "Can you see a problem with that?"

Dumfries' eyes were downcast. "In retrospect, yes."

"But at the time it was more important to protect your financial and political future." MacKinnon made no effort to conceal his disgust.

"I made a mistake."

"Oh, spare me the modern American *mea culpa*. If you accidentally spill your milk, that's a mistake. Forget to carry the one when you're balancing your checking account; that's a mistake. But deliberately hiding a murder victim's body to conceal political malfeasance and then doing your damnedest to shut down the investigation isn't a mistake. It's a crime."

"Chief," Dumfries said in a quiet chastened voice, "can't we come to some sort of understanding about this?"

"How do you mean?"

"I mean, isn't there some way we can settle this here? For instance, the issue of your contract. You're well past due for a pay increase and—"

"Mayor, I know what you're thinking and don't go there. You've got enough trouble as it is, without adding attempted bribery to the list. Don't worry. I'm not going to arrest you tonight, but I am going to file charges with the Commonwealth Attorney's office sometime next week."

"And there's nothing I can say . . . or do . . . to change your mind?"

He shook his head in distaste. "Mayor, don't."

"You're a strong man. You've always stood up to me . . . and I like that."

"Mayor."

"Sometimes I daydream about you." She looked at him with bedroom eyes. "You sitting in that chair and me . . ."

"Stop it! Don't make this any worse than it already is."

She stared at him for a moment and then the pretence of lust vanished instantly from her countenance. She suddenly rose from the chair, pulled her shirt up, and yanked her bra up and screamed, "Oh my God! What are you doing? No! No! Help!"

"What the hell are you doing?" demanded MacKinnon. Curiously, he didn't sound very surprised.

"Don't do that! Stop! Help!" Dumfries shouted toward the door, while pushing the waistband of her sweatpants below her hip.

There was a clatter of footfalls ascending the stairs and Kathy Sayers burst into the office with a portable police radio in her hand. The dispatcher gaped at Dumfries, who was now sobbing and pulling her shirt down to cover her breasts. *It was a performance worthy of an Academy Award,* thought MacKinnon.

In a terrified voice, Dumfries told the dispatcher, "He tried to molest me! Get an officer here immediately. I want this . . . this animal arrested."

Kathy Sayers raised the radio, but before she could transmit a message, MacKinnon said in an amused tone, "By all means, get Deshawn in here, because there's something I want him to see."

"You think this is funny?" shrieked Dumfries.

"No, just pathetic. You know, Mayor, I'm a little disappointed you actually thought I was so stupid I wouldn't want a record of our meeting." MacKinnon walked over to a set of cupboard doors that were open about two inches. He swung both doors fully open to reveal a video camera pointing toward the room. "Smile. You're on 'Candid Camera.' "

Dumfries looked from MacKinnon to the camera and then again at the chief. She started to say something, went pale in the face, and then began to cry real tears.

He scooped the handcuffs up from the desktop. "I've changed my mind. I *am* going to book you into county jail tonight."

It was nearly midnight when he returned home. Slowly climbing from the patrol car, he paused for a moment to look at his dream home and wondered glumly whether he'd just won a small battle and, in the process, lost the war. Victoria and the dogs were waiting for him at the door and he told her the story as he climbed the stairs to the bedroom and got undressed. As he recounted the sequence of events, he noticed his wife clenching her jaw ever tighter and thought: *oh, oh, Houston, we have ignition*. Ninety-nine days out of a hundred, Victoria was a paragon of affable composure, someone who maintained her temper and almost never used obscene language. But, like her husband, on the rare occasions when pushed beyond her limit, she was prone to exploding like a tactical nuke and employing amazingly vivid words and expressions that would make a gangsta rapper blush.

Unable to contain herself any longer, she snarled, "That rotten, miserable . . ."

MacKinnon listened in rapt fascination as his wife delivered a magnum opus of obscenities, vile insults, and vicious fantasies of revenge. When she at last stopped to catch her breath, he said, "Feel better?"

"A little," she grumbled.

"Then let's try to get some sleep. It's going to be a long day tomorrow." He guided her toward the bed.

"Rub my shoulders?"

"Only if you don't complain if your nightgown accidentally comes off."

She flashed him a sly smile. "You're on."

The following morning before breakfast, MacKinnon telephoned the county jail. After a brief conversation with the deputy, he hung up the phone and said to Victoria, "She's bailed out, but our esteemed mayor didn't post bond until after three a.m."

"Serves her right for trying to frame you for sexual assault." Victoria opened the refrigerator to get the carton of half-and-half as the cats began to sing their discordant morning hymn in praise of dairy products. She was an easy mark and, after pouring cream into her coffee, poured a little into each cat's bowl. Stirring her coffee, she said, "My question is, do you think Kathy Sayers was involved?"

"Much as I'd like to believe the worst about her, no, and not because I don't think she isn't capable of lying through her teeth to bury me. She simply wasn't given the chance to be a conspirator. This was something that the mayor came up with on the spur of the moment." He shook his head and smiled. "But, you should have seen Kathy's face after I showed her and Deshawn the videotape. It was priceless."

"And the mayor's defense is that she was taking pain medication and blacked out? How original," Victoria said scornfully. "Who's going to believe that?"

"You might be surprised. Remember the Twinkie defense?"

"Well, at least she's dead politically."

"I wish you were right, but if I know anything about human nature, most of her supporters will remain loyal. They have to. The last thing anyone wants to do is admit they've blindly supported a scoundrel. In fact, I'll bet that the next issue of the *Courier* will have at least one letter from the lunatic fringe claiming the videotape was a fake I had created at Industrial Light and Magic."

The telephone rang and MacKinnon answered it. It was Charles Young, editor of the Talmine *Courier*, and the newspaperman cautiously asked for an interview. *Speak of the printer's devil,* thought MacKinnon. He respectfully declined to talk about the incident and hung up the phone. There was nothing to be gained by helping to fan what he knew was going to be a local media firestorm. The facts would speak for themselves in court.

"So, what's on the agenda for today?" asked Victoria.

"I've got to contact the organizers of that event in Richmond to confirm that Carnes was there. Then I'll knock out an arrest warrant affidavit on Carnes and get that into NCIC. After that, I'm going to visit Greg and then get started on the report."

"How can I help?"

"With the mayor's arrest and you being the victim of the Web posting, it'd probably be best if you kept a low profile. There's no sense in creating the appearance of a conflict of interest."

"Maybe I'll start addressing the envelopes to mail all those pictures we had developed."

"Let's hold off on that for now."

"Why?"

"When we get Carnes into custody, his attorney is going to want to examine all the photos to make sure we didn't overlook Theodore Bundy lurking in the background. Why don't you just work on your quilt and spend some time with Farshee?"

"Oh, we got very well acquainted last night. Did you know that he started climbing the curtains after you left? Then he tried to pick a fight with Roly."

"God, it's a good thing Roly didn't sit on him. We'd have had a flat cat." MacKinnon looked at Roly Polar, who seemed to have understood the deprecating comment and gazed disdainfully back. MacKinnon apologized, "Sorry,

Roly. I know, you aren't fat; you just have big bones."

After breakfast, he dressed for work and, when he came back downstairs, he found Victoria in the backyard, watering the flowers. Hugging her, he said, "I'll see you at lunch."

She put the hose down and hugged him back. "I remembered something while you were upstairs. You have to call the medical center in Fredericksburg and reschedule the MRI."

"I really don't have time for that, honey. I'm fine."

"Steve, you promised."

"Okay." He raised his hands in surrender. "I'll call them this afternoon."

She kissed his nose and said, "Thank you, sweetheart."

As he drove to the police station, he noticed a curious thing. Some people waved at him as if he were a celebrity in a parade, while a slightly lesser number of folks glowered or turned away. The news of Jean Dumfries' arrest had spread quickly through Talmine.

Seeing MacKinnon enter the station, Dispatcher Julie Crozier was cautiously cheerful. "Good morning, Chief. You've got a stack of callback notes on your desk. It looks like the DC papers and a couple of radio stations heard about . . . what happened last night."

"Morning, Julie. Yeah, I imagine the phone lines are going to be busy for the next few days."

"And I just wanted to tell you that I've always been on your side."

"Thank you, Julie."

"Oh, and Mr. Pawling called and made me promise to tell you that he really needs to talk to you first thing this morning."

You don't need to be Nostradamus to know what the town attorney wants to chat about, thought MacKinnon as he went upstairs to his office. He picked up the phone and pressed Norman Pawling's telephone extension. Usually when they spoke there were casual pleasantries exchanged, but not this morning.

"Bottom-line, Chief, how bad is it?" asked Pawling.

"Worse than the mayor's told you. If she's smart, she'll resign now, because I have her on videotape admitting to hiding a murder victim so that she could pursue a dishonest deal to sell the portion of Brookesmith Park that adjoins some acreage she owns. After that, it gets even worse."

"How could it be worse?"

"Well, she just avoided attempted bribery, tried to seduce me, and then made a false accusation of sexual assault. Show that tape to any jury and it's an instant conviction."

"The mayor said you didn't read her her rights."

"I didn't have to. You know that, Norm. It began as a non-custodial interview."

"Any chance you'll lose the videotape at an evidentiary hearing?"

"Not likely. I don't doubt her attorney will make a motion to suppress, but it won't go anywhere. There's plenty of case law that says there's no reasonable expectation of privacy during an interview at a police station."

Pawling sighed. "When can I see the tape?"

"You can come over and watch it now, but I'm not going to let it out of my sight until I have some copies made."

"Don't you trust me?"

"Don't take this personally, Norm, but right now I can't afford to trust anybody in the town government. If that tape suddenly disappeared or came up blank, it would just be my word against hers, and I wouldn't have a case. If you want to watch the tape, let me know."

"I'll call to arrange a time."

"Oh, and you might want to start thinking of some cunning legal arguments to prevent the release of the tape to the media. If this hits the major news services, as I suspect it will, there's going to be some interest."

"God, I hadn't thought about that. Any ideas?"

"For now you can say that releasing the tape might harm the ongoing murder investigation."

"That'll work." There was a pause and then Pawling said, "But Chief, just between you and me, why would you want to help keep the tape away from the media?"

"This is ugly enough as it is, Norm. There isn't any point in making it worse for the town."

No sooner had MacKinnon replaced the receiver than the phone rang again. This time it was Sheriff Jarboe.

"Hi, Mac. Thought I'd call and see what's new," he said innocently.

"As if you didn't know."

"The rumor is she got naked and climbed up onto your desk."

"The rumor is false, but what happened was bad enough. Tom, I hate to cut this short, but I've got to get to work. Come by the house tomorrow night and we'll have a beer and I'll tell you all about it."

"Wouldn't miss it for the world. See you later."

MacKinnon leafed through the stack of messages and decided that none needed his immediate attention. He turned on his computer, accessed the Internet, and found the Web page for the Richmond Civil War Artifact Exposition. There was a telephone number listed and he called. The receptionist transferred him to an executive, who reported that the company did maintain a list of exhibition participants. MacKinnon was put on hold for a few minutes and, when the woman came back on the line, she confirmed that Joseph

Carnes had attended the function as a seller. MacKinnon asked the woman to set the application forms aside and told her that he would come to their offices the next day to collect the document.

Disconnecting from the call, he pressed the interoffice number for dispatch. When Julie answered the phone, he said, "Julie, could you please hold all my calls until further notice? I've got some serious typing to do and I can't be disturbed."

"Yes, sir."

Ninety minutes later, he collected the arrest warrant affidavit from the computer printer and, after reviewing the complicated narrative a final time, walked over to the courthouse. Court wasn't in session and, after a word with the bailiff, MacKinnon was ushered into Judge Gordon Willett's office.

MacKinnon was familiar with the town joke that said the elderly Gordon Willett owed his presence on the bench to his friendship with President Johnson—Andrew Johnson. Willett was a pallid old man with thin hair, thin hands, and a thin temper. He was considered a good judge, but had a reputation for occasionally ignoring laws he considered idiotic. MacKinnon guessed that one of the statutes Willett held in disregard was the Brookesmith County ordinance prohibiting smoking in governmental buildings, because the judge was puffing industriously on a huge and foul-smelling Meduro cigar. He peered at MacKinnon through a shroud of smoke and silently motioned him to have a seat.

When Willett had finished reading the affidavit, he cleared his throat and grumbled, "No eyewitnesses, no physical evidence. This is awfully circumstantial."

"It's all circumstantial, Judge."

"Glad to hear you say that," Willett said grudgingly. "I

don't have any patience for policemen who don't know the law."

"Yes, sir."

Willett signed the warrant and looked up at MacKinnon. "Did you have a bail amount in mind?"

"A million dollars wouldn't be out of line. He's a flight risk, and I need to keep him in custody until I can find the Lost Order."

"Good reasons," said Willett as he wrote the figure on the arrest warrant. He handed the papers to MacKinnon. "Off the record, Chief. What did happen in your office last night?"

"I don't mean to be rude, sir, but I don't think it would be wise for me to discuss the case with you. After all, won't you be the trial judge?"

"Not a chance, son. Jeanie's lawyers will ask for a change of venue to Outer Mongolia before they risk putting her case on in my court." Willett studied the glowing end of the cigar for a moment. "So, did she really take her clothes off and get up on your desk?"

"No, and as much as I'd like to tell you about it, Judge, I just don't think I should until I have a chance to present the case to the Commonwealth Attorney."

"Of course, you're right," said Willett, disappointed. "Okay, Chief, can't sit here gabbing all morning. Good luck finding this Carnes fella."

MacKinnon excused himself and, after filing the warrant paperwork with the court clerk, went back to the police station. He handed the arrest warrant to Julie Crozier and asked her to enter the information into the statewide and NCIC computer systems.

"Any new messages I should know about?"

She looked up from the computer screen. "Lots of calls from reporters. The Richmond paper and the *Washington*

Times. They want to interview you about the business with the mayor last night."

"They can wait. I'm going to go over and say hi to Greg."

A few minutes later, MacKinnon entered the hospital room and saw that Greg was watching a retina-searing, ear-drum-piercing Japanese cartoon on TV while Wendy held his hand. The wounded officer smiled when he saw MacKinnon and then looked embarrassed when MacKinnon glanced up at the TV. Greg fumbled for the remote and, instead of changing the channel, turned the volume up. Wendy took the device from him and turned the TV off.

MacKinnon wanted to tell him that there was no need to be ashamed over watching cartoons. Indeed, the chief's most secret vice was an addiction to "Pinky and the Brain," not that he'd admit the fact to anyone, even under torture.

"Hi, Greg. I thought I'd check in and see how you're doing."

"Thanks, Chief."

"And Wendy, how are you?"

"Fine." There were dark smudges beneath Wendy's eyes, evidence that the dispatcher had cut back drastically on sleep to spend time at the hospital. "We just had some good news. They're releasing Greg tomorrow morning."

"That's great."

Greg said cheerfully, "And the other good news is that Wendy and I are going to get married just as soon as we can get down to the courthouse."

"And we were wondering if you and Mrs. MacKinnon would be our witnesses. We'd both like that."

"I think I can safely speak for Victoria and say that we'd be proud to be there. Just let us know when. I've got to get back to work and, Wendy, you'd better go home and get some sleep."

"Yes, sir."

"I tried to tell her that, Chief, but she wouldn't listen to me."

"If you're going to be married, you'd better get used to it, Greg," said MacKinnon as he waved goodbye.

Leaving the hospital, he drove home for a quick lunch with Victoria and discovered that Farshee's bad habits weren't limited to scaling curtains and gladiatorial exhibitions. Lured by the scent of the Black Forest ham and provolone sandwiches, the kitten boldly climbed onto the tabletop and attempted to help himself to lunch. MacKinnon dumped the cat on the floor, then told Victoria about the impending wedding.

"It's sweet that they want us to be there for the ceremony," she said.

"And I can think of the perfect wedding gift."

"I told you before, we are not giving them the couch from your office." Victoria shook her head in mock exasperation.

"They'd get more enjoyment from it than a toaster."

After lunch, MacKinnon returned to the office and began typing. He completed the arrest report on Dumfries and then resumed work on the murder investigation narrative. When his vision began to grow blurry from too many hours of looking at the computer monitor, he decided to take a break. He checked his watch and was surprised to discover that the day had slipped away from him; it was already past three o'clock. Needing a little fresh air and to stretch his legs, he walked downstairs. However, he paused when he saw that Kathy Sayers was just beginning her night-watch shift. The dispatcher looked up quickly, wearing an expression of dread.

He paused in the doorway and said, "Kathy, I know why you hate me and I wish you didn't, because Ron is a good guy and you're an excellent dispatcher, one of the best I've ever seen."

"But," she said.

"But this war you've been waging against me can't be allowed to go on the way it has for the past year and a half."

"It looks like you won the war."

"Just a skirmish. By next week there'll be something else I've done or haven't done that you'll begin complaining about."

"Do you want my resignation?"

"No. I'd prefer it if you stayed, but from now on it has to be on my terms. You don't have to like me, but I'm your boss and I'm not going to tolerate any further subversion. Is that understood?"

"Yes, sir."

"With that in mind, do you want to continue working here?"

"Yes, sir."

"Good. Then the matter is closed."

After spending a few minutes in the afternoon sunshine, he forced himself to go back to his desk and return to work. The next section to be written was "Victim's History," and he opened the folder containing the documents collected from the Hagerstown Police and Washington County Sheriff. Leafing through the crime reports, he began to examine the elder fiduciary abuse report he'd obtained two days earlier. He scanned the fact sheet, and his gaze was suddenly riveted on the name of the man who'd called the police to report his parents had been victimized.

Telephoning home, MacKinnon said, "Honey, I've got to drive over to the neighborhood of Fredericksburg right now, so I'm probably going to be late for dinner tonight."

"Have they found Carnes?"

"No, and the next time I start acting like I'm Hercule Poirot, would you please give me a swift kick in the ass?"

"What's wrong?"

"I was just reading a crime report listing Christine Norland as the suspect, and I found an ugly surprise. The RP is a guy named Bibbs," said MacKinnon. "He was one of the reenactors who told me that he saw our victim on Saturday morning, and was very definite when he told me he didn't know her."

"So, why did he come forward to tell you he'd seen her?" Victoria sounded puzzled.

"I don't think it was his idea. Bibbs was with another reenactor when he saw Christine. It was that guy—Niles was his name, I think—who approached Ron Sayers to provide a witness statement. And try this on for a motive for murder. Darling Christine wiped out Bibbs' parents' life savings."

"But Carnes—"

"Right now, all we can prove is that Carnes was there to buy the Lost Order, and he's still the prime suspect in the shooting at Blackburn's Antiques. But until I get the truth from Bibbs, we've got to accept the possibility that my carefully constructed case is all wrong and that Carnes didn't kill Christine."

Fourteen:

Into the Wilderness

MacKinnon drove into Fredericksburg, passed through the center of the city, and continued westward. After a short time he came to the town of Spotsylvania, and then the highway took him into a region of gloomy forestland. He didn't believe in ghosts, but he was willing to acknowledge that if there were such things as specters, this pine wilderness was haunted. No matter the weather or season, the atmosphere always seemed melancholy and slightly oppressive—and with good reason. Between May 1863 and May 1864, three large and very bloody Civil War battles had been fought in these vast woods—Chancellorsville, the Wilderness, and Spotsylvania Courthouse. They were vicious affairs that produced an aggregate butcher's bill of over 80,000 dead and wounded men.

Eventually he came upon a brown roadway sign with white letters that read, "Chancellorsville National Battlefield Park" and an arrow pointing to the right. He turned down the two-lane road and parked in front of the Visitors' Center, a boxy single-story building composed of brown bricks and glass. Getting out of the car, he heard iron heel-plates clacking on the pavement and saw a trio of solemn Confederate reenactors walking toward a minivan. The Visitors' Center was constructed on the site where Southern General Thomas "Stonewall" Jackson had been accidentally shot by his own men during the Battle of Chancellorsville and was a place of pilgrimage for the Rebel hobbyists.

There was a park employee standing in front of the

building, and MacKinnon asked her where the Union reenactors were camped. She pointed to the southwest and replied that the Federal living history camp was located only a short distance away, in Hazel Grove. MacKinnon knew the spot. Hazel Grove had been the site of confused and bitter nighttime fighting during the battle. He thanked the park worker and got back into his car.

A few minutes later, he arrived at a large and untidy encampment on the edge of a grassy clearing near a row of silent cannon. The two-man, canvas dog tents were scattered about in no particular order, and some of the reenactors had erected *shebangs,* crude and temporary shelters made from rubber rain ponchos and tree branches. MacKinnon was enormously impressed at the camp's authenticity. At many reenactment events, the faux soldiers erected their tents in neat rows, which was a common practice when the troops were in permanent camp, but that was seldom the case when the troops were on campaign. An infantryman who'd marched twelve miles along muddy or dusty roads, carrying a heavy rifle and thirty pounds of equipment, and who'd perhaps been involved in fighting, was usually too exhausted to worry about the military niceties of straight tent lines. He simply pitched his shelter wherever he could, and that was what the reenactors had done here.

MacKinnon walked into the camp and, despite the presence of tourists, felt himself propelled backward in time. There were men lying inside the tents, some reading letters or prayer books and others snoring. Two soldiers were sitting cross-legged on a rubber ground cloth and playing dominoes, while a third darned a threadbare, gray woolen sock. In front of a regimental headquarters tent, the National Colors and a blue flag bearing the Seal of the State of Pennsylvania hung limply in the still August air. The atmosphere smelled faintly of campfires, tobacco smoke, and horse droppings. Off in the distance, MacKinnon heard a horse whinny and the shouted commands of a sergeant drilling a squad of troops. Nearby, a bearded soldier sat with his back against an old tree stump, strumming a banjo and singing, "The Minstrel Boy," an Irish song popular among the troops.

MacKinnon found Wayne Bibbs standing next to a smoky campfire, surrounded by a crowd of tourists taking pictures and video. The Zouave reenactor was giving a lecture on the sad art of soldiers' cuisine. From the smell and appearance of the debris frying in the grimy pan, it looked as if Bibbs was making *skillygalee,* an awful-tasting and unhealthy meal of pulverized hardtack biscuits cooked in pork fat. The reenactor offered a spoonful of the stuff to a young girl, who squealed and darted behind her mother. Bibbs joined the crowd in laughter; then he saw MacKinnon and turned slightly pale. MacKinnon nodded, signaling the Zouave reenactor to finish his presentation.

After Bibbs showed how the soldiers made coffee—the beans were secured within an old sock, smashed with a rifle butt, and submerged in the waters of a battered coffeepot—he thanked the crowd and excused himself. Then, after pausing to pose for pictures, the reenactor at last detached himself from the tourists and joined MacKinnon.

"Mister Bibbs."

"Chief."

"Let's go someplace and talk."

Bibbs nodded and followed MacKinnon away from the camp and into the trees.

Finally, MacKinnon stopped, folded his arms, and said, "You know why I'm here."

Bibbs' shoulders slumped. "Yes, sir."

"Did you kill Christine Norland?"

"I know it looks bad because I lied to you, but, no sir, I didn't kill her." Bibbs looked at the ground and shook his head.

There was no parsing of words or non-verbal signs of deception, which meant that Bibbs was either a world-class liar or perhaps actually telling the truth. MacKinnon decided to push a little harder and find out. "Any particular reason why I should believe you?"

The Zouave looked up to meet MacKinnon's gaze and firmly replied, "Look, I got scared and stupid and lied to you. But she was alive when I left her, and I'm willing to take a lie detector test to prove I'm telling the truth."

"I may take you up on that offer." MacKinnon sensed the reenactor was indeed providing honest answers. Murderers seldom volunteered to undergo a polygraph examination. "Okay, you didn't kill her. Do you know who did?"

"No, sir."

"Do you own a black-powder pistol?"

Bibbs sighed. "Yes, sir."

"What kind?"

"An eighteen-fifty-eight Remington, .44 caliber."

The gun named by Bibbs was too small in caliber to have fired the lead ball that killed Christine. Nonetheless MacKinnon wanted to know more about the firearm. "Antique or replica?"

"Replica."

"Where is that gun right now?"

"Up in Emmitsburg. I didn't bring it with me on the trip."

"And if I searched your gear and your car, I wouldn't find it?"

"No, sir, you wouldn't, and you're free to look." Bibbs seemed to bristle slightly.

"I will in a little bit. How about a LeMat revolver? Do you own one of those?"

"No, sir. I'm sorry I lied to you."

"Me too."

"How did you find out that I was involved?"

"There was a crime report on file in Hagerstown, listing your parents as the victims of fiduciary abuse and Christine Norland as the suspect. I'd have been out here two days ago, except I didn't get a chance to read it until this afternoon."

Bibbs fiddled with the red sash that encircled his waist, looked into the trees, and finally said, "Christine was a bad woman."

"That's true. The world's probably a much better place because she's gone, but that doesn't mean I don't have a duty to catch the killer. Tell me what happened."

"Mom is seventy-two and Dad's seventy-five," said Bibbs as he removed his blue fez and wiped the sweat from his forehead with a coat sleeve. "Up until about a year ago, my parents were doing just fine. But that winter, Mom fell on some icy steps and broke her hip. Dad took care of her, and then he had a small heart attack. I did my best to help, but they needed someone to keep house and cook meals."

"So you contacted a temp agency, who sent out Christine Norland," said MacKinnon, recalling the report narrative. "Did you ever meet her?"

"Only once, on a Saturday morning. I went by the folks' house and Christine was there, serving them breakfast. She impressed the hell out of me."

"Why was that?"

Bibbs tugged at his coat. "I was in uniform because I was on my way to a reenactment down near Staunton. Christine takes one look at me and says, 'Seventy-sixth Pennsylvania Keystone Zouaves.' Man, you could have knocked me over with a feather. Whatever else about her, that woman did know her Civil War history."

"You ever see her again?"

"You mean before Saturday?"

"Right."

"No."

"You're sure?"

"What are you hinting at?"

"Christine wasn't above using sex to get what she wanted. Did you guys have any sort of romantic relationship?"

"I'm a happily-married man, eighteen years in September. I've never cheated on my wife," Bibbs said angrily.

"I believe you, Mister Bibbs, and I'm sorry for upsetting you. But knowing what I do about Christine, I still had to ask the question. When did you find out about the theft?"

The Zouave took a moment to collect his thoughts and then said, in a calmer tone, "Things seemed to be working out great and then suddenly, one day, Christine just stops showing up. A couple of days go by and my folks called me, and then I called the temp agency. They tried to call Christine, but said they couldn't find her. She'd just dropped out of sight. I got them to give me her home address, and went by there to see if she was okay. The address she'd given was some motel in Hagerstown, and nobody knew her there."

"The Carrollton Inn?"

"How did you know that?"

"She worked there," MacKinnon said. "What happened after that?"

"That's when I discovered she'd cleaned out my folks' bank account. Ninety-seven hundred dollars in savings and checking, every penny of it gone. Money can be replaced, but trust . . . it just about killed my folks to think that someone they barely knew would hurt them so badly."

"And you were feeling guilty because you were the one who'd brought her into your parents' home," said MacKinnon, his tone soft.

"I suppose that's true."

"Which brings us to Saturday morning. What happened?"

"There we are at the reenactment, Eric and me, when suddenly I see Christine at the sutlers'. Even with the fake beard, I recognized her. What were the odds?" Bibbs shook his head in wonderment.

"Did she see you?"

"No. I kinda ducked behind a bunch of uniforms."

"Did you tell Eric that you knew her?"

"No."

"Why not?"

"Because I wanted to handle her myself, and I didn't want Eric to get into any trouble."

"Why didn't you stop one of my officers and have him arrest her?"

"I was going to, but I wanted a little time with her myself before I got the cops involved. I didn't figure you guys would let me talk to her, and there were some things I wanted to say to her. Anyway, the drummers started sounding assembly, and I told Eric I was going to drop the bayonet off in my car. Once he took off for camp, I went after Christine, followed her into the woods."

"Was there anybody else around?"

"No, we were alone."

"And then?"

"I grabbed her by the arm and then she recognized me. I told her that she'd robbed my parents and that I was gonna have her arrested," said Bibbs, mopping his damp forehead once more.

"What did she do?"

"At first, she said that I had the wrong person, got all huffy and told me I was nuts. But then she understood that I wasn't buying her BS and she got all weepy." Bibbs sounded scornful. "She begged me not to call the cops and promised to give the money back, but I knew she was lying."

MacKinnon nodded and silently waited for Bibbs to continue.

The reenactor inhaled deeply and then said, "I asked her what she'd done with the money, and she kept crying and told me that she'd spent it all. So, I told her to come with me and we were going to find a cop. Then Christine says, 'Wait a minute, maybe we can make a deal.' "

"And?"

"All of a sudden she ain't crying anymore, turned those tears off like a goddamn garden spigot. In a snotty voice, she says that putting her in jail won't get any of my folks' money back. She tells me that she'll give me something that's worth more than the money she took."

"And you were interested."

"My parents were left without a dime. Yeah, I could have put her in jail, but that wouldn't help my folks. Christine pulls a plastic envelope from her haversack and gives it to me, says that it's Robert E. Lee's Lost Order."

"And naturally, you didn't believe her."

"Of course not. But when I looked at the papers, they seemed to be authentic."

"How could you be certain?"

"I wasn't, but I recognized the wording, and the papers looked real old. Never did more than a year of junior college, but I *do* know about the Battle of Antietam. I've read everything there is on that fight," Bibbs said with quiet pride. "So, tell me. Is it really the Lost Order?"

"Yeah. Christine stole it from the Library of Congress."

"Well, I won't lie to you. I figured it was stolen from someplace. But not the Library of Congress."

"And so you took the papers, figuring to sell them and use the money to replace your parents' savings."

"I thought about it, thought about it a long time at night while lying in my tent," said Bibbs, jerking his head in the direction of the camp. "And it was real tempting, because there are a lot of people in this world who have more money than they do sense or scruples."

"That's true."

"And there are collectors out there who'll buy anything and don't want to know where the stuff came from. That's why guys slip into the battlefields late at night with metal detectors. An authentic brass belt buckle will pull down as much as four hundred bucks, and even a single gilt button can cost almost twenty dollars. I didn't have to be Einstein to figure I could find someone who'd pay a good price for the Lost Order, maybe ten times the money Christine stole."

"So, what did you decide?"

"I couldn't do it." Bibbs kicked at the ground and emitted a humorless laugh. "And you know why? Because if I did that, I'd be no better than Christine, a damn thief, and that really troubled me. Last night, I decided that when I got home I'd check around and see if there was some sort of reward being offered for the Lost Order. Then, if I came up dry, I was going to call you."

"I wish it had been sooner rather than later. Back to your meeting with Christine, what happened after you took the Lost Order?"

"I let her go and headed toward my car, while she took off in the other direction," Bibbs said. "That was the last I saw of her."

"You see anyone else around?"

"A Reb general was coming down the trail as I was leaving."

MacKinnon assembled the rest of the puzzle in his head. A con artist to the end, Christine had still made her rendezvous with Carnes, hoping to convince the antique dealer to pay for the Lost Order. It was her last scam and she'd paid for her overreaching greed with her life. "Tell me what this Confederate officer looked like, Mr. Bibbs."

"Gray pantaloons, gray frock coat, cavalry boots, and a kepi. He had a beard."

"Could you recognize him if you saw him again?"

"Maybe."

"Last question, Mister Bibbs. Where is the Lost Order?"

"In my car."

"Before we go get it, take me to your tent. I want to search your knapsack and gear."

"Yes, sir."

MacKinnon followed Bibbs into camp and to a stained canvas dog tent. The reenactor pulled his black knapsack from the tent and unfolded it on the ground. After unhooking the leather straps and ties of the two storage compartments, Bibbs removed an odoriferous collection of dirty socks, cotton drawers, and collarless linen shirts. A search of the haversack revealed some hardtack inside a cloth sack, a chunk of salt pork wrapped in wax paper, some wizened carrots, and the stub of a candle. There was no sign of the Remington pistol or the revolver's specialized black-powder ammunition.

After that, Bibbs led MacKinnon toward a group of cars, vans, and SUVs parked on the grass about a hundred yards away. Bibbs pointed to a brown-colored Chevy Monte Carlo that bore a bumper sticker that read, "This Vehicle Stops at All Civil War Reenactments." He unlocked the trunk and removed a clear plastic sheath containing some yellowed sheets of paper. MacKinnon scrutinized the handwritten document which was labeled, "Special Order No. 191," and beneath that were the words: "Army of Northern Virginia." It was the Lost Order.

"I guess you'll want to search the car now," said Bibbs, holding out his keys.

Placing the document on the roof of the car, MacKinnon carefully checked the trunk and then moved to the passenger compartment. He worked slowly, starting with obvious hiding places like the glove box and center console and then checking beneath the seats. Next, he removed the backseat bench and, after replacing it, pulled on the corners of the upholstery, trying to locate a hidden cubbyhole. After that, he opened the hood and checked the engine partition. Bibbs had been telling the truth. He didn't have the Remington.

"So, you gonna arrest me now?" asked Bibbs, sounding both apprehensive and weary.

"Ordinarily I would, but I can't." MacKinnon handing the car keys back. "Whatever your reasons, you were in possession of stolen property and you willfully impeded my murder investigation by lying to me. Either of those crimes could land you in state prison."

"But, I'm not going to jail?"

"Not tonight. You see, you're on Federal land right now and as a state peace officer I don't have any legal authority to take you into custody. I could get a park ranger and have him hold you until I get an arrest warrant, but I've got too many other things to do right now."

"So, what happens to me?"

"I'll write up a report and file it with the Commonwealth Attorney. If he feels that charges are merited, he'll send you a notification letter," said MacKinnon. "But I don't think it's real likely that the DA will issue the case against you."

"Why's that?"

"My report is going to indicate that you voluntarily returned the stolen property and also assisted with my murder investigation. But there's a price. You're going to have to testify truthfully when I catch the murderer and this mess goes to trial. If you perjure yourself or your memory fails, I promise you, you won't like what happens."

"I understand, sir."

"Good. You can go back to camp now."

"Thank you, sir. But before I go, can I ask a couple of questions?"

"No guarantees I'll answer them, but go ahead."

"Was Christine at your park to sell the Lost Order?"

"Yeah, she was."

"And did the Reb I saw murder her?"

"That's the way it looks."

"And that happened right after she gave me the papers?"

"More than likely within minutes."

Bibbs looked off into the shadowy trees and his voice bore traces of sorrow and guilt. "So, did I help kill her?"

MacKinnon paused before answering. "Legally, no. But as far as your moral responsibility goes, you're the only one who can really answer that question."

It took slightly more than an hour for MacKinnon to drive back to Talmine. On the way home, he stopped at the police station to retrieve the mass of paperwork and investigative notes. There was still a great deal of the homicide report left to complete, and he'd try to finish it after dinner. As he passed the dispatcher's office, he paused to tell Kathy about having recovered the Lost Order.

"Good work," said Kathy, sounding genuinely pleased.

"Thanks, but believe me, it was more luck than anything else."

"You want the evidence locker keys?" She pulled a desk drawer open.

"No, I'm going to put it with the videotape of the mayor's interview in my safe at home," he said. "I'll call the FBI and have them come pick it up first thing tomorrow morning. I want this thing out of here, so that Carnes doesn't have any other reason to turn this town into a shooting gallery."

Fifteen:

Finder's Fee

"So the Bureau is going to send some agents tomorrow morning?" asked Victoria.

"From DC. They said they'd be here before noon," MacKinnon said. "I guess they were keeping the theft under wraps, because when I called, the agent got all mysterious and told me he could neither confirm nor deny that a Civil War document had been stolen from the Library of Congress. So I said, 'Hey, bud, I can confirm it was stolen and if you want it, you'd best shag your ass down here.' "

He and Victoria sat on the porch in the dusk, finishing a dinner of thermonuclear turkey chili and cornbread. Tonight the chili had been especially hot, so much so, that after a few experimental sniffs, the dogs weren't even trying to cadge table scraps. Rob Roy exhaled disdainfully and gazed at MacKinnon. It was easy for him to imagine the dog saying: "A dinner we can't share? Is this your idea of a cruel hoax?"

"Honey, that was delicious." MacKinnon put the empty bowl on the end table. "Even if my mouth feels like I've been sucking on the exhaust valve from Chernobyl."

"Thanks. It was good," she said. "So, do you actually think that Kathy will behave?"

"Maybe. Who knows? But I felt I had to give her one last chance."

Victoria shook her head and said nothing.

"Yeah, I know you think I'm being naïve, but maybe she's learned a lesson."

"And maybe they're serving ice cream sundaes in Hell."

MacKinnon took her hand. "Vic, I could have stomped her, but I had to think about how it would have affected the department. Kathy is a good dispatcher, and because of that she's earned one more chance."

"Steve, people like Kathy and the mayor see that sort of altruism as weakness."

"That's probably true, but I still think I did the right thing."

"We'll see." She pulled at his sleeve. "Sweetheart, why don't you change out of that uniform and make yourself comfortable?"

"Because I have a small mountain of paperwork to complete, and if I stay in uniform, it will force me to get it done. Otherwise, I'd be vegging out on the couch watching the Orioles, and I don't have time for that."

He retired to his office and resumed typing the report, while Victoria sat in the living room and worked on her appliqué quilt. About forty-five minutes later, he heard the doorbell ring and the dogs bark. He didn't get up because he knew Victoria would answer the door. Members of her quilting club and the neighbors had been visiting the house and telephoning throughout the day, as word of the obscene computer message spread. The dogs continued to bark, and then were silent as Victoria banished them to the downstairs guest bedroom.

A moment later, she pushed his door open. "Steve?"

"Be with you in a second, honey." He stared at the computer screen. "Let me just finish this paragraph."

"Steve."

This time the tone in his wife's voice required immediate attention. Something was very wrong. Looking up, he inhaled sharply. Victoria was standing in the doorway, and next to her was Joseph Carnes. The antique dealer was holding Victoria by her blonde hair and pointing the huge, black LeMat revolver at her head. MacKinnon half-rose from his chair and glanced toward the corner of the room, where his gun belt lay on the leather wingback chair.

Carnes saw the look. "Don't even think about it, Chief. And don't go for the desk drawer, because I know that gun over there isn't the only firearm in the house."

His experience as a fugitive hadn't agreed with Carnes. The once-spruce Confederate general had dirty hands, his hair was oily and uncombed, and he wore grubby khaki trousers and a faded plaid shirt. But MacKinnon paid the greatest attention to Carnes' eyes. They shone with an unsavory excitement.

For a fleeting instant MacKinnon considered diving for his revolver and snapping off a shot. But the antique dealer's pistol was cocked and there was no way MacKinnon could cross the room, get his gun, and get a shot off before Carnes pulled the trigger. MacKinnon might have chanced it if he were alone, but with Victoria's life at stake he knew he couldn't take the risk.

"Are you all right, honey?"

Sensing the decision her husband had just made, Victoria slowly exhaled. She said in an angry, frightened voice, "Fine, so far. He was the one that rang the doorbell. I opened the door, and he said he would kill me if I made a sound."

"What happened to the dogs?"

"I locked them in the guest room."

"They seem like nice dogs. I didn't want to kill them," Carnes said.

"It's a shame you didn't give Christine Norland the same chance," said MacKinnon.

"She didn't deserve the same chance. She wasn't nice."

"Much as I'd like to, I can't argue that. I know that Christine tried to cheat you, but why kill her?"

"We'd agreed upon a price and I was prepared to pay. I'm not a killer by trade."

"Maybe you missed your vocation."

"She brought it on herself. When we met in the woods, she upped the price by an extra ten thousand and told me she already had another purchaser ready to buy, if I didn't produce the money that afternoon."

"And then you murdered her, because you couldn't come up with the cash and couldn't bear the idea of someone else having the Lost Order," said MacKinnon. "Boy, you must have been fit to be tied when you searched her and didn't find those papers. But tell me something. Why did you take us to the body?"

"When I saw that Christine didn't have the Lost Order, I realized she must have hidden it someplace in town, more than likely her car. There were hundreds of cars at the park and no way for me to know which one to search, so I decided I needed police assistance."

"Clever. We do your legwork and find the car."

"And then I steal the Lost Order from your police station . . . or at least that was the plan. But the document wasn't in the car, either."

"No, it wasn't, and are you ready for the punch line to this bad joke? Just before she was going to meet you, Christine ran into one of her earlier crime victims and gave him the Lost Order to avoid going to jail."

Carnes released his grip on Victoria's hair and motioned her toward the love seat next to the window. "Sit there and don't move."

Victoria sat.

"Now, Chief, before we talk any further, I want you to

slowly move over to the wall near the bookshelves, turn away from me, and put your hands behind your head," commanded Carnes.

MacKinnon did as he was instructed, and from the corner of his eye he saw the antique dealer edge over to the easy chair. Carnes yanked the .357 Magnum from the holster and stuck it into the waistband of his trousers. Next, he took a pair of handcuffs from the leather case and put them on the desk.

"So, Carnes, it looks as if you've been roughing it for the past few days. Where have you been?"

"On a boat out on the river."

"Where did you get a boat?"

"Colonial Beach. The owner didn't need it anymore."

MacKinnon knew what that meant. "What's that, two murders now?"

"In for a dime, in for a dollar, as the old expression goes." Carnes leaned over the desk and opened the top drawer. "Do you have any other guns in here?"

"Just the Springfield." MacKinnon inclined his head toward the antique rifle hanging on the wall.

"I noticed that. Genuine or reproduction?"

"Genuine."

"Very nice."

"Pardon my asking, Carnes, but I know you didn't come here to talk about antiques. Just what the hell do you want?" MacKinnon turned slightly. He could see Carnes continuing his search of the desk, while keeping the pistol aimed at Victoria.

"I'm here for the Lost Order."

"What makes you think it's here? It's locked up in my evidence room at the police station."

MacKinnon heard a soft tread of footfalls on the carpet

behind him and then felt something heavy and metal crash against the back of his skull. He saw stars and staggered forward, slamming into the bookshelf. MacKinnon heard Victoria bite back an angry scream.

"Don't move!" Carnes shouted to Victoria. Then to MacKinnon he said, "That was for lying to me. I know the document is here in your safe."

"What makes you think that?" croaked MacKinnon, who felt something warm trickling down the back of his neck. The blow had broken the skin.

"Because I have every confidence your mayor is a very reliable informant," said Carnes.

Suddenly MacKinnon understood and wished he had stomped on Kathy Sayers. *The little weasel probably called Dumfries about the recovery of the Lost Order the minute I left the office,* he thought. In turn, the mayor had somehow passed the information to Carnes. If he and Victoria survived this encounter, MacKinnon silently swore he would henceforth always remember a bitter fact of life: no good deed ever went unpunished.

"How long have you known Dumfries?" asked MacKinnon.

"Not long, two hours, but long enough to know she hates you with a passion. I've been in town for the past two days and dropped by her house this evening, after I heard about how you'd arrested her. I thought I might find a sympathetic ear, and I certainly wasn't disappointed."

"This information couldn't have been free."

"Of course not. I agreed to kill you."

"And my wife?"

"Actually, just you. Your wife isn't on the mayor's execution list." Carnes glanced at Victoria. "Not because she holds you in any regard. She really hates you too, but she apparently thinks it would be a delicious form of torture for you to go through the rest of your life remembering your husband's murder. She's a most frightening woman."

"That's a remarkable statement, coming from you," said MacKinnon.

Carnes nodded in agreement. "But I must confess, I haven't decided yet if I'm going to oblige your vengeance-minded mayor."

"A sudden attack of conscience?" asked Victoria.

"No. It's because if he kills us, he runs the risk of the death penalty. A lethal injection would prevent him from enjoying the Lost Order," MacKinnon said.

"Correct," Carnes said.

"So take the damn paper and go," spat Victoria.

"The Lost Order and the videotape," Carnes corrected.

"Open the safe, honey," MacKinnon said. "The sooner we give him what he wants, the sooner he's out of here."

"And the sooner I can wring some necks," muttered Victoria. To MacKinnon she said, "It was Kathy who told the mayor about the document, wasn't it?"

"I'm afraid so. She's the only one who knew. I apologize. You were right about her."

"There'll be plenty of time for you two to sort this all out later," said Carnes, his voice eerily congenial. "Open the safe and, if you continue to cooperate, I'll let you both live."

Squinting out of the corner of his eye, MacKinnon saw Carnes grab Victoria's sleeve and pull her to her feet. He escorted her over to the corner of the room, where a small safe rested on the floor. She knelt and began rotating the combination dial, while he brushed the barrel of the pistol against the back of her head. There was a click and she pushed down on the handle and swung the metal door open. She reached inside and retrieved the videocassette and the envelope containing the Lost Order.

"Open the envelope and show me the document," said Carnes.

She bent the brass hasps upward and slid the papers from the envelope.

"Hold them up, so I can see." He leaned forward and peered at the paper. "Good. Now put them back in the envelope and place everything on the desk."

Victoria obeyed the instructions.

"Now get up and go back and sit down," he said. "Chief, I want you to turn around slowly and pick up the handcuffs. Take them over to the door and lock yourself to the handle."

MacKinnon gradually lowered his hands and turned. Carnes had backed away several feet and had moved close to Victoria. The gun was only inches from her head. Understanding what Carnes intended, MacKinnon quietly said, "Take me."

"That's very gallant, but no. You're precisely the sort of man who would try to overpower me. Besides, so long as I have your wife, you won't follow too closely. But I promise you, once I'm out of town I'll release her."

"What if I refuse?"

"You know, I'm growing very, very weary of this." Carnes savagely pulled on Victoria's hair, pressed the gun barrel against her temple, and said, "Put those handcuffs on right now, or I'm going to blow your wife's brains all over the room!"

Fighting his growing sense of helpless dread, MacKinnon picked up the handcuffs, walked over to the door, and secured himself to the doorknob.

Carnes nodded jerkily in approval and released his grip on Victoria. "Much better. Take your key ring and throw it down the hall."

Once more, MacKinnon followed the instructions.

Victoria looked to MacKinnon, who nodded. She rose to her feet. "And what if I don't want to go?"

"Then I'll simply grant the mayor's wish and murder your husband and let you live, knowing that you could have prevented it," replied Carnes in a frighteningly reasonable tone.

"Fine. Let's get this over with."

"I love you, honey," said MacKinnon, wishing there was something he could add to the simple pronouncement.

"I love you, too," she said, as Carnes roughly pushed her out of the room and toward the stairway.

As soon as he heard the footfalls reach the ground floor, MacKinnon reached around to the small of his back and found the handcuff key loosely sewn inside his uniform trousers waistband. Twenty-two years earlier as a rookie cop, he had been taught by his training officer to always keep a key hidden on his person for just such an emergency. The old cop had pointed out that crooks kept spare handcuff keys hidden to assist them in escaping, so it was nothing but good sense for the police to learn from that example. Although he never expected to actually need the hidden key, MacKinnon had religiously sewn a key into his trousers for over two decades.

In seconds the manacle was open and he was free. From outside he heard the Explorer's engine start and he realized there was no time to retrieve the .45 automatic from his bedroom. He raced for the front door, hoping that Victoria would remember the hidden handcuff key.

The lights of the SUV bounced up and down as it backed out of the driveway and onto the street. He could see two shadowy figures in the vehicle, and he guessed that Victoria was driving while Carnes continued to hold her at gunpoint.

Suddenly, the engine roared as Victoria slammed the accelerator of the Explorer to the floor. The truck shot up over the curb and across the lawn. Plowing through a floral barrier of rose bushes, the truck sped directly into the willow oak and there was the jarring sound of a crash. Jumping from the porch, MacKinnon heard a gunshot and saw Victoria tumble into the darkness from the open driver's door.

Oh my God, no! He's killed her, thought MacKinnon.

Berserk with rage, he charged Carnes, who was disentangling himself from the slowly-deflating airbag as he climbed from the Explorer. Carnes raised the LeMat and tried to cock the trigger, but by then MacKinnon was on him. MacKinnon viciously rammed Carnes into the side of the SUV and grabbed the gun. Twisting the heavy pistol inward, MacKinnon stripped the firearm from Carnes' hand and jammed the LeMat's barrel beneath Carnes' left ear.

The antique dealer's pupils were constricted with panic. He raised his hands and wailed, "I give up! I surrender!"

"You kill my wife and think you can surrender?" MacKinnon's voice was emotionless. "In the words of your beloved D. H. Hill: this isn't war, Carnes, this is murder."

"Please! No! God, don't!" shrieked Carnes as MacKinnon's finger tightened on the trigger.

"Steve, don't do it." Victoria's voice sounded from behind him and he felt her hand on his shoulder. "I'm okay. I'm okay."

MacKinnon didn't know if he wanted to laugh or weep. Reluctantly, he lowered the LeMat and roughly turned the trembling Carnes around to search for the stolen .357 Magnum. He couldn't find the revolver, but he did discover the antique dealer's trousers were wet with fresh urine. In the distance, MacKinnon could hear a siren begin to yelp. Apparently the neighbors had called the police and the cavalry was on the way, which was a good thing because MacKinnon had forgotten his handcuffs inside the house.

"Where's the other gun?" he snarled as he spun Carnes around to face him.

"In the truck."

"Get it for me, Vic." He shoved Carnes to the grass. "Face-down on the ground; put your hands out to your sides! Face in the ground!"

"Oww! I can't. The ground's all covered with rose bushes."

"Too goddamn bad. Lie still or I might decide you're trying to escape, and then I'd have to kill a fleeing felon."

Victoria handed him the .357 Magnum. "And if he doesn't I will, you son-of-a-bitch," she said to Carnes. "Look what you made me do to my rose garden!"

Sixteen:

Armistice

The following night, MacKinnon and Victoria walked the dogs along River View Drive past Brookesmith Park. A saffron sliver of new moon hung just above the western horizon, and out on the murmuring Potomac, a tiny cluster of boat lights slid silently down river toward Chesapeake Bay. The floodlights were on at the softball field, and MacKinnon heard the pop of a bat hitting a ball, followed by cheers. An atmosphere of tranquility again enveloped the town and, after the insanity of the past few days, he remembered why he'd wanted to live in Talmine.

"Any word on whether the Colonial Beach cops found their murder victim yet?" asked Victoria.

"Not yet. Carnes said he tossed the body overboard somewhere east of town, so it's probably drifted down river into the bay. Somebody will spot it." MacKinnon stopped walking and allowed Rob Roy to lift his leg and leave some liquid dog graffito on a fire hydrant.

"And tell me again why you can't charge Dumfries with attempted murder," said Victoria. "Carnes told us she put him up to it."

"We can charge her, but we won't get a conviction. Carnes' statement is co-defendant testimony."

"Which means her lawyer will have it suppressed?"

"Right. Even though we know the only way Carnes could have learned about the Lost Order being in my safe was through Dumfries, and he admitted that, we can't corroborate it with any other evidence."

"So she walks?"

"On the conspiracy to murder me, but not on the other charges," he said. "But look on the bright side. Dumfries did resign today."

Victoria snapped the leash as the golden retriever strained to examine a Popsicle wrapper. "She resigned, but supposedly for health reasons."

"But she's dead in the water on the other counts. There's the videotape, and that guy Phillips from the construction company cut a deal with the Commonwealth Attorneys this morning. He's agreed to testify that Dumfries covered up the body, in return for no charges being filed against him."

"Good."

"And we got a tape-recorded statement from him, just in case he changes his mind about testifying."

"Even better."

"And you ought to be very happy, knowing that Kathy is gone."

"You should have charged her too." Victoria's voice was grim.

"At first I was going to, but after I finished interviewing Kathy, I honestly don't think she knew what Dumfries was going to do with the information."

"Oh. Well, that would have made me feel *much* better, if Carnes had killed you."

MacKinnon was silent as he remembered the events of the morning. When the ugly story was revealed of how Carnes had obtained the information on the Lost Order, Ron Sayers had visited the police station only long enough to submit his, as well as his wife's, resignation. As Sayers placed his badge, ID card, and gun on the table, MacKinnon had seen tears in the man's eyes. MacKinnon knew the sergeant hadn't had anything to do with Kathy's misconduct and tried to talk him out of quitting. But the mortified cop had refused to say anything but a disconsolate mantra of, "I'm really sorry."

That meant MacKinnon had to promote a new sergeant and put out a hiring announcement for both a new officer and a dispatcher. He knew he should be home now, hunched over the keyboard, working on the report and those administrative chores. But for the moment, the work could wait. He was enjoying his time with Victoria too much to cut their walk short.

"Oh, and I forgot to tell you," he said. "This afternoon I went by the library to look at the access log for the computer. I had to see who'd posted that message about you."

"And I'll bet you got a lot of help from Emily!"

MacKinnon knew his wife was referring to chief librarian Emily Brewer, a longtime friend and supporter of Mayor Jean Dumfries. "Emily helped, but not intentionally. I asked for the user log and she gave it to me. It's just a spiral notebook and—big shock—the page listing that day's users was gone."

"So, we'll never know."

"Wrong. I know who sent it. It was Jean."

"What? How did you find out?"

"I ran a scam by Emily and she bought it," MacKinnon said with ill-concealed pride. "I told her that I was going to seize the computer as evidence and let the State Police computer techs examine the sent messages file. Then I told her that those techs would be able to match the user password with specific outgoing messages."

"Can they?"

"Beats the hell out of me. But I must have sounded convincing, because Emily believed me and rolled on Jean. The mayor came into the library yesterday and asked to use Emily's computer password to access the Web. Of course, Emily had no idea what Jean was doing."

"Right," Victoria said.

"Then Jean called Emily this morning and told her to shred the page from the sign-in log. And now Emily is my new best friend. She provided me with a written statement and agreed to testify against Jean in the computer-threat case, if it ever goes to trial."

"Very impressive, Chief MacKinnon." Victoria gave his hand a squeeze.

"Not half as impressive as you, my love." He stopped and hugged his wife with his free arm. Victoria rested her head on his shoulder and sighed into his neck. "You were very brave last night," he said softly.

"I was scared to death," she countered. "But I waited too long to be married to you, Steve, and I'm not ever going to let anything separate us. Which reminds me, when are you going to reschedule that MRI?"

"Tomorrow's out. I've got to take that search warrant back up to Hagerstown and return it to the court. Besides, I'm feeling better."

"Steve, you promised."

"Okay, okay. We'll make a day trip of it. We'll go to Fredericksburg for the MRI, have lunch, and you can hit the antique shops—"

"While you visit the battlefield museum."

"You know me far too well," MacKinnon said with a happy sigh.

As he leaned forward to kiss her, his wireless phone rang. He wanted to ignore the damn thing, but he answered.

"Chief, it's me, Wendy, calling from dispatch. Sorry to bother you, but Deshawn has a car stopped on Old Tavern Road and he thinks the driver might be that cat burglar on the BOLO from Lancaster County."

MacKinnon looked at Victoria and smiled. "They need me," he whispered. "I'm en route," he said.

Afterword

There is no such place as Talmine. The town's name derives from a village located on the northern coast of Scotland. Furthermore, Brookesmith County is also imaginary. I created the place by annexing portions of Westmoreland, Northumberland, and Richmond Counties; I hope I'll be forgiven for the land grab. Finally, the town of Sharpsburg, Maryland, does not have a police department; the fine men and women of the Washington County Sheriff's Department provide law enforcement for the community.

About the Author

During his eighteen-year career in police work in Southern California, John Lamb served as a homicide investigator, detective sergeant, and hostage negotiation team leader. He was medically retired from police work in 1997, and this allowed him to pursue his other great love, writing. In 1999, his first book was published: *San Diego Specters*, a nonfiction work of historical research and investigations into haunted sites that garnered praise as one of the most intelligent and readable books in recent years about ghost phenomena. *Echoes of the Lost Order* is his first novel and he's at work on a sequel, *Echoes of a Lethal Magic*. Additionally, he's the author of *The Mournful Teddy*, the first in a series of mysteries scheduled for release in May 2006.

When John isn't writing, he's still very busy. He's an instructor and consultant with a private firm that provides training to law enforcement organizations all over the country on death scene analysis and cold case homicide investigation. On weekends, he's out in the field in his blue uniform with Sykes' Regulars, a Union Army reenactment unit. Finally, John is very happily married to Joyce, a retired police department fingerprint expert. Much like the main characters in *Echoes of the Lost Order*, in 2004, they moved from California to a rural home in Virginia's Shenandoah Valley, where they live with their two golden retrievers and six cats.